Crafting Love

Coastal Dreams Book Three

ALEXA ASTON

USA TODAY BESTSELLING AUTHOR

OLIVERHEBERBOOKS

Cover art by Dar Albert at Wicked Smart Designs

Published by Oliver-Heber Books

0 9 8 7 6 5 4 3 2 1

Prologue

DEVONWOOD ACADEMY—
CONNECTICUT—EIGHTEEN YEARS AGO...

Sullivan Shepherd's liberation would come in five hours and forty-five minutes.

Then he would be free for the summer.

He knocked on the open door of Mr. Kellogg's office. "You wanted to see me, sir?"

"Come in, Mr. Shepherd."

Taking one of the seats in front of the teacher's desk, he wondered what this summons was about.

"Is there a problem, Mr. Kellogg?"

The history teacher smiled fondly. "Not in the least, Mr. Shepherd. I wanted to tell you not to come and sit for your final examination this afternoon."

"But...why?" he asked, puzzled by this odd request.

Kellogg chuckled. "Because it would be a waste of your time and mine. You would spend two hours composing essays, which would be perfectly outstanding. I would then take time grading something that is better than anything I could ever write. You know more world history than any student I have taught during my thirty-five years at Devonwood Academy.

From the first day you entered my classroom, I knew you were special."

He felt his cheeks grow warm. "Thank you, Mr. Kellogg. I really enjoyed your lectures. I feel I learned an awful lot."

"I hope when the time comes, you will ask me to write one of your letters of recommendation in regard to your university applications. I guarantee it will be glowing. And I do wish that you would consider majoring in history, Mr. Shepherd. You would make for a fine professor."

His favorite teacher's words meant the world to him. Hearing them also crushed him.

Because becoming a teacher was the last thing Oliver and Jacqueline Shepherd would allow. No, that wasn't right. An educator would be next to last.

Last on his parents' list of professions would be the thing Sullivan most wanted to do—and would never be allowed to pursue.

Instead of dumping his problems on Mr. Kellogg, Sullivan merely said, "Thank you for the compliment, sir, and I appreciate knowing you will be willing to write a recommendation letter for me in the future."

The teacher rose and offered Sullivan his hand. He rose and accepted it. "You have a fine mind, Mr. Shepherd. Whatever you decide to pursue, I am certain you will meet with rousing success."

He left the office, mulling over what his future would hold. His parents were obsessed with money and position in society. His mother's family could trace their lineage back to the Massachusetts Bay Colony. She had been educated at the finest private schools and been given everything she ever desired before she knew she wanted it. On the other hand, his father came from very humble beginnings, but he was smart and determined. He'd won a scholarship to Harvard. Learned to blend in with the blueblood crowd. Made friends with Alexander Wagner, another brilliant scholarship student from Texas. Today, Oliver Shepherd was the number two man at Wagner Enterprises.

To put it mildly, expectations for Sullivan were high. Beyond high. Especially because his older brother had drowned. From what he gathered, his mother had been unable to have any more children after giving birth to Sullivan. He became an only child, and he sometimes felt as if he carried the weight of the world on his shoulders. He was expected to have exceptional grades. Perform at the highest athletic levels.

And he definitely was destined to take his place in society while he made a ton of money.

He returned to his dorm room and sat at his desk, opening his Latin grammar book. Most students complained that they were all studied out at this point, but Sullivan enjoyed his studies. He also liked that he went to boarding school, so he wasn't around his parents all that much. Even better, Pawpaw and Memaw would pick him up this afternoon, and he would spend a glorious eight weeks with them in Baker's Cove, a small coastal town in Maine. Those eight weeks each summer were his favorite time of year. His grandfather was a carpenter, and he had taught Sullivan from a young age how to craft wood, starting with whittling and then moving up to large projects.

If he had his heart's desire, he would become a carpenter and build cabinetry and furniture just like Pawpaw. It was all he wanted to do, but his parents would never allow that. His father was embarrassed by his humble roots, and his snobbish mother openly loathed her in-laws, referring to them as common laborers. Sullivan loved his paternal grandparents, though, and he believed he took after them in personality and looks. He also ascribed to their moral beliefs, meaning he treated others kindly and didn't worship at the altar of money.

Zane came bounding into the room, his face flushed, his T-shirt soaked.

"Been out on a run?" he asked his roommate and best friend.

Peeling off the shirt, Zane said, "Yeah. Trying to get in shape for the Fourth of July run."

Zane referred to the annual run in Driftwood Bay, a Texas coastal town where his grandparents lived. Every summer, Zane spent a little over a month in Driftwood Bay, his father's small hometown. Alexander Wagner was proud to have come from humble beginnings and encouraged his son to spend time with his parents in Texas. The couple owned the Driftwood Diner, and Zane put in a few hours each day, working as everything from busboy to dishwasher to short-order cook. The rest of the summer, Zane spent with his dad, traveling the world on business for Wagner Enterprises. His friend had seen far-flung places such as Japan, Germany, and Brazil. Sullivan couldn't help but envy Zane a little bit. Not just for the travel but the close bond he had with his dad.

"What's Harris doing this summer?" he asked.

Zane snorted. "Just because he's my brother doesn't mean I know anything that's going on with him."

Harris was two years their junior and had been kicked out of four different schools. He was supposed to attend Devonwood next year, and Zane was dreading being in the same place with his brother.

"I'm grabbing a quick shower, then we can head over for the Latin exam," Zane said, peeling away his running shorts, shoes, and socks. Grabbing a towel, he padded from the room, stark naked, heading to the communal bathroom at the end of the hall.

Sullivan looked through his Latin textbook and finally closed it. He knew his verb conjugations were spot on and felt confident he could translate any passage thrown at him during the final exam.

He opened his trunk, adding the last couple of items to it before closing the latch. Already, he was itching to see Pawpaw and Memaw and make the drive to Baker's Cove. It was about four hours away, but they would stop for a bowl of clam chowder and a lobster roll on the way, an annual tradition. Sullivan was grateful he had his grandparents in his life and wished he could see them more often. Summer was the only time he did, however. Other school breaks, his mother planned things for him. Still, he wrote his grandparents once a week and received a letter from them in reply. It would great if he could text or FaceTime them, but Devonwood's headmaster didn't allow cell phones on campus. In a way, he was happy about that, knowing how people were wedded to their phones and addicted to social media. He would leave school well-versed in the art of conversation, as well as clinging to the tradition of letter writing.

Zane appeared again, tossing off his towel and dressing hurriedly in their school uniform of dress shirt and pants, striped tie, and navy jacket. He ran his fingers through his jet-black hair.

"Ready?"

Sullivan nodded, picking up a couple of pens and slipping them into his inside lapel pocket. Blue books would be waiting for them. None of Devonwood's staff allowed computers or tablets in classrooms, regardless of the activity, so students learned to take notes by hand, using the Cornell method, and they wrote their essays in longhand. And cursive. Thank goodness he'd already learned cursive, a dying art, before he arrived at the Connecticut boarding school.

As they went downstairs, they said goodbye to a few boys who were already being picked up by parents. Stepping outside their dormitory, he saw several cars awaiting students. His grandparents wouldn't be here until after the world history exam was over. Even though he wasn't sitting for it, he didn't mind waiting for them to arrive. In fact, he'd probably sketch a few ideas for some of the furniture he wanted to tackle with Pawpaw this summer.

Then his gut flipped over, as he spied Bates, his father's longtime driver, leaning against a black Lincoln Town Car. The chauffeur spotted him and stood, closing the gap between them.

"What are you doing here?" Sullivan demanded, not caring that his tone sounded rude. "Pawpaw and Memaw are picking me up this afternoon."

"There has been a change of plans, Master Sullivan."

He hated being addressed that way, but Mother insisted that all their servants refer to him in that manner.

"What change?" he asked, tamping down his suspicions. He glanced to Zane, who merely shrugged.

"You're to accompany me home once you finish your exams. I just spoke to the headmaster and was cleared to take you back to Manhattan."

"But...when would I go to Maine?"

Bates looked apologetic as he said, "I am not certain as to the exact schedule for the summer, Master Sullivan."

His gaze pinned the driver's. "Come on, Bates. The staff knows everything. You hear and see and talk about everything among yourselves. Please. Clue me in."

For a moment, Bates hesitated, then he said, "You are fifteen. Old enough to be included in these conversations. Mrs. Shepherd has decided that you won't be going to Maine this summer." He paused. "Or any future summer."

"Not go—at all?" he asked, anger rippling through him.

Bates nodded. "I know you are to take a PSAT prep course. You also have riding lessons scheduled. And—"

"But I want to go to Maine," he protested. "I *need* to go there. It's what recharges me. Can you understand that?"

The chauffeur looked at him sympathetically. "It isn't for me to say, Master Sullivan."

He cursed under his breath, frustration filling him. He should have known this day was coming. His mother had put up a fuss last year when he had gone to Maine, saying he was wasting his time in such a pedestrian place.

In that moment, Sullivan hated his mother—and his father. Hated their phoniness and twisted values. Hated that they were keeping him from the two people he loved most.

Sullivan glanced down at his hands. These were the tools he loved. Pawpaw had taught him to work magic with them. They were supposed to build a China cabinet together this summer. A toy chest. He also had plans to work with a friend of Pawpaw's on a sailboat.

Glancing at Bates, he reined in his rage. The chauffeur didn't deserve any blame for this decision. He was simply the middleman, sent to bring Sullivan home.

Except that he wasn't going there.

"I've got to get to my Latin exam," he said. "You can go upstairs to my dorm room and bring down my trunk. My initials are on the top."

He told the driver what room he was in, and Bates said he would place it in the car's trunk.

"Come on," Sullivan told Zane.

As they walked off, he said, "I'm not going home. And you're going to help me."

Zane flashed him a look of understanding. "Any way I can. I wish I could sneak you down to the Bay with me."

On the way, Sullivan began devising a plan on how to make his escape. They reached their Latin classroom, and he parted from Zane, going to his assigned seat. Two minutes later, the teacher closed the door and passed out the blue books. Sullivan dutifully wrote his name on the front of his. He accepted the exam the teacher handed him and raced through it. He knew the two translations he completed had no errors in them, and he was familiar with every verb and conjugated them appropriately, flying through deponent and semi-deponent verbs with ease.

Once he completed his exam, he looked over everything, making one change, then stood and walked to the teacher's desk, creating the stack since he was the first to finish.

"Enjoy your summer, Mr. Shepherd."

Sullivan left the classroom, pushing Latin aside so that he could concentrate on how to get to Maine. Though his grandparents were no longer on their way, he couldn't necessarily make that assumption. Knowing Mother, she would have deliberately kept the plans she had made for her son quiet and would think it amusing that her in-laws drove four hours to retrieve their grandson, only to find him already gone.

He went upstairs, where several teachers had their offices, and went into the first one. Locking the door, he called the familiar number. His heart sank as he heard Memaw answer.

"Hello?"

"Memaw, it's Sullivan."

"Oh, my dear boy, I'm so grateful to hear your voice. Honey, Sullivan's calling. Go get on the other phone."

He heard the extension click and said, "Hey, Pawpaw."

"Well, we weren't expecting to hear from you."

"I ran into Bates on my way to my Latin final. He told me I'm not coming to Maine this summer."

A long pause occurred, and then Memaw said, "Your

mother thinks that it's best if you stay in the city. She has some plans for you."

"I don't want to do anything that woman has planned. I'm fifteen. She can't decide my life for me."

"She can, Sullivan," Pawpaw said gently. "She's your mother. Like it or not, you're still a minor. Don't worry. We'll see you sometime. Hopefully, soon."

"Not if she has anything to say about it," he said bitterly. "You know what she's like. The only reason she hasn't kept me from you before now is that she and Father travel a lot during the summer. All you are is a babysitter to her." He sighed. "I want to see you. Be in Maine. Make things with my hands. That's what I'm meant to do."

"Oh, Sullivan, you aren't meant to be a carpenter. You'll go to college like your daddy," Pawpaw said. "You're even smarter than he was."

"I don't want to go," he said stubbornly. "I want to craft in wood."

"No, you will go to college," Memaw said firmly. "It's an advantage not everyone has. Get your degree. By then, you'll be an adult and on your own. You can decide what your future will be when that time comes. Don't rock the boat now, honey."

"I better go," he said. "I'll see you soon."

They just didn't know how soon.

Sullivan hung up and left the office. He went downstairs and sat on a bench, waiting for Zane to finish.

Five minutes later, his friend appeared. "So, what's the plan?"

Quickly, he explained how he didn't have to take his world history exam.

"I'll get in the car with Bates. Have him raise the privacy window. Then when we get to the gate, he'll have to roll down his window and return the laminated visitor placard to the guard. That's when you show up. Knock on my window. I'll open the door. Make up some reason you need to tell me something. Then when Bates turns back to the guard, that's when I'll bail."

"And then?"

"He'll drive off. It's at least three-and-a-half hours back to the city. I'll tell him I'm gonna sleep, so he won't bother me."

"Where will you be instead?" Zane asked.

"Hitching a ride to Maine," he replied.

"You know they'll come after you."

Glumly, he said, "Yeah. But at least I can see Memaw and Pawpaw before I'm caught in Dante's Nine Circles of Hell."

His friend laughed. "I say go for it. I'll do my part."

They walked back to their dorm, seeing more fellow students leaving. Sullivan told Zane goodbye and then walked up to the car where Bates waited. The chauffeur tucked his cell into his pocket.

"I have your trunk, Master Sullivan."

"Could I at least be Sullivan when Mother and Father aren't around?"

The driver bit back a smile. "Of course."

He got into the town car, knowing that Bates would be in big trouble once his parents found out Sullivan wasn't in the car. He doubted they would fire the driver, though. He'd been with them too long and knew too much dirt about the family.

Bates got behind the wheel and started the vehicle, heading toward the gatehouse at the edge of the property.

"Could you raise the privacy screen, Bates? I was up way late studying last night. I'm going to try and catch up on my sleep on the way back."

"Of course, Sullivan."

The chauffeur touched a button, and the screen began

rising. Sullivan's heart began beating in double time. He knew what he was doing was dead wrong.

But he was going to do it anyway.

The car slowed, and he prayed that Zane was ready to step in and do his part. Suddenly a rap sounded on the window, and he opened the door. He couldn't see Bates, but Zane stood there.

"Here. I forgot to give you my grandparents' new number in case you have a chance to call this summer so we can catch up."

As Zane spoke, Sullivan rolled from the car and dropped to the ground, moving behind the car, even as he heard the security guard telling Bates goodbye. He raced to a nearby tree with a broad trunk and heard his friend say, "We'll talk soon. Bye!"

Leaning around, Sullivan watched Zane close the door. "Okay, Bates," he called. "Bye!"

The town car pulled through the gates which the security guard had opened. He hadn't thought about having to scale the fence. His gaze met Zane's, and his friend seemed to know what to do.

Zane hurried to the security window, standing so the guard's vision was blocked. Sullivan took off, managing to get through the gates just before they closed. He scrambled to the right, praying Bates didn't look in his rearview mirror as the town car sped down the road to the left. Keeping to the wall, Sullivan moved alongside it, hugging it until he knew he was out of sight.

Then he began walking along the road. He planned to hitchhike to Baker's Cove. In every movie he'd seen with hitchhikers involved, that was always a mistake, but he didn't care.

Fortunately, he'd only walked about two miles when an eighteen wheeler approached from behind him. He held out his thumb, hoping the truck's driver would stop.

He did.

Relief swept through Sullivan as he approached, and the driver rolled down the window.

"Where ya off to?"

"Maine."

"Going that way myself. Portland."

Eagerness filled him. "I'm heading to Baker's Cove. It's a few towns before Portland."

"A-yuh. Know it. Have a brotha who lives there. Get in, kid."

Sullivan did.

The trucker was friendly. Had a son a year younger than Sullivan. They had a decent conversation before a natural silence blanketed them. When they got to Baker's Cove, the trucker stopped at a light.

"I'll get out here."

"Take care of yourself, kid."

"Will do. Thanks again."

He walked the two miles to his grandparent's house, a cottage near the water. As he approached the shop which sat next to the house, he could hear the whine of a sander. Sullivan paused in the open doorway, breathing in the scent.

The shop smelled like home.

For a moment, he drank in the sight of Pawpaw, then he stepped inside. He doubted he would be in Maine for long.

But he was here now.

Chapter One

KANSAS CITY

Piper Roberts was going to make the most of this performance. She had been touring the country in this current production for nine months now. After ten years on the road, she had worked her way up from the company to featured roles to that of lead actress with top billing. She was living the dreams of her youth. Yet she had come to realize she was both happy and incredibly miserable at the same time.

Because of that, she had decided to go home.

Driftwood Bay had begun calling out to her a couple of years ago. Her hometown on the Texas Gulf Coast had been a sweet place to grow up. Swimming and fishing. Riding her bike everywhere. Singing in the choir at church and school. Dancing on the drill team and serving as editor of the *Pirate Press*, the school's newspaper.

But she had yearned for a life outside the Bay. One of performing. Traveling the US and singing in both classic and contemporary musicals. After only two years, she broke out of the chorus and gained supporting roles in G*rease*. *Mamma*

Mia. *School of Rock*. Then had come lead roles. Christine in *Phantom of the Opera*. Satine in *Moulin Rouge*. Galinda in *Wicked*. And finally, Roxie Hart in *Chicago*.

It was hard to reconcile how much she enjoyed performing with how lonely life on the road could be. Constant travel. A different city every few weeks, one you never really got to see. While travel and performing had appealed to her at twenty, when she had dropped out of college to join a traveling production of *Hairspray*, suddenly her twenties were gone. At thirty, she had no permanent address. Everything she owned fit into two suitcases and a backpack.

More importantly, she longed to put down roots.

Her closest friends since preschool, Mila and Layne, had done just that. All three girls had been eager to escape the small confines of the Bay and spread their wings. Eventually, Mila returned, serving as their alma mater's head volleyball coach. She had married a fellow coach last Thanksgiving and was a stepmom to Lily. Layne, who'd had a dazzling business career in Dallas, had also returned to the Bay, inheriting her parents' Bay Breeze Inn, and finding love with Keaton, a local artist.

Layne and Keaton would be in today's audience, cheering on Piper's final appearance on the stage. She would then accompany them back to Driftwood Bay and figure out what she wanted to do with the rest of her life. While doing so, she would serve as temporary manager of the Bay Breeze. She looked forward to being in her hometown once more, spending time with her closest friends.

Piper finished applying her makeup and donned the wig she wore to play Roxie. She glanced in the mirror a final time, ready to give this last matinee her all.

Minutes later, she was onstage. As Roxie. Not Piper. Piper was an actress who could immediately immerse herself into a character. During a performance, she never had a Piper thought in her head. Everything from her posture to her mannerisms to what she was thinking was that of whatever role she had taken.

She sang and danced her way through everything from *Funny Honey* to *We Both Reached for the Gun* to *Me and My Baby*. It was only when she began to sing *Nowadays* that it almost seemed like an out of body experience. She had read stories of severely injured people dying on the operating table and rising above, watching as medical personnel tried to save them, and then returning to their bodies.

That was what this number felt like as she heard herself singing, her voice rich and full of emotion. It was almost as if she were a separate person, watching someone else perform.

And thinking she was pretty darn good.

Roxie and Velma finished the song, and Piper seemed to float back into her body. The reprise ending the musical became a blur, and she took her bows along with the cast, then a separate bow recognizing her own performance. She floated off-stage into the wings, adrenaline rushing through her, bringing a natural high.

Waiting for her was Eric, who had played Billy Flynn in the production. He gave her a quick kiss.

"One for the books, Piper."

She smiled. "It sure was."

She and Eric had been a couple for the last two months. Attachments formed on the road and could be swift and heady. These relationships fizzled quickly, though, as actors moved on to new productions and cities. Piper liked Eric. She thought him witty and fun to be around, but they both knew last night had been an end for them.

"You going back to New York?" she asked.

He shook his head. "LA. I just landed an audition for Fiyero!"

"Ooh, a featured role in *Wicked*?" Piper threw her arms around him, hugging him tightly. "I hope you get it, Eric. No, I know you will. Your voice has never sounded better. When would touring begin?"

"In ten days. The guy they cast was hit by a car on the way to rehearsals. He broke both his legs. The understudy had just left to take another role, so they're in a bind. I'm flying out tonight and will read for the role tomorrow afternoon."

"Break a leg," she said. Grinning, she added, "But not two."

Eric brushed his lips against her cheek. "I had fun with you, Piper. See ya."

She left for her dressing room, realizing that Eric hadn't even asked what she would be doing next. Their relationship had been very surface. Trying a new restaurant. Bingeing something together on Netflix. And great sex. Conversation hadn't really played into things. These temporary road relationships rarely grew serious. And now that Mila was married and Layne was getting married soon, Piper wanted more than surface. She wanted a deep dive, where she really got to know someone. Although she doubted the dating pool in the Bay would be large, hopefully, she might find somebody she had something in common with and get to know them. Share things with them.

And maybe find love.

Quickly, she removed her stage makeup, always glad to get it off her skin so it could breathe. She'd just taken off her Roxie costume when she heard a knock at the door and threw a robe on so she could answer the door.

Layne was on the other side, and Piper threw herself at her friend, clutching her tightly.

"I'm so glad you're here," she said.

"You were fantastic!" Layne declared. "We loved your performance."

She released her friend and smiled at Keaton. "You're even better looking than on FaceTime," she teased, giving him a hug. "It's nice to meet you in person."

"Good to meet you, Piper," Keaton said. "You're electrifying on stage."

Piper glowed at the compliment. "Thank you. Come on in. Let me change."

She stepped behind a screen, tossing on a shirt and her favorite pair of jeans as they talked about the musical. Emerging, she put on socks and boots.

"You still have those boots?" Layne asked. "They look like they're in great shape."

"I enjoy wearing them. They're fifteen years old. Once I broke them in, they felt like house shoes. Besides, they take up a lot of room, so it's easier to wear them than pack them."

Layne touched her forearm. "How are you feeling about coming back to the Bay? Leaving the theater world behind?"

She sighed. "Honestly? I've got mixed emotions. This has been my life for a decade. That's a long time. My entire twenties were spent on the road. I've enjoyed professional success." Her gaze met Layne's. "But you know something about that."

Her friend had helped build a business in Dallas, only to see it bought and find herself out of a job. Worse, Layne discovered on the same day that her longtime boyfriend had been cheating on her and that her parents had died by suicide.

"I do," Layne said quietly, reaching for Keaton's hand. "Fortunately, this guy came into my life, and I'm the better for it. He's not only helped me restore the Bay Breeze, but he's saved me in every way."

Keaton lifted their joined hands and pressed a kiss to

Layne's knuckles. "We saved each other," he said, his voice low and rough.

For a moment, the couple drank one another in, and Piper felt the palpable heat between them. A bit of envy stirred within her. She was happy her friend had found a partner, but she longed for a relationship herself.

"Let's get out of here," she told the pair.

"Need to say your goodbyes to anyone?" Keaton asked as they left the dressing room.

"Actually? No. Most of those were said last night after the performance. Theater people can be odd ducks. We have tight bonds, but once a show's run is done? We move on and don't make a big deal of a production being over."

"Any friendships you're leaving behind?" Layne asked. "Or a romance?"

Piper smiled mysteriously. "You'll never know."

She rode with them the few blocks to the hotel where the cast and crew were staying. Keaton checked them in, while Layne accompanied Piper to her room.

Glancing around, her friend said, "It looks as if you've pretty much got everything packed."

"I told you I travel pretty light."

"Are you sure you want to manage the inn?" Layne asked. "You don't have to."

"I want to. It'll be nice, being useful, as I try to figure out what I want to do when I grow up."

They both laughed, and Piper added, "You know I'm taking the job simply because it comes with that big suite. That way, I don't have to be thirty and moving back in with my parents. I still can't believe Mom and Dad are going to retire at the end of May."

"I was a little surprised by that," Layne admitted. "I don't think of your parents as old. Or Mila's. But Dr. Perry has already given his notice to the schoolboard that he'll wrap up his career in June. They'll have to start the hunt for a new superintendent."

"What about Mrs. Perry?" she asked.

"She's going to keep the boutique. For now. Just not go in as often. I have the feeling that Dr. P will want to travel some, along with your parents. Mrs. Perry will need to hire a full-time manager for Coastal Charm."

"Hmm. Who knows? If I'm good at this managing thing, maybe I can run the boutique for Mrs. Perry."

Layne's phone chimed. She glanced at her cell. "Keaton has us checked in and is waiting in the lobby, ready to take us to dinner."

"Great. I'm starving. I usually am after a performance."

They met him in the lobby, and he asked where they might want to go for dinner.

"Do you mind if it's somewhere quiet?" Piper asked. "I'm hungry, but I'm also coming down from an adrenaline high. Any particular food you like, Keaton?"

"He's a great cook," Layne said. "He probably likes what he cooks himself the most. But we're open to anything."

"There's a great Italian place about four blocks from the hotel," she told them. "It's a little pricey, though."

"I'm buying," Keaton said. "To celebrate your last performance."

"I appreciate that. Let's walk. It's not worth driving such a short distance. Plus, I don't think we'll run into anyone from the touring company there. At the end of a run, a lot of people go back to the hotel and crash. Order takeout. Or they actually fly out tonight, ready to begin their next job."

Layne slipped an arm around Piper. "I'm glad you're taking a break and coming back to the Bay to decompress."

"It's not just a break," Piper told her friend. "I don't think

I'll ever go back to musical theater. It's so transient. Don't laugh—but I'm ready to sink my roots back into the Bay. You and Mila have already done so."

Her friend squeezed Piper. "I'm so glad you're coming home."

They arrived at the restaurant, and Keaton eagerly scoured the menu. The two women told him to order appetizers for the table, and soon they were dining on toasted ravioli and fried calamari, with garlic cheese bread reserved for their entrees. Piper got an Italian potato dumpling pasta with vodka sauce, and she took her time savoring it. Usually, meals were rushed affairs, so it was nice to slow down and truly enjoy her food.

Keaton insisted they have dessert, so she ordered an Italian risotto cheesecake topped with baby strawberries. They lingered over their desserts, sipping coffee, as Layne and Keaton caught her up on various individuals in the Bay.

As they strolled back to their hotel, Keaton said, "I'm not rushing you, but you might want to explore some of the job opportunities that will be available once Tidewater opens."

"Oh, the new resort?"

"The new resort for the über rich," Layne said. "It's going to draw a wealthy crowd who will want to be catered to. They're still a ways from hiring staff, but there will be a ton of jobs available. We can ask Sullivan about it."

"Sullivan?" Piper asked.

"He's a friend of mine," Keaton said. "The architect of Tidewater. Works for Wagner Enterprises, which builds luxury resorts around the world. He'll have the inside track on the kinds of jobs available. When recruitment and interviews will start."

"You'll like him, Piper," Layne said. "Sullivan is smart and funny and a really nice guy." She paused. "Maybe we could set the two of you up."

"No," she protested. "No setups. Just let me move back to the Bay and start figuring out my life. Once I know what I want to pursue, then I might think about stirring a guy into the mix. Besides, I'm finally ready to go long-term in a relationship. I'm sure Sullivan will simply move on from the resort once Tidewater is completed."

"Well, you'll wind up meeting him anyway," Layne said. "We see a lot of him, Mila, and Carson. In fact, we can have everyone over for dinner this next week."

"Aren't you planning your wedding?" she asked.

"There's not much to plan. We're keeping it super-simple. Besides I've got your mom and Mila's organizing everything. We'll have time to have people over for dinner."

"I am looking forward to seeing your house. I remember riding my bike past it and thinking how cool it would be to live there, right on the water. And I'm definitely eager to see the B&B and all you've done to it."

"You'll recognize it. We tried to retain its charm while updating it," Layne said. "I'm really proud of how it turned out. And reservations are already pouring in."

"Good. I'm going to like keeping busy. Even if you are insisting I take cooking lessons."

"Cooking's actually fun," her friend said. "Especially if you have a great teacher like Keaton."

They entered the hotel and made plans to meet downstairs at six. Keaton had suggested getting on the road early in order to avoid Kansas City's morning rush, then they would stop somewhere after an hour or so to have breakfast. The drive would be long, but they planned to make it in one day.

"See you in the morning," Piper said, giving both a hug. She was already comfortable with Keaton. It helped that he had joined in some of their FaceTime chats and she had already begun to know him, but in person, he was really a terrific guy.

Piper returned to her hotel room for the final night of sleep. She lay awake a long time, wondering what her thirties would bring. Her twenties had been professionally fulfilling and full of adventure, but she was ready for a slower pace and more personal satisfaction.

Hopefully, she would decide on new dreams—and find them in Driftwood Bay.

When Piper went to the lobby the next morning, she found Layne waiting.

"Keaton's gone to get the truck," her friend said. Her cell chimed, and Layne glanced at it. "Okay. He's outside. Here, I'll roll one of your suitcases for you."

She followed Layne out the front doors of the hotel, a little sad to be leaving her old life behind. She had become comfortable with it, but she was ready for new challenges.

Keaton lifted her two suitcases with ease, placing them in the bed of the truck. Piper kept her backpack and climbed into the back of the cab as Layne joined her husband in the front.

They talked for a few minutes, and then she noticed the direction they were headed. It was in her nature to be organized, and she had called up the directions to the Bay on her map app last night, wanting to see where they would pass.

"Uh, Keaton. Wait. I think you took a wrong turn."

"Nope," he said cheerfully. "The airport is this way."

"Airport?" she said. "I'm confused."

Layne swiveled around. "Keaton knows the trip is about

fourteen hours, and that's with no stops. We took two days to drive up so we wouldn't be so exhausted." She glanced over, smiling. "So, he decided to fly you and me to Corpus."

"Wow! You *are* a keeper. If Layne hadn't already laid claim to you, I think I'd want you for myself," Piper declared.

"You just ended a long tour," Keaton told her. "You're exhausted. You and Layne have a lot to do and go over regarding running the inn. Plus, there's the wedding next week. I thought it would be easier to fly you ladies home. I'll drive straight through, just stopping for gas and grabbing a few snacks. If I have smooth sailing, I should be back in the Bay by nine or ten tonight. I'll bring your luggage. Why don't you stay with us tonight? That way, you can see the house, and if I get home later than planned, Layne will have some company, and she can even loan you some PJs."

"This is amazing. You're the best, Keaton."

They entered the airport, and he dropped them at their terminal. Layne kissed him goodbye, and Piper hugged him tightly.

"I've already arranged for a ride home, so you ladies don't need to rent a car or do a ride share."

"Okay, where can I clone this guy, Layne? I want one just like him," she joked.

"I shared your boarding passes to your wallet," Keaton told Layne. "Also forwarded the email confirmation. Holler if you need anything." He kissed her. "See you late tonight."

Check-in was a breeze since neither of them carried any luggage. Piper even left her backpack in the truck, feeling footloose and fancy-free. They went through security and found a place to grab coffee and croissants, which they took to their gate.

Once they settled into their seats, she said, "Not that I had any doubts—but if I did—Keaton dispelled every one of them with such thoughtfulness."

Layne smiled. "He's been like that from the beginning, Piper. I was the lowest I've ever been. I swear I cried more the day I ran into him than I had in the previous thirty years total. Keaton rolled with everything. He's smart. Nurturing. And talented as hell. Sometimes, I wonder how I could get so lucky."

"You deserve every good thing that comes your way," Piper insisted. "You're going to have a wonderful, strong marriage with an amazing man. I hope I'll get to know him well enough to call him friend."

"He can be a little on the quiet side, but he's really opened up around you. I know you didn't get to come to Mila's wedding because of touring, but you're going to see how great she and Carson are together, too. And we're going to find you a terrific guy, Piper. Maybe he'll be a teacher at the high school with Mila and Carson. Or a cop from your dad's police department. It could even be someone new to the Bay who lands a job at Tidewater. The manager. The chef. A hot tennis pro."

"I hadn't thought about all the staff which will be needed at the new resort. I might need to look into it. See what might be available. After all, I'll be coming from hospitality myself, managing a B&B," she teased.

"Sullivan can help you there, "Layne said. "As the architect, he'll know every nook and cranny of Tidewater. Plus, he's designed several resorts for Wagner Enterprises. You can pick his brain at dinner."

"I plan to do that."

They boarded their flight, and Piper pulled up her Kindle app on her phone.

Layne leaned over. "What romance novel are you reading now?"

"I'm on a Regency kick. I was reading romantasy for a while, but I cut my teeth on Regency historicals back in high school. No matter how many times I read a romantic suspense or a small-town romance series—or even a medieval or historical western—I always seem to loop around to my beloved Regencies. Give me a hot duke in a *ton* ballroom, and it's like I'm addicted all over again."

She buried herself in her novel, only pausing to order a sparkling water and accepting the biscotti the flight attend passed to her. The plane made a stopover in Dallas, but they didn't even have to deplane. Some passengers got off, while other ones got on. Then their flight left for Corpus. By the time they reached their destination, the total trip had only been a little over three hours.

Layne called Keaton the moment they hit the tarmac, learning he was in Oklahoma City. She told him they had just landed and that she would wait up for him, no matter how late he arrived.

"Love you, too," Layne said, ending the call. "I wonder who he has picking us up. It's a school day, so it won't be Mila or Carson. Maybe Sullivan."

They left the plane and went through the doors separating the gates from the rest of the terminal, and Piper squealed, running and throwing herself in her dad's arms. He lifted her off the ground, swinging her around.

"How's my little girl?" he asked.

"Better, now that I've seen you. Oh, Dad. I'm so glad you're here."

"Not half as glad as I am, baby. Hey, Layne."

"Hi, Chief. I'm glad Keaton called you. He didn't tell us who'd be picking us up. This is a nice surprise."

"It was fun cooking it up."

Dad slipped an arm about each of them. "Come on, girls.

Maybe if you're lucky, I'll use the lights and siren and get us home faster."

They laughed, accompanying him to his department-issued vehicle. On the way home, he asked a dozen questions about her last few months.

"I'm glad your mom and I flew out to see you perform in San Diego. Are you gonna miss singing and acting, honey?"

"Probably," she admitted for the first time. "But right now, I'm running on empty. I needed a break from the stage. Being a nomad isn't all it's cracked up to be."

"Layne tells me you're gonna manage the Bay Breeze for her."

"I am. I'll be living there. The manager needs to be on site." Piper made sure to mention this so there'd be no talk about her moving home. "But tell me about retirement. Do you and Mom have any trips planned?"

"Two," he said, grinning at her. "We're going to go to Yellowstone. I've always wanted to see Old Faithful and all the other geysers and hot springs. We'll do a little hiking and even some horseback riding."

"You know, Keaton lived in the Grand Tetons," Layne said. "I don't think that's too far from Yellowstone. You might want to talk to him and extend your trip a little."

"Not a bad idea. We don't have a timetable. Except for going with Bill and Laura on a river cruise."

"Ooh. Where? When?" Piper asked.

"It's something your mom and Laura cooked up," Dad explained. "Bill and I are just along for the ride. We'll be gone the first week of December, cruising along the Rhine River. It's Christmas market time, so the ladies want to see all the markets and do their Christmas shopping. It's mostly in Germany, but we will also see a little of Switzerland and France."

"Boy, I'm already jealous of this retirement," she said. "Two fun trips planned. I'm glad to hear it, Dad. You and Mom never really go much of anywhere. And that's crazy, with Don being a travel writer."

Her brother was ten years older. Because of the age gap, she and Don had never been close. Still, she followed him online, where he wrote a travel blog. He'd also authored numerous travel guides, concentrating mostly on Asia and Eastern Europe.

"Your brother is actually going to meet us in Basel, where the cruise embarks. We're coming in a few days early, and he'll take us to Lake Lucerne. It'll give our bodies time to acclimate to a new time zone seven hours ahead, plus we'll also get to visit with Don."

Dad looked to Layne. "Tell me about the Bay Breeze. I know you've been working hard to finish the renovation."

"It'll open soon. We painted the entire interior and exterior. All new furniture. The floors have been refinished. It's got a new HVAC system. The bathrooms and kitchen were pretty much gutted and redone. It's fresh and modern, yet it still retains all of its small-town charm."

Piper began asking questions about the inn, and Layne easily answered them. They were still talking about it when they arrived in Driftwood Bay. It had been years since she had been here, and she fell silent, studying the passing scenery.

"Some things have changed, but I still recognize most of what I'm seeing."

Layne nodded. "I was the same way. I hadn't come back often to visit. My fault. Jeremy didn't like it here. He thought it was too boring, and I let him influence me. You'll see a few new shops on the square. The Sonic has expanded some. They've also added on a new wing to the high school. Other than that, the Bay is the Bay."

She liked that. It was good to come home and be familiar

with where she was. Piper rolled down her window and took in a deep breath, catching the scent of salt and sea.

"Oh, I've missed the water," she declared.

Of the three friends, Piper had been the one who most enjoyed living near the beach. The Gulf seemed to run in her blood.

"I feel centered," she said.

"Keaton is the same way," Layne said. "He grew up in Dallas before moving to the mountains. Had never lived near the water, yet when he arrived in the Bay, he said it spoke to his soul. It calms him. Helps him to focus. That's why he was so eager to find oceanfront property and move permanently to where he could wake up and see the waves washing onto the shore."

"I'm gonna drop you girls off at your house, Layne," Dad said. "Ellen will make a beeline over here as soon as she gets out of school since I told her I was picking you two up."

"Why don't I order pizza?" Layne suggested. "You and Mrs. Roberts can come for dinner. I'll ask Mila, Carson, and Lily to come, too."

"Pizza is always fine by me," Dad said as he pulled into the circular drive in front of the house. "I'll head over here when I get off work."

They got out of his SUV and waved as he drove off. Layne was already texting Mila, who answered right away, saying they would come by around five.

"I'll go ahead and put in an order with Pizza Perfecto," Layne said, unlocking the door and leading them inside.

Piper was impressed with the house. Not just because it was large and had a wonderful floor plan, but it already looked like a home.

"I can see your touches here," she told her friend. I know you haven't lived here long, but it's homey."

"We'll gradually add to each room. We don't want to rush it."

She walked to the wall of floor to ceiling windows, which overlooked the water. "This is a spectacular view!"

"It's nourishing for Keaton's soul. He's itching to get back to painting after all the work he did on the inn. Though he had enjoyed getting his hands dirty again, with placing backsplash and sanding floors, he's definitely ready to begin his next series of landscapes. Let me call in our order, and then I'll give you the grand tour."

Once she had seen the entire house, Piper said, "I would live outside. This outdoor kitchen. This view. And it's great that Keaton has a studio which is separate from the house."

"He likes the space. The light." Layne chuckled. "And the commute."

They returned to the great room and talked some about the wedding and the honeymoon.

"We won't go unless you feel perfectly comfortable running the B&B," Layne said.

"I'm going to be fine. Your honeymoon sounds amazing. While I've been all over the country with touring, I never got to really see any of the places I performed in. I may have to see the US first, then I'll work on Europe."

"Keaton and I have never left the country. That's why I'm excited about seeing Italy and France." Layne sighed. "Actually, I'm just happy to be wherever Keaton is. We could stay home, here in the Bay the rest of our lives, and I'd be perfectly content."

"Hey, go and do while you can. Before kids come." Piper paused. "Unless perhaps there's already one on the way?"

Layne laughed. "Not yet. But I think we'll be trying soon. We're ready to fill this house with little Maxwells."

"And Auntie Piper will spoil every last one of them."

The doorbell rang, and Piper said, "Let me get it."

She opened the door, finding her mom on the porch. They hugged one another tightly.

"I can't believe you're here, Piper. You're finally here."

"Hopefully, I'll be staying, Mom. Come on in."

"In the kitchen," called Layne.

They entered, and she saw Layne had opened a bottle of wine and was now taking out crackers and cheese.

"We can nibble and talk," she said.

They did so for the next hour, and Piper's gut told her coming home had been the best move. Especially with her parents retiring soon, she would be able to spend more time with them. While the Bay Breeze would take up some of her time, she didn't think it would be like a full-time job.

Soon, her dad returned, and the Andrews' family arrived right after him. Pizza Perfecto delivered five pizzas with varying toppings, and they all grabbed slices as Layne poured iced teas for everyone.

As she sat eating and talking with her parents and friends, Piper knew she had been meant to return to Driftwood Bay.

Now, she was eager to see what this next chapter in her life brought.

Chapter Three

Sullivan finished polishing the coffee table, the first piece of furniture he had crafted in years. Bitterness swelled within him, thinking how much he had enjoyed the summers he spent with Pawpaw and Memaw in Baker's Cove.

And how his mother had put an end to all of it.

Jacqueline Shepherd had insisted that her son stop going to Maine to see his paternal grandparents, putting him in all kinds of activities that she believed would benefit him socially. He'd appealed to his father, but Oliver Shepherd stood united with his wife on the issue. He explained that during Sullivan's teen years, he needed to prepare for college and beyond. It was important to participate in the right activities. Be seen with the right people. Do the right things. Mother constantly reminded him that since Thurston wasn't around to do these things, Sullivan was doing everything for the both of them.

Since he was a minor, he had no say in the matter. That summer, instead of making furniture with Pawpaw and canning fruits with Memaw, he'd done a PSAT prep course. He began taking lessons in Mandarin and sailing. His parents had been gone during all of June and July, but they had returned in August, taking him to Martha's Vineyard. He was forced to go to the country club and parties. Sullivan did it all with a smile on his face, plotting ways to return to his grandparents the next summer. He even took up running, saying he wanted to train for a marathon, just so he could be out of the house and not around anyone.

It hadn't mattered. By the next summer, both his grandparents were dead.

He rubbed his hand along the smooth wood, thinking the hours he had put into making the coffee table had been some of the best he had spent in years. It felt right to hold wood in his hands again. To make something from nothing. Crafting furniture filled a place in his soul which had been starving for a long time.

He cleaned up the shop, setting the coffee table next to the door. Pulling out his phone, he snapped a few pictures of the table from different angles. Then he created an album on his phone.

Sullivan's Furniture.

He might never create another piece again, but at least he had this coffee table to be proud of.

Taking one last glance around the shop, he turned off the lights and locked the door. He decided to stop by the Driftwood Diner and return Neville's key since his time in the Bay was drawing to an end. The last surge of work would pick up in the next month, and then he'd leave the Gulf Coast.

For a while, he had toyed with the idea of staying in Driftwood Bay, liking the friendliness of the small, coastal town. He'd become close to a local artist, Keaton Maxwell, and the high school's basketball coach, Carson Andrews. He had even volunteered to draw up the plans for a house for Carson, which he and Mila would move into soon once it was completed in a couple of weeks. He'd even thrown out a name —Sullivan Design Studio. He had thought he might be able to build furniture for a living, while putting his architecture degree to use on the side and design a home every now and then.

Then he'd had second thoughts. It seemed foolish to waste his degree, staying in the Bay. He also worried that he might come to resent giving up his position with a renown, world-wide company. Sullivan had designed resorts in the US, as well as ones in Thailand, South Africa, and Japan. Wagner Enterprises had given him opportunities that allowed him to use his imagination. He flexed his creative muscles and challenged himself with each new, multimillion dollar project. To go from a career which paid him an ungodly amount of money and kept him fulfilled and busy to a quiet life in a small town seemed ridiculous. Maybe one day, far in the future, he could retire to a spot such as Driftwood Bay. Tinker around and carve the occasional piece of furniture. Sullivan Design Studio was just a pipe dream. He'd leave here and get caught back up in his professional life.

Sadness filled him, knowing he didn't have much of a personal one waiting for him in New York. He shook it off, though. Everyone had to make trade-offs in life. Most people would envy him, with his high-profile job and luxury apartment. He needed to appreciate what he had—and not hanker for something that probably wouldn't satisfy him.

He drove the few blocks to the diner and entered. Zane's grandparents, Neville and Nellie, had run the place for decades. It was interesting how his best friend's summers had paralleled his own, with Zane coming to Driftwood Bay for several weeks once school let out. Zane had fond memories of this small town, and he had been the one to push for one of Wagner Enterprise's upscale resorts to be built just off the coast of

Driftwood Bay. It had also been Zane who approved Sullivan's request to remain here during construction of Tidewater.

Usually, Sullivan designed a resort over several months, visiting the site so he could take into consideration where the property would be built and incorporating the area into his design. Once the design had the green light, he would again travel to and be onsite in the early stages when they broke ground. Once things were underway, he returned to his apartment in Manhattan, one he shared with Zane. The Wagner corporate office was located in the city, and he could walk to work. Zane was rarely home, usually halfway around the globe, scouting locations for future resorts or office buildings. When they were in town together, Sullivan treasured those times, especially since Zane had been briefly married. The marriage was a disaster from the beginning, and his friend had moved back in with Sullivan as soon as it ended.

He parked and entered the diner. Nellie greeted him with a hug.

"How's my coffee table coming?" she asked.

"I finished it." He fished out his cell and brought up the pictures. "What do you think?"

She studied the photo. "Honey, you did a wonderful job. I can't wait to show it off to my friends! Now, you're gonna need to make me two end tables to match. I can put 'em on each side of the sofa."

Sullivan wanted to say he probably wouldn't be in town long enough to complete a pair, but he didn't want to have that conversation right now.

"I'll check my schedule and see," he told her.

"You want some coffee? A bite to eat?"

"Maybe a coffee to go. I need to get over to Tidewater. Just wanted to let you know I was done. I think I'll go say hi to Neville."

"Coffee coming up," Nellie said cheerfully.

He went to the kitchen, where Neville was frying bacon in one pan and eggs in another.

"You done?" the old man asked.

Holding up his phone, he allowed Neville to study the photo.

"Damn fine job. Better than I could've done. Your granddaddy taught you well."

"He sure did." Fishing out the key to the shop, he handed it over. "I want to thank you for letting me tinker in the shop. It felt good, working with wood again."

"You can keep it for now," Neville said, flipping the eggs over as he refused the key. Then he studied Sullivan. "Unless you're leaving soon."

"Probably. The resort is coming along. They're about to start posting positions."

"Well, you're welcome to use the shop whenever you like, for as long as you like. I guess Zane'll be coming into town soon if things are wrapping up."

"Not for a bit. But you're right, he'll arrive before the resort opens. He'll want to see into every nook and cranny. Learn everyone employee's name. Test out items on the menu. Sleep in a few rooms and see how the maids clean them. I may be gone by the time he arrives, though."

Neville scooped up the eggs and plated them, along with the bacon. He transferred a generous pile of hash browns to the plate and then set it in the window, tapping the bell which sat nearby. A server retrieved it.

"We've enjoyed having you in the Bay, Sullivan," the old man said, his eyes misting over. "You're our honorary grandson now."

Sullivan grinned. "I should be. I've eaten enough meals here. I appreciate how you and Nellie have looked out for me while I've been here. Even rented me the room above the diner."

"You're welcome to stay as long as you like. And keep the shop key."

"Order up!" a server called out.

"You're busy. Talk later," he said, leaving the kitchen.

Nellie handed him his coffee. "One sugar and plenty of cream."

"Just as I like it. Thanks, Nellie."

He left the diner, returning to his car and driving to the water. Tidewater sat on an island almost two miles off the coast and was only reachable by the local ferry. Sullivan had factored in that some people might want to fly in by helicopter, though, and had made certain a helipad was a part of his final plans for the resort. The island didn't have room for a runway, so guests would either fly to Corpus and have a member of the resort transport them to Driftwood Bay and then arrive by ferry, or they could land in Corpus and take a chartered helicopter from there. He had recommended having two company helicopters, seating six each, remain at the Corpus airport. It was something Zane would arrange.

After he parked, he walked toward the ferry. While it was large enough to hold about eight or ten cars, he could simply use one of the golf carts at Tidewater and leave his rental on this side. This way, he could sit on the top level of the ferry and enjoy today's sunshine. It was already in the mid-sixties this morning. Considering New York had gotten snow three days ago, Sullivan thought he could get used to living in such a temperate climate. He chastised himself for the thought, telling himself he needed to get in the mindset of leaving soon.

"Hey, Kylie!" he called, waving at the blond whose family ran the ferry and also did charter boat runs for fishing, diving, and sightseeing.

"My favorite regular," she said. "Work calling you?"

"As always. Did just finish making a coffee table for Nellie Wagner, though."

"You made it? That's really cool. How on earth did you learn how to do that?"

He climbed aboard. "My grandfather taught me when I was young. He died years ago. I hadn't crafted anything since then. But Neville mentioned he had a shop he monkeys around in, and I asked if I could use it. That's how Nellie now has a new coffee table."

"Don't let Mom or Dad hear you say that. I'm sure they'd want to put you to work."

"I'll be leaving the Bay soon. Gotta march forward. New resorts to conquer."

She laughed. "Danny will push off in five."

Sullivan took a seat outside. He was joined by two others. The woman wore a navy pantsuit and had a mane of auburn hair. The guy had on a suit and tie and appeared nervous, fidgeting in his seat. He looked vaguely familiar.

"Going to Tidewater to interview?" he asked.

"Yes," both responded. They looked at one another and then began laughing.

"I'm Sullivan Shepherd. I work for Wagner Enterprises. I designed Tidewater."

"You do nice work," the woman said. "I'm Quinn Walker—and hope to be the spa manager for Tidewater."

"Where do you work now?" he asked as the ferry began to slowly move away from the shore.

"At a resort in the Hill Country."

"They've got some fancy places there."

She laughed. "Not half as fancy as a Wagner property."

He looked to the man, who said, "Barry Blaise. Coming from the same spot as Quinn. I'm the tennis pro."

"The courts were just finished last week. Same with the three pools. Good luck to you both."

"Any advice on landing a job at Tidewater?" Quinn asked.

"Just be yourself. If you've been asked to interview in person, then you've got the bona fides to be here."

"I've already been through two interviews on Zoom," Quinn said.

"I've done three," Barry confirmed.

"Wagner doesn't bring you in unless they're serious. Simply tell them why you're the best candidate for the job. Why you are a better choice than someone else."

Quinn sighed. "I've studied Wagner websites. I probably know more about their spa programs than whoever interviews me does."

Barry looked sheepish. "I didn't get online and look at anything. I wanted to be me. I can sell myself."

Sullivan realized where he knew Barry from. "Men's doubles, right? I saw you play at Arthur Ashe Stadium once. The US Open."

Barry nodded. "That was me. I played doubles and mixed doubles."

"You have a mean backhand. You're a lefty, aren't you?"

"Actually, I'm ambidextrous. I can play with either hand equally well, but in competition? I learned back in junior tennis that it was easier to play—and win—if I did so left handed. Not many players face a lefty opponent, so that gave me an advantage coming out of the gate."

"You medaled at the Olympics, didn't you?" he asked.

"I did. That was ten years ago. Most people don't follow doubles competition, though. I was able to leave the tour with two good knees and elbows. Not every player can say that."

"Why Tidewater?" Sullivan wanted to know, curious.

Barry laughed. "My wife's from Driftwood Bay. She's

always wanted to come back and raise our kids in a small town. Be close to her parents. I thought that would be impossible until I heard about Tidewater being built. It would be a dream job working for a Wagner resort, plus it would make for happy wife, happy life."

"How about you, Quinn? Why Tidewater?"

"Because Wagner resorts are premier places," she responded. "I would be able to hire the best of the best. Have sleek, modern facilities. Offer superb services. Their reputation speaks for itself."

"Well, good luck to you both," he told them. "Bill Lonsdale will be the guy interviewing you. He'll head up HR at Tidewater."

Immediately, Quinn whipped out her phone, and Sullivan knew she would know everything the internet knew about Bill by the time she sat for her interview.

They arrived, with Bill actually being at the group of golf carts. He introduced himself to the two job candidates and waved at Sullivan, who went to one of the carts and headed to the construction manager's trailer. Craig Small was at his desk, sleeves rolled up, a frown on his face.

"What's up?" Sullivan asked.

Craig launched into a long explanation, which Sullivan interrupted.

"I'm better at seeing. Let's go."

They went to the area Craig was concerned about, calling over a few construction workers and talking things through. Sullivan pitched an idea, and both construction workers agreed that it would solve the problem.

"You're a lifesaver," the construction manager praised. "It's good having you on-site, Sullivan."

"I'll be wrapping up soon," he said, feeling wistful as he did so. He would miss Driftwood Bay.

"Let me know when you're leaving," Craig said. "I'll start composing a list of questions that I'll want answered before you get out of here."

"Fine with me," he said, laughing. "And I'm always just a text away once I do leave."

Sullivan went back to wait for the ferry. As of now, the city of Driftwood Bay paid the Mayfield family a monthly fee to run the ferry free of charge to its citizens. With the influx of people at Tidewater, both guests and workers, he knew Wagner Enterprises was in talks regarding transportation to the island. Whether Wagner chose to pay for an additional ferry and staff to run it or kept the Mayfields employed with an additional ferry was something he would need to ask Zane about. Maybe he could talk his friend into coming down soon so they could spend some time together before Sullivan took off for New York.

Danny Mayfield greeted him once the ferry pulled up to Tidewater.

"Kylie told me you made Nellie a coffee table."

It still surprised him how everyone seemed to know everyone's business in the Bay, especially coming from the family he did. His mother had been tightlipped about everything, even though she gossiped ferociously, while his dad never spoke of business at home. Because of that, he really felt as if he didn't know his parents well—and probably never would. They had their skewed values and only thought about making more money and impressing as many people as they could, another reason he had been so at home with his grandparents, who valued kindness and hard work.

"Nellie's wanting end tables to match it," he said.

Danny laughed. "That doesn't surprise me. You have to be careful when it comes to women, Sullivan. Give them one nice thing, and they'll want two more. When Denise and I moved into our house, she thought the interior could use a new coat of paint. I did that. Then she decided the floors needed to be sanded. It's five years later, and she's still finding projects for me to do."

He laughed. "And you love her even more for it."

Danny shrugged. "I have to. She brings home treats from the bakery for me. I'm a sucker for a sweet."

Denise Mayfield owned Seaside Sweets Bakery, and Sullivan had become a frequent customer. He craved the black and white cookies and Danish.

"Besides," Danny continued, "Denise is right all the time. I'm not joking. She's got a great eye for things. Probably should've been an interior designer if her mom hadn't left her the bakery. I think the house is just about perfect now. Of course, we'll be moving Amber from the nursery and into her own bedroom once the baby comes in August. If it's a boy, I can tell you now that we'll be redoing the nursery. Maybe we can talk you into making a new bed for Amber."

"Maybe," he said, being noncommittal.

Danny looked at his watch. "Time to push off. Hey, Kylie, ready to roll."

"Roger that," his sister called out.

This time, Sullivan had the ferry all to himself. He enjoyed inhaling the sea air and watched a school of dolphins pass, capturing a few shots with his phone.

Once they arrived, he got in his car, ready to head home and put in some more work on the new resort on land Wagner Enterprises was thinking about purchasing.

His phone rang, and he saw it was Layne. He was supposed to have dinner with Keaton and her tonight. One of Layne's friends had come to town and would be managing the Bay Breeze, and they wanted the two of them to meet.

"Hi, Layne. Dinner still on for tonight?"

"It is, but I need a taste tester now with an honest opinion."

"Well, I'm your man," he teased. "What am I sampling?"

"Breakfasts. A lot of breakfasts."

"What?"

"Just come to the inn. Hopefully, you'll bring your appetite."

"I just got off the ferry. I missed lunch, so I'm definitely hungry. I'll head your way now."

"Thanks, Sullivan. I appreciate you taking out time to eat and give some constructive feedback."

"Be there in ten," he told her, ending the call.

Curiosity filled him.

Why on earth would he need to eat more than one breakfast at two in the afternoon?

Chapter Four

"Are you sure I'm ready for this?" Piper asked, nerves rushing through her at the thought of cooking for someone she had never met.

"You are definitely ready," Layne assured her. "In fact, I can't believe you've caught on so quickly. Then again, you've always put your mind to things and succeeded. Remember how you learned to write all your capital and little letters before Mila and me? And how you learned all the verses in *The Star-Spangled Banner* before anyone else did? Or how you could recite the times tables up to twelve without making a mistake? Boy that made Danny Henry so mad. He thought he was the best in math. Heck, I still can't remember what eleven times twelve is—and I'm great at math."

Despite her qualms, she smiled. For the past two days, Keaton had patiently walked Piper through how to make various breakfast foods. He was a thorough teacher, and he hadn't made fun of her lack of knowledge in the kitchen. Thanks to his detailed demonstrations, her confidence in the kitchen had soared. Now that she was to try her new skills out on a stranger, though, she found her heart racing.

"Do you think Sullivan is someone who will be good as a taste tester?" she asked. "Maybe I should have asked Mom and Dad to come over first."

Layne shook her head. "They love you too much to be critical. Not that I think Sullivan will criticize your cooking, but we need an honest opinion. He can do that. Just be yourself. Take your time. You've got this." She paused. "And if you do wind up lacking on any dish, you've got more than a week to keep practicing until the Bay Breeze is open for business again."

Piper consulted her list of breakfast items, mentally going over the ways to prepare each as Layne scrolled through her emails. Then her friend's cell chimed with a text.

"Denise wants me to come by to sample the icing she wants to use for the wedding cake," Layne said.

"Now?" she asked, a bit of panic seeping into her tone.

"Yes, now. Piper, you've got this," Layne assured her. "It's just scrambling some eggs and frying up a few pieces of bacon. Even I can do that now, thanks to Keaton showing me how simple it is."

The doorbell rang. "Sullivan's here. Let me introduce you to him, and then I need to head over to the bakery."

They both went to the door, and Layne grabbed her purse sitting on the table before she answered the door, ushering in one of the hottest guys Piper had ever seen. He was a couple of inches over six feet, with a lean, athletic frame. His hazel eyes were set off by his rich, dark brown hair. His lips were movie star sensual, and she had a wild urge to kiss him.

"Hey, Sullivan," Layne greeted. "This is Piper Roberts, my wonderful, talented friend who's just moved back to the Bay."

"Hi," she said casually.

"Hey, Piper," he replied, his voice low and steady. He

offered her his hand, and she shook it, aware of the tingles that danced up her arm with the contact.

"I've got to go handle something about the wedding," Layne explained. "You are here to sample Piper's breakfasts. You don't have to eat everything. Just a few bites." She looked at Sullivan steadily. "She needs unbiased feedback. You're an objective bystander. Don't sugarcoat anything. And save room for dinner tonight," Layne cautioned.

"Will do," he said. "See you later."

Layne left, closing the door behind her, and Sullivan turned to Piper.

"So, what's up first? And why exactly do I need to critique your breakfast-making skills?"

She swallowed. "I'm sure you've heard that I'll be managing the B&B for Layne. At least through Labor Day. She's gone through everything with me about how to run the inn. I'm familiar with spreadsheets. The website's booking system. How to clean each room, including making a bed with hospital corners. Part of the responsibilities include preparing breakfast daily for our guests."

Piper smiled ruefully. "And before Keaton got a hold of me, I didn't even know how long to boil an egg."

"You've spent your time out on the road, right?" he asked. "In touring companies?"

"Yes," she said enthusiastically, realizing he was trying to put her at ease by asking her about something she would be comfortable talking about. "I left college after my sophomore year because I had an opportunity to join a professional tour. Other than appearing in a few plays and one musical, I felt I was just marking time in college. To have a chance to perform on a daily basis—*and* get paid for it?" Piper shrugged. "I couldn't pass it up."

"So, you never went back to school?" he asked.

Although he was merely making conversation, Sullivan had hit upon something that still bothered her. Not having a degree would limit future employment opportunities. She pushed aside her feeling inadequate.

"No. I worked my way up from the chorus to secondary roles over several years. Then I finally broke out with my first lead. I have a solid work ethic and a strong voice, and my reputation proceeded me when I auditioned for roles. For the last five years, I've been the headliner of the musicals I toured in across the country."

"You must be really talented. I'd love to hear you sing sometime."

Piper felt herself blushing. "I think my performing days are over."

He grinned. "Maybe you can sing me something from *Wicked* while you're scrambling eggs for me."

"No!" she cried, panic filling her. "I need to focus. Cooking is so new to me. Singing would just mess me up."

Sullivan studied her a moment. "I don't think so. Singing was your life. Don't you find yourself singing when you're in the shower or getting ready? Puttering around the house?"

She laughed. "For your information, I never sing in the shower out of habit. I always needed to rest my voice when I wasn't rehearsing or actually performing. And I haven't had a house to putter around since before I left for college. I've lived out of a suitcase for ten years, Sullivan. Of course, I suppose I can always sing while I'm changing sheets and cleaning bathrooms for our guests."

"Once cooking becomes second nature to you, you might find yourself singing while you fry up bacon."

"Maybe. Right now, I'm feeling pretty good about what Keaton has taught me. We'll see."

"Then let's go into the kitchen and get started," he suggested. "What am I going to be eating?"

He followed Piper into the kitchen, where he took a seat at the table.

"I wonder if I should have you sit in the dining room," she fretted. "That's where I'll be serving our guests."

"Let me stay in here so we can talk."

"Okay," she said, reluctant to send him away. She liked his easygoing manner. She definitely liked his looks. Even though she knew he wouldn't be in the Bay much longer, he intrigued her. As it was, she was used to short-term relationships. Not that she was planning to have one with him, but if she did? She knew how to let go, with no regrets.

"Layne was right when she said you don't have to eat the entire dish. Just a couple of bites. And I need your true opinion. Don't be nice just because I'm Layne's friend."

"Got it. What's up first?"

"Eggs," she decided. "Keaton has drilled into me the differences between over easy, over medium, and over hard. And I can cook them other ways, too."

"Okay, let's get started." He rose and came to stand beside the stove, leaning against the counter. She caught the scent of his cologne, which had a bite of spice to it.

"We'll start with sunny side up. It's got a runny yolk and fully-cooked whites."

She dropped butter into the pan and set the temperature for medium low, dialing it back to low after a minute.

"Tell me what you're doing as you do it," Sullivan said. "I'm not a cook and am in awe of what Keaton whips up. Maybe I can learn something from you and it'll reinforce Keaton's lessons at the same time."

Piper laughed. "Who would've thought I'd be the one teaching someone how to cook an egg?"

She cracked open the egg and talked him through the process, explaining that fresher eggs kept their shape better.

"Non-stick pans make moving eggs around a little easier. Cast iron skillets are better at producing crispy whites, though. And a nylon spatula is better with a non-stick pan, while a fish spatula is best for a cast-iron skillet."

"Wow, you do know a lot," he praised, causing her cheeks to heat.

For the next half-hour, she made Sullivan every kind of egg which she had practiced with Keaton. Boiled. Poached. Soft and hard scrambled. She talked about the subtle differences in an over easy, medium, and hard.

"Even though I probably won't make anything other than scrambled eggs for the breakfast buffet I'll put out in the mornings, Keaton wanted me to be prepared in case a guest had a special request regarding eggs."

He took a bite of the last egg dish. "You've really nailed eggs. I've actually learned a lot from what you're saying. Who knew there were different ways to scramble eggs? Not me. But when I order them in a restaurant from now on, I know to ask for soft scrambled. I like the texture better."

"Restaurants almost always serve hard scrambled eggs because they're easier to do in bulk. In case you were wondering, I'm quoting Keaton now," Piper said, smiling. "He says they're good, but they can verge on being dry. Soft scrambled eggs have to be nursed since eggs cook quickly. You want them runny, but they still need to look wet once they're done."

"What's next?" he asked. "I don't think you'll be putting out hard boiled eggs on a breakfast spread."

"This is all I know as far as egg prep goes. Keaton said not to worry about omelets. I may actually try them, though, at some point. I've always enjoyed eating breakfast for dinner. I'm not very hungry in the mornings. Just a little yogurt and fruit or a protein shake does it for me, but I love all kinds of breakfast foods. I may actually test adding different things to eggs. Ham. Mushrooms. Green peppers. Cheese. I think I could whip up a nice omelet for myself in the evenings with a little practice."

"Well, you've perfected eggs," he complimented.

"Then let's move on. I only have a few other items to test out on you. After I talked it over with Layne and Keaton, we've decided I only need to put out a different breakfast every four days. That'll give short-term guests, weekend guests variety each day with no repeats, while those who stay a week or so, the summer guests, won't get bored easily by our offerings. I suggested that we place a small fridge in the dining room, so it can hold cartons of yogurt, milk, and juice. Keaton just bought a deluxe toaster for the dining room, and that way, guests can make their own toast or even English muffins."

"Great ideas. So, what are the non-egg days like?"

"One day will be French toast. Another is pancakes. And I'll also offer oatmeal."

"Why are you frowning?"

"That's been the hardest thing to conquer. I think I have it down, though. Oh, and I also need to try out sausage and bacon on you. Bacon is a little tricky."

Over the next two hours, Piper walked Sullivan through how to make the remaining dishes on the Bay Breeze Inn's breakfast menu. She found as she explained what she was doing, she really had mastered all these items. He was complimentary about everything, even the oatmeal, though he admitted he really had never eaten it before.

"To be truthful, I'm not fond of it," he admitted. "I think it's the texture. It's just...not me."

"I get that. I had never eaten it either, but it's good to know how to make it."

The only thing he had not liked was the way she fried bacon.

"It's not you. It's me. Memaw made bacon every single morning, and she called it greasy bacon. Most people make it crispy. Actually, your bacon is really good. It's crisp without being hard. I just have a preference for bacon that's a little undercooked. It reminds me of Memaw and Pawpaw."

She saw his eyes mist with tears. "You really loved them."

Sullivan nodded. "They were my favorite people in the world. Good, kind-hearted, hardworking. I spent every summer in Maine with them until I was fifteen. They lived in a small town that reminds me a little of Driftwood Bay. It was in Maine, though. Baker's Cove. On the coast and just south of Portland."

"I'm sure the temperature of the water was different," she joked. "The Gulf here is so warm."

He laughed. "The Atlantic is pretty darn nippy. Of course, I'd go swimming with Pawpaw. He said cold water put hair on a man's chest—and I believed him."

She laughed. "I can see eight-year-old little Sullivan, shivering in the waves, longing for hair on his chest."

Her eyes went to his chest now, wondering what grown-up Sullivan looked like beneath his clothes. Then she raised her eyes, her gaze meeting his, and she saw the heat in his eyes. They had now gone green.

Swallowing, she crossed her arms protectively. "Well, I guess I need to thank you for your time. You were quite the guinea pig, and I appreciate your feedback. I better start cleaning up."

"I can help with that," he said, his voice low and rough, sending a chill dancing along her spine.

"That's okay," she said quickly, turning away, her belly fluttering with unexpected butterflies.

His hand caught her elbow, turning her so that Piper faced him.

"Are you feeling this?" he asked.

She met his gaze, seeing his eyes now blazed a brilliant green. "Yes. But we shouldn't."

"Why not?" he countered.

"Because you're leaving the Bay soon."

"That doesn't mean we can't enjoy the time I have left."

Piper bit her lip. "I don't know," she said hesitantly, wanting to kiss him. Wanting more than kissing. But she had come home to start a new life and hopefully find love, just as her friends had. Jumping into a fling, even if Sullivan was smoking hot, wasn't who she wanted to be anymore. She'd had her fill of quick, passionate affairs. What she was looking for now was a permanent relationship.

Yet this man tempted her.

"Can I at least kiss you, Piper?" he asked, his voice smooth as silk. "Because if I don't, I feel I might regret it. Forever."

Against her better judgment, she heard herself whisper, "All right."

Sullivan framed her face with his large hands, his thumbs stroking her cheeks. He studied her a long moment, causing her pulse to jump.

"You are beautiful."

"No," she said firmly. "I'm not. I'm pretty. Even vivacious."

"Nope," he disagreed. "I'm calling it. You're beautiful."

Then he bent and pressed his mouth to hers. His scent surrounded her, a mix of spice and maleness, causing her heart to race.

He kissed her softly, breaking the kiss and returning again and again. She looped her arms about his neck, moving closer to him. One of his hands stayed, cupping her cheek, while the other moved to the small of her back, his palm pressing her so that it caused her body to be flush against his. She felt the heat emanating from him and wanted to burn in it.

Though she thought he would demand more from the kiss, he didn't. His kisses grew firmer, but he didn't push her for more. She opened to him, hoping he would, but he didn't accept the invitation. Still, the kisses were hot, causing her temperature to rise.

Then he broke the kiss, his forehead resting against hers.

"That was nice," he said, his voice rumbling low.

"It was," she agreed, trying to steady her breathing.

He raised his head and gazed into her eyes. "I'd like to see you, Piper. Take you out. For dinner. A walk after."

"Okay," she agreed.

"Okay? Really?"

He sounded like a teenager who'd just been granted his first date, and that thought warmed her.

"Really. I think I'd like to get to know you better, Sullivan."

His smile caused her heart to skip a beat. "That's good. Because I definitely want to get to know the real Piper Roberts."

Chapter Five

Sullivan showered and shaved before heading over to Keaton and Layne's house for dinner.

Because of Piper Roberts.

He knew beginning a relationship with someone was the last thing he should do, especially since his time in Driftwood Bay was winding down. Yet from the moment he caught sight of Piper, something called out to him. A whisper in his ear that nudged him. It told Sullivan that this was someone worth getting to know.

It had surprised him when he asked to kiss her. He wasn't an asking kind of guy. Not that he had ever forced himself on a woman before. The women of his acquaintance usually gave him very readable signs that they wanted to be kissed. Even bedded. He simply gave them what they wanted. He had never been in love. Never even thought about love. At thirty-three, he was in the prime of his life. Had a thriving professional career. Made an obscene amount of money for work he was very good at.

Yet during his time in the Bay, he had seen a different kind of life, one which reminded him of Baker's Cove. A simpler, satisfying pace reminiscent of his grandparents' lives. Pawpaw having been a carpenter. Memaw, employed as a retail clerk at the sporting goods store. Neither had any formal education beyond high school, yet they had been happy in the work they'd done and in their love for one another.

Sullivan had witnessed love between Keaton and Layne and also Carson and Mia. He enjoyed spending time around these couples and had begun to wonder if it might be time for him to slow down his carefree bachelor life and consider settling down.

"Whoa, buddy," he said aloud as he gazed in the mirror, combing his fingers through his hair. "Just because you're taken with Piper doesn't mean you've got to marry her."

He did want to get to know more about her, though. She intrigued him. Piper was unlike anyone he had met before. Maybe because she had lived a nomadic life on the road for so many years. Even though he traveled frequently for work, he had a home base in New York, a place he considered his anchor. Yet more and more, he was realizing that his life there wasn't the one he desired. He was tired of shallow people and fast talking and being judged by what he wore and who he knew.

Sullivan did not want to become his dad, but he feared he was on his way to that kind of life if he didn't put on the brakes and make a radical change.

Once again, he thought about how he had been tempted to remain in Driftwood Bay.

Was that even feasible?

"Put it on the back burner, bro," he told himself, claiming his wallet, car keys, and the bottle of wine he was bringing to dinner before he headed out the door. He liked that the apartment over the diner had a separate staircase that allowed him to come and go without having to go through the diner. It had afforded him a bit of privacy.

Tonight was going to be enjoyable. Dinner with friends. No pressure. He didn't need to make any earth-shattering decisions right now. It was all about putting one foot in front of the other and staying the course.

But was the course one he wished to remain on?

Feeling out of sorts, he drove toward the water. Getting out of his car, he inhaled the salt-scented air, feeling a sense of peace wash over him as he did so. He used to sit with Memaw on the shore, watching the waves roll in and out. Sullivan wondered if that might be something Piper might want to do.

He was about to ring the doorbell when the door opened. Keaton stood there. He took the bottle of wine from Sullivan.

"Thanks for bringing this. Could you do me a favor and go get Piper? She doesn't have a car yet, and we forgot to pick her up. She said she'd walk, but Layne told her to stay put."

"Sure," he agreed, glad to be able to spend some time alone with her. "Be back in a few."

Returning to his car, he drove down the beach road and turned left, heading back toward town. The Bay Breeze Inn was about two miles away, and he turned onto the gravel road leading up to it. It looked remarkably different from when he had first seen it. The work Keaton had put in, coupled with the construction crew Layne had hired, had restored the tired beauty into something regal and charming.

Piper sat on the porch. She rose, quickly going down the steps and approaching his car. Before he could get out, she had opened the door and climbed into the passenger's seat.

She glanced at him. "Oh, boy."

He frowned. "Oh, boy? What?"

She smirked. "Just noting how you're dressed, Prepster."

"How do you know I went to prep school?"

She waved her hand up and down. "By the way you're dressed. Casual to you means a starched, button-down shirt, neatly-pressed slacks, and..." She paused, glancing at the floorboard. "Loafers." She leaned over, hiking up his trouser leg slightly. Chuckling, she added, "No socks. I should've known."

Releasing his pants leg, she leaned back and fastened her seat belt.

Sullivan glanced up and down at her. "I see casually dressed to you means a light sweater, faded jeans, and boots."

"Yes. Casual. Texas casual. Do you even own a pair of jeans?"

"Of course, I do," he protested, thinking maybe he did. Then again, maybe not.

"I see that look of doubt in your eyes," Piper said, her own eyes gleaming with mischief. "Admit it. You don't own a pair of jeans."

"They're back in New York," he said, trying to keep the irritation from his voice.

He threw the car into reverse and headed back to the water.

"I'm sorry to give you a hard time," she apologized. "I don't know you well enough to tease you like that." She paused. "But you do look preppy in that stereotypical way. So, where did you go to school?"

"A boarding school in Connecticut. Devonwood Academy. And yes, we wore uniforms. White shirts. Khaki slacks. Blazers and ties."

"Was it fun, living with a bunch of guys? Or was your school coed?"

He laughed. "Heaven forbid my parents send me to a coed school. That would have been...*so inappropriate*." The last two words he said in a snooty, aristocratic tone. "In case you were wondering, I was quoting my mother."

"So, Mom wasn't a fan of the coed life. I can't imagine

going to an all-girls school. Then again, no one in the Bay went to private school. You grew up and attended public schools here. Knew everyone in your graduating class."

Curiosity filled him. "What were you like in high school? What were you involved in?"

Piper smiled. "Naturally, I was big in choir and drama. I also danced on the drill team. Was an officer, so I learned how to be bossy in a nice way. I also loved journalism and was the editor of the *Pirate Press*, our school newspaper. I wasn't sure if I wanted to pursue journalism or theater when I graduated and left for college."

"That was your résumé. What were you like?"

"Pretty much the way I am now," she said breezily. "Friendly. Outgoing. I worked hard in school. I wasn't as disciplined as Layne was, but I got pretty decent grades. What about you?" she asked as he turned onto the beach road.

"Reserved. Zane, my best friend, was the outgoing one. I played sports. Enjoyed cross country the most. In fact, I still run today." He paused and then, letting his guard down, revealed, "Running was my escape."

She took that in and asked, "Were you a good student?"

He smiled. "I was our valedictorian. Pissed Zane off. He came in second in our class. If he had applied himself more, he would've challenged me more for that top spot. He's remained the outgoing one, and I'm still more likely to sit back and observe others before jumping in."

Sullivan turned into the driveway and cut the engine. "Don't touch that handle," he warned, getting out of the car and coming around to open her door.

"Ooh, a gentleman. I guess that was driven into you at your posh prep school."

"Nope, that came from the cotillion lessons." When she

looked puzzled, he said, "You don't want to know. Let's just say in cotillion, you learn how to foxtrot and which fork to use."

He placed his hand on the small of her back and guided her toward the house, liking the light, floral scent coming from her skin.

They reached the door, and Piper opened it, going right in. Even though he knew this was a common behavior in small towns, he had yet to conquer the feeling that it was something wrong. Maybe he had more of his mother in him than he was willing to admit.

"Hey, we're here!" Piper called out.

"In the kitchen!" Layne shouted.

Sullivan followed Piper to the kitchen, where Keaton was pulling something out of the oven.

"What's that?" Piper asked, going over and inhaling deeply. "It smells delicious."

"Beef Wellington," Keaton answered. "Tenderloin wrapped in a puff pastry. You'll ladle red wine sauce over it."

"Wow, it smells heavenly. I've never had it before."

Hearing that let Sullivan know just how different the worlds that they came from were. He had grown up eating the fancy entrée, along with other traditional dishes which were commonplace in his parents' household. He mentally chastised himself, trying not to be the snob Piper thought he was. He was used to fine dining in New York, as well as eating at various Wagner Enterprises properties, every meal upscale, with Michelin star chefs leading the kitchens.

"You'll like it," Layne said. "Keaton has made this for me before. He's really spoiling me."

"Glad I brought the wine I did," Sullivan commented. "Thanks for letting me know to bring a red."

Piper glanced around. "We aren't eating in the kitchen?"

"It's so mild tonight, I thought we could eat on the deck," Layne said. "If you get chilly, I can lend you a jacket."

"Sounds wonderful," Piper replied. "Let's carry dinner outside."

With all four of them pitching in, it only took a single trip to bring everything to the table outside.

"Oh, this view," Piper said wistfully. "I am so jealous."

As they placed dishes on the table, Layne told Sullivan, "Piper was our water sprite. She would spend every waking moment in the water if she could."

"Really? Did you miss the water while you were touring?" he asked, pulling out her chair and seating her.

"I didn't realize how much I did until now." She inhaled deeply. "The tang in the air. The sound of the waves gently washing ashore and back out again. This is heaven on earth."

"Well, you're welcome to come over anytime and swim," Keaton said. "The beach in front of you is private. It's fenced off on both sides, so we don't have anyone who's not supposed to be here."

They served themselves, and Sullivan was glad to see Keaton had included roasted root vegetables. He particularly liked the beets and carrots.

"Oh, these veggies are crunchy," Piper said, her enthusiasm brimming over. She seemed the most positive, upbeat person Sullivan had ever encountered.

"They're root vegetables," he said automatically. "Memaw used to make them for me. She liked to include beets when she did so. They were her favorites. She always said root vegetables were sweet, earthy, and crunchy. They complement the Welly's complex flavors."

"My, aren't you the cuisine expert." Piper looked at him. "Care to comment on the potatoes?"

Sullivan took a bite of the scalloped potatoes. "Onions. Cream. And definitely Gruyère."

"You have excellent taste buds," Keaton complimented. "And great taste in wine."

The conversation bounced around, with no lulls. They talked of the upcoming wedding and the grand reopening of the Bay Breeze. How Carson's basketball team had done this year. Then the conversation turned to Tidewater.

"So, when will Tidewater be opening?" Layne asked.

"July first," he said. "They've started interviewing staff. In fact, I rode the ferry with two prospective employees today. One was up for the position of spa manager. The other was looking to be the tennis pro. They both work at the same resort in the Hill Country and seemed sharp. I'd actually seen Barry Blaise compete at the US Open several years ago. I have a feeling both of them will land jobs at Tidewater."

"Speaking of jobs there," Layne said. "I know you have a good idea of the different positions at Tidewater that need to be filled. Since Piper is looking for what she wants to do, maybe you could discuss what's available with her and see if she might be a good fit."

"No," Piper immediately protested. "If the resort is opening at the beginning of July, that's high season at the B&B. I'm not going to cut and run on you, Layne. I told you I'd help manage the inn until at least after Labor Day, possibly through the fall. I can't break my promise and abandon you like that."

"Who's to say there isn't something you'd be good at that might be part-time?" Layne countered. She glanced at Sullivan. "Are there part-time jobs open?"

"Not really," he said. "At least that I know of. Then again, I'm not involved much in HR and their decisions."

"See?" Piper said. "Case closed."

"I still think you could talk with Sullivan and see if something might appeal to you," Layne said stubbornly.

"You're not at a debate, Layne Larson," Piper replied, looking mulish herself. "Drop it."

"But I was just—"

"Why don't I take you over to see Tidewater tomorrow?" Sullivan interjected, not wanting the two friends to remain at odds. "We can walk through the resort. Give you an idea of its layout and the jobs that need to be filled."

"I told you that I never finished college," Piper said. "I doubt there would be anything for me, other than in housekeeping. And even though I'm going to be cleaning rooms at the B&B, I don't want to do that forever."

"You should still go," Keaton encouraged. "You never know. Opportunities show up when you least expect them."

"Keaton's right," Sullivan agreed. "What does your schedule look like tomorrow, Piper?"

"Layne and I were going to finish up discussing bookkeeping."

"That won't take but an hour or so," Layne said. "We can do that first thing in the morning, and you'll be free the rest of the day."

"Good," Sullivan said. "How about I pick you up at nine? We could make the nine-thirty ferry."

He saw Piper flush, looking uncomfortable. "Unless you really don't want to investigate any job opportunities there."

She took a long breath and blew it out slowly. "I suppose I could at least go see everything. Not that they're looking for someone like me."

"Good. It's settled," Layne said. "Now, who's up for dessert."

"Not me," he said. "I'm stuffed from dinner. Which was excellent, by the way. Hats off to our cook."

"It was delicious, Keaton," Piper said. "Maybe you can teach me how to make a few dinners. I may need to add some to my repertoire."

"Have someone you want to impress?" Keaton asked, grinning.

"I just like to be prepared," Piper said. "That's all."

"Let's clean up," Sullivan suggested.

"Nope," his friend said. "If you're not having dessert, we can just have another glass of wine and talk."

"If you don't mind, I'd like to head home," Piper said. "I've got a few things to do. I can walk home so you can stay, Sullivan."

"No, I'll take you," he insisted. Looking to their hosts, he said, "You two can have another glass of wine."

"That sounds like a plan to me," Layne said. "And I'm sure we'll have a little dessert, as well." She flashed a smile at her fiancé.

"Let's get out of here now before they start making out," Piper said good-naturedly. "Again, thanks for a wonderful dinner. I think Beef Wellington may be my new favorite main course. Not that I'll find it anywhere in the Bay."

Keaton and Layne walked them to the car. Sullivan opened the door for Piper, and then they waved goodbye.

"They're really good together," she said wistfully as he pulled out of the circular drive. "Layne was with a real loser for a long time. I worried that she would marry Jeremy, but he's gone and she's the happiest I've ever seen her."

"Well, I haven't known either of them for long, but they do seem perfect for one another."

"I'm sorry if I gave you a hard time about your background," she said suddenly. "I'm usually nicer and never tease anyone." She grinned. "Besides, you can't help it that you're rich. Or should I say wealthy? Rich is such an...*inappropriate* term."

Sullivan couldn't help but laugh. She had remembered what he had said and mimicked his mother exactly, without having met her.

"No offense taken."

"I'm just a small-town, middle-class girl. I haven't had the experiences you've had. I also wanted to say that you are not obligated to take me to Tidewater tomorrow. I think Keaton and Layne kind of strong-armed you on that one."

He turned down the road leading to the inn, coasting before he came to a stop and cut the engine.

"I really can't think of any particular skill I have that would be handy at an elegant resort, Sullivan. Besides, not finishing college is really going to hold me back. I'm going to have to find something to do which doesn't require a degree. At least I'll have plenty of time to research that this spring and summer. Breakfast will only be served from seven to nine each day. Then I'll check out guests and clean the rooms. I've practiced with Layne, using her mom's techniques. I can do each one in thirty minutes or a little less. Yes, I'll also have to handle some paperwork and do check-outs, but it'll still give me time to look into other jobs, mostly online."

Piper faced him. "So, I don't really need to go to Tidewater tomorrow. You're off the hook. I'll just tell Layne that we talked about it and that you didn't think there was anything for me there."

Anger stirred within him. "Don't go putting words in my mouth that I never said, Piper. Who knows if there's something for you at Tidewater? The least you can do is go and see it."

He paused, reining in his temper. Losing the sharpness in

his tone, he continued. "Actually, I'd like you to come and see it. My design."

"Really?" she asked. "I would like to. I can't imagine dreaming something up, putting it on paper, and then seeing it come to life in stages."

He nodded. "It is pretty amazing. No matter how many times I conceptualize something new for Wagner Enterprises, it's still a thrill when construction is completed. Please, say you'll come with me tomorrow."

She smiled. "Yes. I'd like that. A lot."

Then without warning, Piper threw open her door. "Thanks for giving me a ride, Sullivan. See you tomorrow at nine."

She scampered up the steps and unlocked the front door. Turning, she waved goodbye and then disappeared inside.

Sullivan would have liked to have gone into the inn with her and continued their conversation. Piper intrigued him. It had been a long time since any woman had. Actually, no one had. He was a man who lost interest quickly in a woman, always ready to move on after a date or two. For once, his restlessness seemed to have vanished.

He started the car again, eager for tomorrow to come, so he might get to know more about Piper.

Chapter Six

Piper found her attention wandering as Layne spoke about things they had already gone over several times. Her thoughts kept straying to Sullivan Shepherd.

She couldn't deny there was an attraction between them, but he was so different from her, much less any man she had ever been involved with. For one, he was rich. No, *wealthy*. He came from a family of privilege and had attended an elite boarding school. Even though she didn't know where he had graduated from college, it had to be one of the top schools in the country. He worked for a multibillion dollar corporation which built luxury resorts around the world, so he was guaranteed to be highly compensated for his efforts.

Sullivan's world was unfamiliar to Piper. Growing in the Bay, everyone seemed to be on fairly equal financial footing. The banker's daughter, who had been a grade ahead of Piper in high school, did have more clothes than any other girl in school. Besides her, everyone had appeared to be lower to middle class. The few who owned homes along the shore were outsiders to the Bay, only coming in to vacation in these second homes.

The only native to Driftwood Bay who had been known for having made a fortune was John Smith, the guy who'd previously owned Keaton and Layne's house. Mr. Smith had been the geeky tech middle school teacher and had only been able to purchase the waterside estate because he hit it big with some dating app he'd developed. Piper had been in high school at the time, and Smith had been the talk of the town. Smith's children had already flown the nest, and she had thought it decadent for only two people to live in the huge house on the water. She had enjoyed riding her bike by it from the time she was young, even though she wasn't able to picture herself living somewhere so grand. While it was a nice house and she knew Layne and Keaton would enjoy raising their family there, the house was probably small compared to what Sullivan was used to living in. When she thought generational wealth, she pictured luxury apartments in Manhattan and summer houses on Martha's Vineyard.

Piper reminded herself that the architect was strictly a visitor to the Bay and would be gone soon. She shouldn't consider getting close to him. And no hookups. She was ready to find what Layne and Mila had.

True love...

"Earth to Piper. Where are you?"

Layne had broken through her meandering thoughts, and Piper defensively said, "Why, I'm right here. Where else do you think I would be?"

"I don't think you've heard a word I've said for over five minutes," her friend protested.

She placed a hand over Layne's. "I'm ready to do this, Layne. You don't have to worry about me. I've got the computer programs and spreadsheets down and will be able to handle the paperwork. I'm familiar enough with the website now and can add to it when necessary. I know the exact formulas your mom used to make her various cleaning supplies that are natural and do the job. I even mastered the art of cooking breakfast. You can marry Keaton and go on your fabulous honeymoon without having to worry about the B&B—or me as I manage it."

She paused. "Except for one thing. Your mom and dad were a great team and ran the inn with ease. Since it's only going to be me, I may need some occasional help. While I can do all the tasks I just mentioned, I'm not handy with tools. If a doorknob becomes loose or a picture falls from the wall and damages a baseboard, I don't know how to repair those kinds of things."

"I don't want you to call on Keaton to make any repairs," her friend said. "He spent enough time fixing up the Bay Breeze, and I know he's going to be inspired by what we see in Europe. I'm hoping he'll come back with all kinds of ideas and paint up a storm."

"Then I'll look for a good handyman while you're gone. In fact, I may call that guy who headed the construction crew you used for restoring the B&B. What was his name again?"

"Joey Jordan. He's terrific. I'll leave his number with you. I'm not sure he would do small jobs, but if he doesn't? He would know someone who could."

Layne hugged her. "I'm just so grateful that you're going to take over the inn for now. You talk about having to figure out to do with the rest of your life, but you have to remember that I'm in the same boat. I left a very high-powered career back in Dallas. I want to find something to do which is rewarding, challenging, and satisfying, same as you."

"I guess we'll both have to figure out our futures," Piper said. "Maybe you can create some cool app like you did before and start your own company. I could be your personal assistant and help you run the business."

Layne laughed. "We'll have to see. In the meantime, I'm glad that you're going over to Tidewater with Sullivan. And I mean it, Piper. If there's something available that you want to do and they need you start when the resort opens—or even before—take the job if it feels right to you. Keaton and I will be gone the rest of March and all of April, but we'll be back by the beginning of May. I could manage the B&B on my own if I need to. Eventually, I want to hire someone to take over full-time, but I don't want to keep you from anything interesting you may find. Promise me you'll make *you* the priority and not the Bay Breeze."

"I promise, but I don't think Tidewater will have anything for me. You know I'm smart and pick up things quickly, but the lack of a college degree is going to hold me back. Besides, they'll have experts to run all their departments, from the front desk, HR, and accounting to the various restaurants. The spa. The water sports. I can't think of any marketable skills I possess that they might need. It will be fun, though, to see what a luxury resort looks like, even if it's not completely finished. I'll admit that after having dinner with Sullivan and y'all last night, I went home and looked up Wagner Enterprises."

Layne chuckled. "I did the same thing after meeting Sullivan. Impressive, right?"

"Boy, talk about luxury. The people who book rooms in their resorts are way different from what we know. Definitely not the clientele who books a stay at the Bay Breeze. I doubt I'll ever set foot at Tidewater after today. Not with the price of those rooms."

Layne eyed her speculatively. "You do look nice."

Piper glanced down at the crisp, white shirt and tailored black slacks she wore with low black heels. "Not that I anticipate landing a job there, but just in case I do run into anyone important who might interview me at some point, I wanted to make a good impression. And not embarrass Sullivan, of course."

"Your personality is what will win over any future employer. Besides, you've really grown into your looks, my friend. You were always cute when we were in high school, but your beauty has matured."

She felt her cheeks heat with the compliment, remembered how Sullivan had called her beautiful.

"I think it's just because I know how to carry myself now," she explained. "Plus, after all my years working in the theater, I've also learned an awful lot about hair and makeup. I use that knowledge to my advantage and know what to play up."

"I may have to ask you to do my makeup for the wedding," Layne mused.

"I would love to help with that," she said enthusiastically. "How about letting me practice a few palettes on you this weekend?"

"You're on."

Piper's phone buzzed, and she looked down. "Sullivan is on his way. I think I'll go and sit on the porch and wait for him. Soak up some sunshine. I do love being back in the Bay and having such great temps for early March." She giggled. "You do *not* want to be in Chicago or Pittsburgh or Minneapolis this time of year. All my traveling taught me that I needed to settle down in a climate just like the Bay's."

"I'm going to miss Sullivan," Layne said. "So will Keaton. They're both quiet men, but they've become fast friends and open up around one another. I think some of that has been Carson's influence since he's more outgoing. He's been good for both of them."

"See you later," she said, standing.

"I'll head out with you," her friend said.

They returned downstairs, and Piper locked the door behind them. She took a seat on the porch in a rocker and waved as Layne pulled away.

She noticed her mouth was dry. She wanted to go back and grab a bottle of water, but she saw Sullivan's car coming down the long drive and didn't want him to have to wait for her. Standing, she headed down the porch stairs to meet him, taking a few deep breaths and expelling them slowly.

He pulled up next to her, and Piper got into the car.

"Hey," she said, buckling her seatbelt.

"How was your meeting with Layne?" he asked.

She chuckled. "Layne is like a mother hen, hovering over me. She wanted to go over the same stuff we've talked about all week. I kept telling her that I've got everything under control and just encourage her to head out on her honeymoon as planned."

"Well, I'll be around if you need any help with something," he offered.

Piper laughed aloud.

"What's so funny?"

"Somehow, I can't imagine Mr. Prepster scrubbing toilets."

"I could," he said defensively.

She eyed him, biting back a smile. "Have you ever swished a toilet in your life, Sullivan?"

"Not that I can recall," he admitted, causing them both to laugh. "We had a maid who cleaned everything. I did make my bed every day, though."

"Ooh, brownie points for you," she teased. "Did you have to do that at boarding school? Make your bed?"

"Yes, it was a requirement. Every student's bed had to pass inspection each morning before we went down to breakfast.

We had communal bathrooms, though, and the school had staff who cleaned those."

"What about college? Where did you graduate from?" she asked, curious as to where he went and his experiences there.

"I had my heart set on Princeton because of their renown architecture school. Zane and I made plans to room together. He didn't care where we went because he knew he had a place waiting for him at Wagner Enterprises. Both our dads met at Harvard. The only thing Mr. Wagner insisted upon was that Zane attended an Ivy League school with an active Greek life because of the connections we could make. Since Princeton didn't allow fraternities on campus—and neither of us wanted to follow our fathers to Harvard—I decided on Yale. It had a terrific architecture program. Zane majored in finance, like a ton of other Ivy Leaguers. First, we roomed together in the dorms and then again after we pledged in the fraternity house."

"I should've known you were a frat boy."

"You say that as if it's a bad thing."

"Let's just say during my two years in college, my path didn't cross much with those of fraternity and sorority members. I hung out with people in the drama department and those who operated the radio and TV station. Those weren't majors Greeks typically pursued."

"Fraternity guys don't always date girls in sororities," he told her. "I'm surprised no frat guy asked you out."

Piper looked at him, her brows arched. "How many non-Greeks did you go out with at Yale, Mr. Shepherd?"

He was silent a long moment. "I can't think of any," he said sheepishly.

"Point made," she said. "I'm sure you weren't as rowdy and drunk as most of the guys in your frat, but those were still the guys you hung out with."

He nodded in agreement. "You're right. My parents—especially my mother—always wanted me to be seen in the right company. To go to the right schools. Pledge the best fraternity."

"You said you spent summers in a small town with your grandparents. I assume they were your dad's parents and not your mom's?"

"My father came from pretty humble beginnings. Pawpaw was a carpenter, while Memaw worked as a retail clerk at the local sporting goods store. Father was brilliant, though, and earned a scholarship to Harvard. He met Zane's dad there. Believe it or not, Mr. Wagner came from Driftwood Bay. His parents are Neville and Nellie Wagner."

"They own and run Driftwood Diner!" she exclaimed. "I've known them forever. Hmm. I didn't even know they had kids."

"Only Mr. Wagner. He left Texas and set pretty lofty goals. Wagner Enterprises is a multibillion dollar operation with resorts worldwide. Our fathers found kindred spirits in one another, being bright scholarship students from small towns with big dreams. They became best friends who learned how to fit in with the wealthier students. Mr. Wagner wasn't ashamed of his parents, though, the way my father was of his. My mother abhorred having in-laws who were blue collar. That's the biggest reason they stopped me from going to Baker's Cove each summer once I turned fifteen."

She heard bitterness in his tone. "I'm sorry," she said quietly. "I know you speak of your grandparents fondly. That must have been tough."

"It was. I even ran away and hitchhiked to Maine so I could see them."

He laughed, and she saw him loosening up a bit.

"I won't begin to tell you how much trouble I was in when I got carted back to Manhattan."

"Do you at least see your grandparents now?"

"No," he said abruptly, going quiet for a moment. "They died that next summer in a boating accident. Even all these years later, I miss the hell out of them. I accomplish something and immediately want to share it with them—and then remember they're no longer here."

He pulled his car into an empty parking space, and Piper saw the local ferry heading toward them.

"I can't imagine what you've gone through," she said. "I had very loving grandparents. Loving parents, too. They supported everything I ever wanted to do. I don't know if you've met Mom or Dad."

"I've met Chief Roberts. He's one of those salt of the earth guys. He and Pawpaw would've gotten along well."

They fell silent, watching the ferry make its approach. It was steered into the slip, and she said, "Why, I think that's Kylie Mayfield."

"It is," Sullivan confirmed. "She's not always on the ferry runs. A lot of times, she's running one of the charters for her family. Neville and I went on one of her deep sea diving expeditions not too long ago. I'm living in a room above the diner. Neville and Nellie have sort of adopted me as an honorary grandson."

"Kylie was a year ahead of me in school. She was a cheerleader and ran track. The most popular girl in school, and yet she was friendly to everyone."

"You say that as if that's something odd," he noted.

"That's right. You didn't go to a coed school. Let's put it this way. Even in a place as small as the Bay, you've got your popular clique, which is composed of mean girls, for the most part. I pretty much ignored them because I had Mila and Layne. Mila played volleyball and hung out with the other players some. Layne did the same with her soccer team and fellow debaters, while I was tight with the other drill team officers and my newspaper staff. When we weren't around those groups, the three of us were thick as thieves. Have been since kindergarten. Thank goodness for technology because we have FaceTimed a few times a month all during college and our twenties. In a way, it's really remarkable that we've all returned to the Bay as adults and are still friends."

"Let's get out," he suggested.

They both exited the car, and she waved at Kylie, who waved right back, a big smile on her face.

"Piper Roberts! I can't believe it's you."

They boarded the ferry, and Kylie enveloped her in a tight hug.

Kylie released her and said, "I heard you'd come back to the Bay. That you were a big-time performer."

"I don't know about that, but I did make my living appearing in musical productions all around the country."

"You always had an amazing voice. I remember that talent show where you sang *Defying Gravity*. Your voice soared to the rafters, and you brought down the house. It was like hearing an angel."

She had forgotten about winning the talent show her junior year and smiled fondly at the long-ago memory.

"I haven't had the pleasure of hearing you sing," Sullivan said. "You'll need to do that for me."

Kylie smiled at him. "Didn't mean to ignore you, Sullivan." She glanced around. "Looks like it's just the two of you for this run." She hollered, "Danny, go ahead and cast off."

"Rodger that," her brother called.

They took seats on the deck, and Kylie joined them, saying, "I'd really love to catch up with you, Piper. Mila and Layne, too. It's wild that you Three Musketeers have all returned to the Bay. Maybe we can do dinner one night soon."

"I'd really like that," she said, wondering why a girl of Kylie's looks and intelligence was back in the Bay, working for her family's business. She would ask Mila what Kylie's story was before they got together.

"Let's trade phone numbers," she suggested. "I'll text the others about when we might be able to meet up. You do know Layne is getting married next week, don't you?"

"I'd heard something about it," Kylie confirmed. "To that handsome artist who opened the gallery by the water last year."

"Yes. Keaton Maxwell," Piper said, providing his name. "They're going on a honeymoon to Italy and France, so if we don't get together with her before, we can catch up with her once they're back. Mila will be around, though."

"Mila has really created a strong, competitive volleyball program," Kylie said. "The town turns out for volleyball matches as much as they do for basketball and football these days."

"I'm proud of all Mila's accomplished," she said.

"So, what takes you over to Tidewater?" Kylie asked, looking at her speculatively.

"Sullivan designed it. He's going to show me a little of his work today," she replied, not wanting to discuss her plans regarding seeking future employment at the resort.

"Once Tidewater opens in July, we're going to be mega-busy," Kylie said.

"I heard that a second ferry might be in the works," Sullivan said.

Kylie nodded. "We're in early negotiations now regarding that. I've taken too much of your time."

"Give me your phone so I can input my number." She handed her phone to Kylie, who passed over her cell before they traded back. "Enjoy seeing Tidewater. Hope to hear from you soon, Piper."

Sullivan looked at her. "Even though Kylie is friendly, we've only said a few words in passing. You really know how to draw out people, Piper." He smiled shyly. "Even me."

She shrugged. "I just like being around people."

"Don't sell yourself short," he told her. "It's a gift."

They pulled up to the dock, and Sullivan got off the ferry first, holding out a hand to assist Piper. Kylie called goodbye to them, and Sullivan led her to a golf cart.

"This is how we get around. Climb aboard."

She did so, and he started the cart, moving away from the water.

"How did you decide on this particular property?" she asked.

"It was all Zane's idea. He still makes a point to visit his grandparents once a year. On a trip to the Bay two years ago, he learned the island was finally for sale. Things snowballed from there. We came down so I could see it in person. I like to view the site if I can before I begin to draw up plans. Of course, I meet with a committee of people and garner specifics as to how many rooms the resort will need to have. The number of restaurants on the property. That kind of thing. Then I'm pretty much given the freedom to design what I want. I try to envision what I create in its environment and bring elements of the surroundings into my designs."

They crested a small hill, and Piper gasped. "You designed… all *this*?"

Sullivan smiled proudly. "This is one of my babies. It may be my favorite creation to date."

He pulled the golf cart close to a set of others lined up. "Let's go see Tidewater."

Chapter Seven

Sullivan heard Piper's reaction and couldn't help but feel pleased by it. He wanted to impress her, something he had never thought about doing with any other woman. There was something about her that spoke to his soul. Piper had a purity about her, a zest for life, and a boundless energy which he had rarely witnessed in others.

Every woman he had dated from college and beyond had been jaded. They acted bored by everything around them and showed no interest in much of anything. Piper was the exact opposite, interested in everything around her, and he couldn't wait to show his latest project to her.

"This is incredible!" she declared. "It also looks as if it were meant to be here, as if it's a part of the landscape."

"That's something I really work on doing," he said with pride. "After I'm given certain parameters regarding the design, which I mentioned, Wagner Enterprises has learned to give me the freedom to create what I wish. Zane is the one who locates and purchases the properties, and it's my job to envision something which needs to blend in as a part of the surrounding area.

This is only the second beach resort I've designed, and I think I did a decent job with it."

"More than decent," she said, her eyes sweeping over the main facility and then around to other visible buildings. "I only came out to the island a few times. The couple who owned it ran a small hotel, but it had a good-sized ballroom. Our senior prom was held in it. I attended a few weddings and receptions here, as well, with my parents."

He nodded. "They were reaching retirement age and knew they were sitting on a goldmine. Zane had been after them for almost five years to sell, and he finally persuaded them that they needed to sell while they still had their health and could enjoy the money the sale would bring. Naturally, we razed the previous structure and then started from scratch. Fortunately, we had a lot of room to work with. Let's look at a few of the bungalows first and see the outside features before we head into the main establishment."

They entered a bungalow, and she said, "I'm surprised this is completely furnished. It's very tastefully done. It's got that beach vibe, but it still looks sophisticated." As she walked through it, she added, "This is as big as a lot of houses in the Bay."

"The bungalows vary between fifteen hundred and two thousand square feet," he shared. "Each will come with its own butler to attend to guests' needs."

She shook her head in disbelief. "I don't ever see myself staying at Tidewater."

"You say that, but we always like to have a few people come in and do that very thing, Zane among them. He likes to sleep in a bed to see what the mattress, sheets, and pillows feel like. He wants to watch and see how the room is cleaned. He'll eat meals in the various restaurants and give feedback on the dishes. I can make sure you're on the list, and you can be a part of that process a couple of weeks before Tidewater opens."

Her eyes lit up in surprise. "That would be incredible, Sullivan. Thank you. It would be a real treat to experience such luxury."

He didn't mention that he was usually gone by that time, and these were things which Zane did on his own. A prickle of jealousy rippled through him, thinking of his best friend escorting Piper about the property, letting her sample items from the menus and sleep in a suite. He shook it off, preferring to live in this moment with her and take all the enjoyment he could from it.

Her hand ran along the sofa. "This material is sumptuous. Of course, I realize a professional decorator has come in and pulled the look together."

"We used Kaitlyn Banner on this project. She's done interior design work for Wagner for several years now, from suites to restaurants. She's in her mid-thirties. Bright and creative."

"Well, if you talk to her, tell her the rooms capture the feel of the beach. They're luxurious and inviting and in a wonderful palette."

Piper sat on the sofa. "Everything is comfortable, and yet it's obvious that it's a cut above the usual hotel experience. Are all the bungalows already furnished?"

"Not yet. While the outside of every building has been completed they're working on the insides. Painting. Flooring. Furnishings. They like to decorate various types of rooms to see if the design works. Once it's approved, then they'll order large runs of items, such as the duvets and curtains."

"Let's go see more," she said excitedly, her eyes sparkling.

Sullivan took her by the three different pools, noting their swim-up bars. He also showed her the outdoor restaurant which would be used for breakfast and poolside service, along with the cabanas. They walked down to the tennis courts, and he explained that guests could play sets and also sign up for lessons with the pro.

"We don't have to go over now, but on the back side of the island is a golf course." He named the golfer who had designed it, and she nodded in recognition.

"Even I've heard of him."

"Once we knew the dimensions of the hotel and surrounding bungalows and amenities, work on the golf course began first. It takes time to lay it out and have the grass grow in properly. I'm curious as to whom they'll hire for the golf pro."

She laughed. "Well, it won't be me. I've never held a golf club in my life. Or a tennis racket."

Those were two sports that children in his social world were exposed to from a young age. Sullivan bit back a smile, thinking what it would be like to introduce Piper to his mother. She would be appalled at Piper's modest background and small-town upbringing and shocked that she had dropped out of college, never finishing her degree.

"You're smiling. That means you play both golf and tennis."

"It's something I grew up doing," he admitted. "Sometimes, business is conducted on the links. I don't want to be left out of those talks. And I'm competitive enough that I want to shine."

"What else did you do as a boy that I have no experience with?"

"I took horseback riding lessons and competed in dressage. Sailing lessons, too."

"Finally, something I'm familiar with. I love being on the water. Dad has both a sailboat and a small fishing boat. Sometimes, I think I'm most myself on the water."

"I've never been fishing," he revealed. "Pepaw hated the

smell of fish. He worked summers from the time he was thirteen at the fishery in town. It was where his dad and uncles worked. Pepaw despised the taste of fish, too. The family almost went to war over him choosing to apprentice with the town carpenter. He was happy, though, doing what he loved."

"Then I'll take you fishing," she said eagerly. "We can catch dinner and bring it back for Mom to fry it up. She's got an amazing recipe for fish batter."

He grimaced. "Would this catching include cleaning fish?"

She smiled widely. "If there's one thing I know, it's how to clean a fish. You can watch and learn, Prepster."

He thought Piper had a lot she could teach him about how to live life.

They continued through the beautifully landscaped grounds, stopping at two of the tranquil outdoor spaces meant for guests to meditate or relax in. Going down to the water, he pointed out the various water sports which would be offered, from kayaking and paddleboarding to snorkeling.

"Let's head to the main building now," he suggested. "I think you'll find the lobby interesting."

Sulivan had them walk around the hotel so they could enter from the front and get the full effect. As he anticipated, Piper was thoroughly impressed.

"It's simply gorgeous, Sullivan," she praised. "Even though we're inside, your design makes it seem as if we're outside. You've really brought the island to life in here."

They went upstairs to one of the sample indoor suites.

"It's hard for me to imagine having all this room. I lived on the road the last ten years, and we were booked into rooms which were no larger than shoeboxes. Every room here has sitting rooms. Some even have dining rooms. The bedrooms are larger than the apartment I shared with three other gals in New York."

"I live in New York," he told her. "Zane and I share an apartment. I can walk from it to the office in mid-town. It's got a great view of the park."

"I'm sure my entire Brooklyn apartment would've fit into your closet," she joked. "I finally gave it up because I was traveling so much, going directly into rehearsals for a new musical after wrapping a run with the current one."

"You really did live out of a suitcase," he marveled, unable to imagine everything he owned fitting into what he could carry.

"Let's keep going," she said cheerfully.

He took her to the spa area, which had treatment rooms and a large relaxation center, as well as hot and cold plunge pools, a hot tub, indoor swimming pool, and a Nordic ice room. Opening the door to it, they stepped inside for a moment.

"Brr! This is freezing even with my clothes on," Piper declared. "I can't imagine being wet."

Immediately, he pictured her without clothes, and desire rippled through him. He told himself she wasn't a one-night stand kind of woman. Or even someone who would be interested in engaging in a brief affair. His time in the Bay was limited, so Piper Roberts should be off-limits.

Yet he wanted to spend every waking moment left with this woman.

"Where to next?" she asked.

They explored the fitness center, which was located on the same floor as the spa.

"Even this is luxurious for a locker room," she said as they walked through the women's changing rooms and shower facilities before heading into the fitness center itself, stopping first in the weight room. "All these sparkling weights."

Piper moved into the room filled with machines, from exercise bikes and treadmills to lat pulldowns and leg extension machines. "Everything you would need for a complete workout."

They entered a large room, and she asked, "I assume this is for classes? I see yoga mats and medicine balls."

"It is. They'll be hiring instructors to teach those."

"That's actually something I'm qualified to do," she mused, her face thoughtful. "Living on the road, it's a little hard to eat as you should, so I became devoted to working out. Over the years, I earned certificates as a yoga and Zumba instructor and would hold daily classes for those in the company who wanted to get in a daily workout. I usually held classes on the stage of whatever theater we were performing in, but sometimes, I would hold outdoor classes if there was a nearby park if the weather was good."

"Is that something you'd be interested in? I could facilitate a meeting between you and Bill Lonsdale. He's the manager for Tidewater and hiring staff now."

"I do enjoy getting up and moving every morning and really had fun leading others through a class. So, do you think rich people would actually sign up for classes even though they're on vacation and want to be pampered?"

"Lots of guests take advantage of various exercise classes in our fitness centers." Sullivan thought if men got a look at Piper, they would sign up in droves.

"Let's continue the tour," she said, but he could tell she was more contemplative now, as if she might actually be considering applying for a job at Tidewater as a fitness instructor.

They visited the nightclub, which would be a main gathering center each evening.

"Usually, we have a few different performers entertain

guests here. A pianist. A singer or two. One night a week is devoted to karaoke. Also on this floor is a dance club."

He took her back downstairs for the last stops, saying, "We'll have three main restaurants. One features Asian fusion. Another Mexican cuisine. The third will spotlight continental cuisine."

Sullivan led Piper through the first two restaurants and then an area which would offer a breakfast buffet before entering the final restaurant, which had elegant chandeliers and tables and chairs.

"This looks so fancy. What do people even wear at a luxury resort?"

Thinking back to his own vacations at exclusive beach resorts, he said, "Guests go for mostly neutral colors. You won't catch anyone walking around in T-shirts and shorts or swimsuits and cover-ups except by the pool. For the most part, men wear dress slacks and collared shirts."

"I'm sure the women dress up more, though."

"True. They dress simply but chicly. Maxi dresses. Silk blouses and tailored slacks. Dressy sandals."

"I don't mind dressing up on occasion, but on vacation? I want to be comfortable. Give me shorts and flip flops any day. Besides, I'm sure one night at Tidewater would cost me a month in salary." She paused. "Would you mind if we cut through the kitchen? Now that I'm interested in cooking, I'd love to see what a restaurant kitchen looks like."

They entered the kitchen, a large space of gleaming, stainless steel countertops and tables and pots and pans which hung from the ceiling. A man unfamiliar to Sullivan sat at a table, pen in hand. It flew across the page of his notebook as he frowned in concentration.

"Ty?" Piper asked.

The man looked up. "Piper? Piper Roberts?"

He quickly came to his feet, beaming at her. She moved toward him, and he enveloped her in a bear hug.

If Sullivan had thought jealously coursed through him at the thought of Zane dining with Piper, it now poured through him as he saw how familiar the two were with one another.

The man released her, and they both said at the same time, "What are you doing here?"

"You first," she said. "Although I have a sneaking suspicion you work here."

"I do. I just drove in from New Orleans yesterday."

"That's right. You were the chef at a restaurant there. Mom told me about that."

"I was. The lure of returning to the Bay was too great, however. Wagner Enterprises came knocking on my door with an offer too sweet to pass up. I'm going to not only be the head chef for one of the restaurants at Tidewater, but I'll oversee its entire food and beverage program."

"That's great, Ty," Piper said. "And a heckuva lot of responsibility."

He chuckled. "It really is. Sometimes, I wonder if I'm crazy to bite off as much as I have." His eyes flicked to Sullivan, and Piper spoke up.

"Meet Sullivan Shepherd, the architect of Tidewater. He's giving me the grand tour of the resort."

Sullivan offered the chef a hand.

"Tyler Chastain," the other man said. "Thank you for leaving the kitchens' design up to me."

When Piper frowned in confusion, Sullivan said, "I've learned to reserve a set amount of space for a chef's kitchen and restaurant. While Kaitlyn designs the interior of the restaurant, whether it's tables or banquettes, I leave the entire kitchen space up to the chef to design as he sees fit."

"You don't know how I appreciate that, Sullivan," Tyler

said. "Every chef wants to put his mark on his food, but I believe that starts in the kitchen itself, with its design and workability. I've never had the luxury of creating a kitchen from scratch, but Wagner allowed me to do so in all the kitchens here. I've spent a good amount of time on Zoom calls, getting all the details just right, but this is perfect. Now, all I need to do is create the perfect menu."

"Have you hired the chefs who'll run the other restaurants? Or is that a Wagner thing?"

"Wagner asked me for a short list of chefs I would recommend, then they approached them individually. I was able to sit in on those Zoom interviews, and then I made my recommendations to HR. I'm pleased with the talent they've hired. Each chef has been guaranteed the ability to hire his own staff. Like me, they'll bring a few others with them whom they've worked with in the past. I stole my sous chef from my NOLA restaurant. She's simply incredible. We have a great shorthand in the kitchen. She's hoping a step up to a Wagner resort on her résumé will allow her to run her own kitchen someday soon."

"I've actually learned to do a bit of cooking myself, Ty," Piper revealed. "You remember Layne?"

"I sure do. Mila, too. The three of you were inseparable."

"Mila came back to the Bay a few years ago. She's the volleyball coach at the high school, and she married the basketball coach last Thanksgiving. Layne is getting married to a local artist next week. She inherited her parents' B&B, and I've come home to manage it. At least for a few months." She chuckled. "I'm trying to figure out what I want to do when I grow up."

"What have you been up to? I lost touch with most everyone after I left the Bay and went to cooking school in Paris. After that, I stayed in Europe for almost five years, soaking up all the knowledge I could. Then I came back to New York and worked at two different restaurants there before

I was tempted by a great offer to go cook in NOLA. Now, that's a place which knows how to make incredible food."

"I left college early and began touring in musicals around the country," Piper explained. "That's what I've done for the last ten years. After so long on the road, though, the appeal had waned. Plus, Layne and Mila had come back to Bay. I missed them and my parents terribly. As eager as I was to leave Driftwood Bay, its siren song has brought me home. Now, I just have to decide what it is I want to do. Managing the Bay Breeze will give me time to investigate other avenues of employment."

Piper glanced to the table. "I see you're really busy."

"Working on creating the menus for Le Point Idéal." He grinned. "French for The Sweet Spot."

"Then we'll let you get back to that. It was good seeing you, Ty."

"Same, Piper. Why don't we catch up more? We could meet for a drink tonight at the Pelican Porch. Dad would also love to see you."

Before Piper could respond, Sullivan said, "Piper's busy tonight. Maybe another time."

His gaze met the chef's, and he hoped Tyler Chastain received the message he was sending.

"Okay, maybe another time then."

"Let's trade numbers," Piper suggested. "I know Mila and Layne would love to see you now that you're back in the Bay."

They exchanged cells and typed in their contact information for one another.

"I'll text you soon about that drink," Piper promised.

They said their goodbyes and left the kitchen, making their way through the restaurant's dining room again. Once outside, though, Piper came to a halt. She scowled at him, her glare one which could freeze water on a summer day.

"What the hell was that about?" she demanded.

Chapter Eight

Heat rose within Piper, and not the sexual kind. She did her best to keep a lid on her anger as she continued to glare at Sullivan, waiting for an answer.

"Well?" she asked, the one word biting and caustic.

"Not here," he said gruffly.

She looked around, seeing two construction workers heading their way and knew it would be wrong to confront him at his place of work. Instead, she turned and headed to the golf cart he had parked nearby. Getting into it, she sat silently. He did the same, driving it down the main drive, back toward the water. Neither of them said a word.

Unexpectedly, he veered off onto another path and brought the cart to a halt. They had total privacy now, and she wasn't going to hold back.

Facing him, Piper said, "What on earth got into you, Sullivan? You acted like some rutting dog who'd staked his claim. I don't go in for that kind of apish behavior."

"Look, I'm sorry," he said, and she caught the glint of regret in his eyes.

"I don't get it. All I was doing was arranging to have a drink with an old friend whom I haven't seen in more than a dozen years."

His gaze met hers. "I was jealous. Okay."

"Of Ty?" she asked, slowly putting the pieces together.

"I didn't know that you were just friends with him. For all I knew, he was the great love of your life in high school, and you had parted ways, moving on to different lives. I apologize, Piper. I don't know what got into me. I've never been jealous before in my life, much less acted on it."

She could hear in his voice that he was telling the truth. Part of her was flattered, but the greater part was still mad at him.

"Even if you and I were dating exclusively—which obviously isn't the case—I wouldn't want my boyfriend to prevent me from seeing a friend, male or female. That's possessive, controlling behavior, and it doesn't sit right with me, Sullivan."

"You had said you would go out to dinner with me. Take a walk afterward. I know we hadn't firmed up an actual night, but I was hoping tonight would be it." He raked his hands through his hair, clearly frustrated with himself. "I blew it, Piper. Totally blew it. I don't know what got into me. I'm more of a gentleman than that."

She felt herself softening and said, "I know we said we would go out. I'm not sure if that's a great idea now. Like I mentioned before, you're going to be leaving the Bay soon. I've already gone through enough upheaval in my life recently, and I don't really want to invest any of myself in you, only to see you walk out of my life and never come back. I know that you're around Layne and Keaton a lot. Mila and Carson, too. Why don't we just agree to be friendly toward another and leave it at that?"

He placed his hand over hers, causing tingles to dance up her arm.

"I can't change the fact that I don't live in Driftwood Bay, but I want to make the most of my time remaining while I'm here. I'd like to spend as much of it as possible with you, Piper."

No man had ever pursued her in this manner. It was flattering, yet Piper knew she must guard her heart. Then again, what could a few, harmless dates involve? Sullivan Shepherd would be leaving the Bay, while she had made a commitment to stay here because of family and friends. She would never have an opportunity to be with him again.

She couldn't help but think back to the kiss they had shared. How she had yearned for more from him. She was the master of the fast, casual relationship. Piper supposed she could do it one more time with this man, whom she was really attracted to, and then she promised herself that when the next guy came along, things would be different.

Even if he wouldn't be Sullivan Shepherd.

"All right," she began. "I'll go out with you for that dinner and walk. That's all it'll be. Understood? And I can't promise anything beyond that."

He squeezed her fingers, a smile playing about his sensual lips. "Understood," he echoed. "I just want the chance to know more about you. You're different from any woman I've ever been around, Piper."

She chuckled, trying to make light of things. "I may not be one of your blue-blooded beauties, but I'll do my best to keep our conversation lively. Deal?"

His gaze met and held hers. "Deal."

He started the golf cart again and drove to the area where they had retrieved it.

Bringing them to a halt, Sullivan said, "I'm sorry we never made it by Bill's office. I wanted to introduce you to him."

"I need to think about things," she told him. "And if I do decide to pursue an open job opportunity at Tidewater, I'll do it on my own. I don't want you to smooth the way for me."

He nodded. "I understand. You want to make your own impression. Land the job on your own terms."

They sat in the golf cart in silence until the ferry appeared. Climbing from the cart, they walked down to the dock to meet it. Danny Mayfield steered the ferry into the slip and left his pilot's station, attaching the ropes to hold the ferry in place.

"Hey, Danny," Piper greeted. "Where's Kylie?"

"She had a last-minute fishing charter come up. You're stuck with me, Piper. How have you been?"

"Trying to get back in sync with the rhythm of the Bay. How's Denise? You have any kids yet?"

Danny beamed proudly as he took out his phone and showed his lock screen. "This is Amber. She's three and her mom's mini-me. Denise is due again in August. We'll have a sonogram done next month to see who's up to bat next." He laughed. "Amber wants a little sister—or a puppy."

She caught sight of a golf cart coming down the path and turned to see a man driving it.

Sullivan said, "That's Bill, the manager of Tidewater. He was the assistant manager at one of our resorts in the Bahamas. This is the first time he'll be in charge of a Wagner resort on his own."

Bill shook hands with the man accompanying him, who then exited the cart and joined them on the ferry.

"How did your interview go?" Danny asked.

The man smiled widely. "You're looking at the new head of water sports."

Sullivan spoke up. Offering his hand, he said, "I'm Sullivan

Shepherd, the architect for Tidewater. This is Piper Roberts. She manages the Bay Breeze Inn in Driftwood Bay."

The new hire introduced himself, "I'm Greg Delaney," he said, offering his hand and shaking Sullivan's enthusiastically before turning and doing the same with her. "Nice to meet you both."

Greg asked a couple of questions, which Sullivan answered with ease. Piper liked listening to his voice, which was soothing. She hoped she was making the right decision in agreeing to not only be friends but to go out with Sullivan. She reminded herself that if she did choose to get involved with him, it would be a temporary relationship. After all, there was nothing wrong with having a bit of fun with a good-looking guy as she discovered who she would become in this next chapter of her life.

Danny cast off, and the two men continued talking about Tidewater, so she pulled out her phone in order to text Mila and Layne.

> Need to catch up with both of you. Coming back from Tidewater now. It's truly impressive. Saw Kylie Mayfield on the ferry ride over. She suggested having dinner sometime with all of us. Know everyone's busy, but she seemed eager to connect. What's her story? Why's she back in the Bay? Any night good before the wedding?

Immediately, Layne suggested Sunday evening and offered to host, saying she would send Keaton over to see Carson. A few minutes later, Mila chimed in, texting that Sunday worked for her. Piper sent back a message, saying she would check with Kylie and get back to them to confirm if Sunday worked or not. Even if Kylie couldn't make it, Piper said she wanted the three of them to get together. She sent Kylie a text, not expecting a quick reply since she was out on the water with customers.

They reached Driftwood Bay again, and she waved goodbye to Danny, telling him that she would stop by the bakery soon to see Denise. She got into Sullivan's car, and they drove back in a comfortable silence. She was glad she had put her anger aside and was able to be in his company without things being strained between them.

He pulled up to the B&B and turned to her. "Fresh start?" he asked.

Piper nodded. "I'd like that."

"Then how about dinner tonight? If that's not too pushy. Something casual, such as Backyard Bites."

"My mouth is already watering, thinking about their spinach artichoke dip," she told him, smiling. "What time?"

"It's a Friday night, so it'll be a little busier."

"Let's say six," she said. "Although that's probably early for rich people to eat," she teased.

"You don't have to be such a smart-ass," he fired back good-naturedly. "How about I pick you up at a quarter till so we be there by six?"

"Sounds like a plan. Thank you for taking me over to Tidewater and showing me around, Sullivan. I didn't have a chance to say this before, but I'm really proud of you and impressed by your work. It's a beautiful design."

"I accept your generous compliment and will see you tonight."

Piper unfastened her seat belt and got out of the car, heading up the porch steps. At the top, she turned and waved. Sullivan waved back. She unlocked the door to the Bay Breeze and entered, feeling better about how things stood between them. Then she retrieved her laptop, checking to see if any new reservations had come in. Two had, and she marked them on the calendar and sent confirmation emails to both guests. One party had included in their note that they were longtime visitors to Driftwood Bay and were excited about the inn's makeover. She made a note to herself regarding that, wanting to acknowledge them for their return business when they checked in.

She couldn't help herself after that and googled Sullivan. Several articles came up about his association with Wagner Enterprises, and she was also able to see a few of the other Wagner properties he had designed. She dived deeper, finding a handful of pictures of him during his college days at Yale. He looked like the typical Greek she remembered from her own days in college. Something told her that he was much nicer than most frat boys, however.

The last picture she found of him was when she googled his name along with Baker's Cove, Maine. It was one of him with his paternal grandfather in the local newspaper. Sullivan looked to be no more than eleven or twelve in the picture, but she could definitely see signs of the man he had become in this boy. He stood almost as tall as his grandfather, and they were showing off a bookcase the two had crafted together.

Her heart stirred, feeling sympathy for the boy who had adored his grandparents and how that relationship had been stolen from him. Piper couldn't imagine her own mom keeping her away from her paternal grandparents. She hoped she would never meet Mr. or Mrs. Shepherd because if she did, she would give them a piece of her mind about how they had hurt their young son. Though Sullivan displayed a confident manner to the world, she knew he had a sensitive side to him and that he'd been greatly affected by being cut off from the grandparents he loved, especially for such a ridiculous reason.

She decided to call Joey Jordan and dialed his number. He answered on the second ring, and Piper introduced herself.

"I'm going to be managing the Bay Breeze for Layne, but I know little things crop up which need repair. Layne's told me how you worked on restoring the B&B. She didn't know if you had someone on your construction crew that I might be able to call upon as a handyman."

"We don't really offer that service, but Layne and Keaton were so good to my crew and me. We'd be happy to be on-call for you, Piper. If anything comes up, just text me. Either I'll stop buy or send one of my guys to handle it for you. Hopefully, nothing will go wrong for a while. The Bay Breeze is in tip-top shape right now."

"I agree, but I just wanted to line up someone in advance since I'm not handy with tools."

Changing the direction of the conversation, she said, "I see where you and your wife are going to be our guests in a couple of weekends."

"Yes, ma'am. We're really looking forward to it. Layne insisted we take a free weekend on her for all the work we put in."

"If there's anything I can do in advance to make your stay more pleasant, just let me know. Right now, I have you down for the Lilac Room."

"That's right. I choose it because my wife's favorite color is any shade of purple. Looking forward to meeting you, Piper," Joey said.

"Same. See you soon."

After their conversation, Piper puttered with small tasks until it was time to get ready for her date with Sullivan. She took a quick shower and then dressed in jeans and a blouse. Since they would be eating at a restaurant near the water, she decided to leave her boots behind and went with tennis shoes. She had a feeling he might want to walk along the water's edge, and boots weren't conducive for a walk on the sand.

Her phone buzzed, and she saw it was Kylie responding to the earlier text.

> Sunday is great. Just tell me what time to be at Layne's and what to bring.

Excited that she would be getting together with her friends, as well as Kylie, she placed them all on a group text and sent a message saying everyone could do Sunday. Layne immediately replied, telling everyone to come at five for a glass of wine and that they'd eat at six. She'd provide everything. Kylie chimed in, saying she would bring cupcakes from Seaside Sweets for dessert. Everyone hearted that message.

Piper still wanted to ask Mila why Kylie was back in the Bay. Her friend would have a better idea since she'd lived here a few years now. Piper had always thought Kylie Mayfield was destined for a bigger life than one lived in their small hometown. Then again, look how she and her besties had returned to the Bay, along with Ty.

Ten minutes before he was supposed to arrive, Sullivan texted that he was on his way. She locked up the inn and went to wait for him on the porch, leaving on a few lights for her return. When she saw his car approaching, she moved down the steps and climbed into his vehicle.

"Hey," she greeted, noting he wore a crisp, button-down shirt of pale blue paired with khaki slacks. She caught the whiff of his cologne and noted that he must have shaved, seeing no stubble along his jawline. Her fingers itched to stroke his face, but she kept them firmly in her lap.

"Hey, yourself. Y'all look really nice."

She grimaced at his words. "You're totally using y'all wrong," she told him. "Y'all is plural. There's just one of me."

Sullivan's eyes glinted with mischief. "I'm just teasing you, Piper. Even I've gotten down the correct usage of y'all since I came to the Bay." He glanced at her. "Your blouse is a pretty color. Like the color of bluebonnets. It really brings out your blue eyes."

She blushed at the compliment. Most guys she had gone out with rarely noticed what she wore, but she supposed Sullivan, being an architect, was a man who always noticed details.

"Thank you. I love bluebonnet time in Texas. I've missed it."

"I'll miss it myself. I've never seen such a rich blue in a flower. It's almost a purple-blue. And fields of them that go on and on. Their time blooming was pretty brief, but bluebonnets definitely made an impression on me." He paused. "Just like you."

Now, her cheeks burned. "Okay, Prepster. Quit laying it on so thick," she chided gently. "You got your date with me tonight."

They reached Backyard Bites and this time, she let him come around and open her door for her, liking his gentlemanly manners. He didn't take her hand, which was a good thing, but he did press his palm to the small of her back in order to guide her to the front door. The warmth burned through her clothing, and she licked her lips, thinking about if he slipped that hot hand under her blouse.

Sullivan opened the door for her, and Piper entered the familiar restaurant. It was three-quarters full at the moment. The Bay did a good job of supporting local merchants, and that included restaurants and bars. Of course, on a Friday night during the summer, the line at this time would already be out the door. There were advantages to being in the Bay during the off-season.

The hostess, who looked like a high school student, greeted them and seated them in a booth. They had just opened their menus when Betty Chastain appeared. Piper stood and hugged the restaurant's owner.

"Ty told me he saw you today," Betty said. "I'd heard you'd come back to the Bay when your mama and daddy were in here two nights ago. They were bursting at the seams to have you here again."

"It's good to see you, Betty. And yes, they are very happy this bird has returned to the roost. Do you know Sullivan Shepherd?"

Betty smiled. "I sure do. Sullivan has been a good customer while he's been in town. Nellie is beside herself, knowing you're leaving soon."

"Well, Zane will be here before she knows it. Then she'll have her real grandson to dote on and not her substitute one."

"Sit, honey," Betty told Piper. "What can I bring you to drink?"

"Just iced tea for me," she replied, and Sullivan asked for the same.

"Coming right up. Your server will be with you soon."

They enjoyed an appetizer of the spinach artichoke dip Piper had missed so much, and Sullivan said he was a convert to it. They each ordered burgers, bacon cheddar for him and Swiss mushroom for her. They agreed to share a basket of fries, which would have fed at least one more person if not two.

"That was a great meal," she said when they had finished and were waiting for their check.

"Agree. Actually, I haven't had a bad meal in the Bay," he said. "Do you have room for dessert?"

"I wish. What I do need is that walk you promised."

"Good. Would you mind walking along the beach? I see your ever-present boots were left behind this evening."

"I didn't think sand and boots mixed very well."

He handed his credit card to their server. She ran it and

handed Sullivan the small machine for him to place a tip and sign the bill, giving him a copy of his receipt. They waved to Betty on their way out the door.

"So, she's Tyler's mom," Sullivan said as they left Backyard Bites. "That means Ben from the Pelican Porch next door is his dad."

She nodded. "Ty grew up around the food business, so it didn't surprise anyone when he announced he wanted to be a famous chef in fifth grade. I knew he'd gone to culinary school in Paris after he graduated from high school, but he was a year ahead of me. I was focused on all my activities senior year, and then I went away to college. Ty is just one of the friends I lost touch with. It's great he's back in the Bay."

He threaded his fingers through hers, walking toward the water. Piper's heart sped up at the touch. She hadn't felt this giddy since her first kiss in eighth grade. Sullivan really appealed to her physically. It didn't hurt that he was also smart and kind. She warned herself silently not to get too attached to him.

And had a feeling that caution would fly out the window if he kissed her again.

Chapter Nine

Holding Piper's hand felt right.

Sullivan was feeling things he had never expected to experience with any woman. Because of the household he had grown up in, he had always guarded his emotions carefully. He played everything close to the vest. Never let others know what he was truly thinking. He didn't want to play any games with Piper, though.

They shuffled through the sand, the dunes thick and hard to slog through. Once they reached where the water had washed ashore, however, the tightly packed sand was hard and much easier to navigate. He kept Piper's hand in his as they strolled along the beach in silence for several minutes, the only sound being the waves moving in and out.

Then he said, "I want to get to know the real Piper Roberts."

"You think I'm going to reveal all my secrets to you?" she asked, her eyes twinkling with mischief. "Then you'll have to do the same, Mr. Shepherd. So, what's your favorite color?"

"Gray," he responded.

Her nose crinkled. "Gray isn't a color. Colors are vibrant. Rich. My favorite is teal. It's bright. Electric. Eye-catching."

"Gray is a color," he insisted. "A neutral one. It's soothing to me. Actually, soft, muted colors are who I am. The colors I'm drawn to."

"I would say that you're drawn to the colors of the sea," she observed. "You should commission Keaton to paint a picture of the bay, showing all those colors."

"Not a bad idea. It would be a nice reminder of my time in Driftwood Bay. What's your favorite food?" he countered.

"Seafood," she replied without missing a beat. "Let me tell you, when you order it in places such as Kansas City or Phoenix, it's not the seafood you get here in the Bay. I never knew how spoiled I was growing up, eating the freshest shrimp. The most tender grouper and different varieties of snapper. What do you like to eat?"

He paused, wistfulness spreading through him. "Anything from Maine. Memaw was a terrific cook. Maine produces the most blueberries in the US, and she made an amazing blueberry cobbler. She could also fry up oysters like nobody's business, and she baked the best brown bread and cooked the sweetest chowder I've ever eaten. I'd give anything to sit at her kitchen table one more time and feast on everything she cooked."

"My mom is a great cook. She can whip up something delicious out of only a few ingredients. I really love her fried chicken and meatloaf. And her pancakes are the fluffiest ever." Piper laughed. "You're making me hungry, and I'm still stuffed from dinner."

"What kind of movies do you enjoy watching?" he asked.

"Mysteries. Or crime dramas. Most of the productions I've appeared in have been musicals, with just a few plays thrown in. I never had an opportunity to act in a mystery. Not many have been written for the stage. I like to see how they unfold.

Try to put the pieces together and solve the puzzle before the big reveal."

She studied him. "That sounds more like what you might lean toward. As an architect, you plan things on paper. I can see you enjoying trying to construct a timeline and figure out who the murderer is. Am I right about that?"

He grinned. "Nope. Not even close. I'm into science fiction and dystopian novels and movies. I guess I'm curious about what our future holds and how mankind always seems to screw everything up. What do you like to do for fun?"

"Being on the road all the time, I couldn't pursue hobbies. No painting or crafting. It would've been too hard keeping supplies on hand. We had to keep our luggage to a minimum. So, I spent a lot of time reading. I also love to dance, but I couldn't take dance classes while traveling. That's why I got into fitness and made dance part of my exercising, especially Zumba. I like the energy exercise brings, plus it helps with stamina, having to stand onstage for hours. I didn't have a lot of time to myself as I traveled, though. I tended to be around others so much that I valued the time I had away from them. Reading allows me to get lost in different worlds. Then again, I've been a reader since I started school."

"Do you have a favorite book, Piper?"

Sullivan watched her face, seeing it flush at his question, and she said, "I like to read romances. I have since high school. I enjoy the struggle of two people coming together. Learning about one another. Figuring out how to solve the obstacles which keep them apart. I find satisfaction when they reach their HEA—the happily ever after. It's a nice payoff and just makes me feel good."

"I've never read a romance novel before," he admitted.

"Not many guys have. They could probably learn a lot from them if they did so. How to treat a woman. How to really listen to her. How to be a good partner. How small, simple gestures mean the most. Women read romances because they don't have any romance in their own lives. My favorite genre is Regency romance."

He frowned. "Why? What's it about?"

"It's a time in England's history when King George the Third was experiencing bouts of madness. His son became Prince Regent and ruled in his stead. It's set against the background of the Napoleonic Wars." She smiled shyly. "I guess I'm a sucker for a pretty gown and a heroine who dances in a ballroom with a handsome rogue she's secretly pined for."

He squeezed her fingers. "So, you're telling me you're attracted to bad boys?"

"Only on a fictional page. In real life? I suppose I'm looking for someone who's steadfast. Loyal. Honorable. Actually, that's what those rogues turn out to be in the romances I read. The heroine doesn't just tame the wildness in a rake. She brings him to his knees. The hero figures out she's what's been missing in his life, and he falls head over heels in love with her."

"Have you ever been in love, Piper?" he asked, preparing for whatever her answer might be.

"No," she said wistfully. "Maybe it's because I've read too many of those romances. Real life doesn't stack up. Sure, I had crushes on guys growing up. Mostly, I've had relationships with fellow actors over the years because they're the only men I've been around. But love? I haven't been lucky enough to be touched by it."

She worried her lip, causing desire to flicker in him. He wanted to take her into his arms and give her that storybook romance she craved. He fought the urge and kept silent, though, allowing her to unburden herself to him.

When she spoke again, he saw tears misted her eyes. "Layne and Mila have been my closest friends—my sisters of the heart

—since forever. I'm thrilled they've found real love with partners they not only care for, but men of good character. It's a little tough, though, to be left out. It's as if they got invited by their Prince Charmings to the most magical ball ever, while I'm sitting at home alone."

Sullivan wished he could be that hero in real life for her, but her future was in the Bay, while his was anywhere but on the Texas coast.

"You'll find the man you're looking for," he told her, hating the fact that she would someday.

And that it wouldn't be him.

"You're a wonderful person, Piper," he continued. "Exuberate. Outgoing. Caring. Smart. You'll find the right guy, the man who deserves you."

"Have you ever been in love, Sullivan?" she asked.

"Not even close. You're right about me. I live in a different world from others. Most women I've dated—no, gone out with because dating implies a relationship—have been pretty shallow. They care about how much I make. Who my parents are in society. It's a false world."

"Then why do you stay in it?" she asked, frowning. "It sounds really depressing and disappointing. You're never going to find happiness if you're stuck doing things you don't want to do with people who don't interest you."

He didn't have an answer for that. Piper was exactly right.

In a moment of rare transparency, Sullivan said, "My grandparents were my rock. My touchstone with what the world was truly like, not the limited society I was exposed to in Manhattan. After they died, I told myself to simply go along to get along, as far as my parents were concerned. I did everything they wanted. In return for not rocking the boat, they pretty much ignored me. Left me alone. Father worked long hours and traveled a great deal. Mother had all her charity affairs to organize and lunched with ladies. I was more an afterthought to them, not a reality. They went their ways. I went mine."

She looked at him, obviously shocked. "You're right. I can't relate to that at all. I'm so close to my mom and dad. They're two of the best people I know and still madly in love after decades together. I guess I've witnessed the example they've set—and it's what I want for myself and the man I love. I want to find someone who's values are similar to mine, a man who enjoys his job but enjoys coming home to his family even more. I need someone to share the big and little things in life. A guy who is a good husband and an even better father. I think that's why I was drawn to returning to the Bay. Because if I'm going to find that, it'll be here."

She took a long breath and released it. "I'm not someone who needs to go travel the world. I learned that *Wizard of Oz* lesson and know what I truly want in life is in my own backyard. My bucket list is small, and at the top of it? Vacationing in the mountains. We drove through them several times over the years in Denver and few other places, but I would've loved to stop for a week. Hiked. Fished. Just sit on the porch of a cabin and enjoy the majesty of the mountains.

"I'm a simple woman at heart."

He couldn't agree more. Women he knew wanted to attend runway fashion shows in Paris. Rub elbows with princes in Dubai. Take a villa in Rome or Venice and shop, spending thousands of dollars on things they might not ever wear. That kind of woman didn't appeal to Sullivan.

His gaze met hers.

This was the woman he wanted. Desperately. Hesitancy filled him, though. He would be heading back to his life in New York soon. He couldn't dally with her feelings, yet every fiber in his being told him he would be making a mistake if he didn't spend as much time as possible with her.

He steered them so that they headed back in the other direction now. A comfortable silence blanketed them, something he wasn't used to when he was in the company of another woman. Sullivan believed he had never been his authentic self in the presence of any other woman. Being with Piper was like coming home, coming to a place he hadn't known existed, and yet it was one both familiar and special to him.

"What's your biggest regret?" he asked.

She mulled over his question and then said, "The biggest is not finishing college. At the time, I was twenty and college classes seemed like a waste of time, mostly just a rehash of what I'd done in high school. Mila told me those first two years were all about weeding out people. That those who stayed the course were rewarded when they earned their degrees. All I really enjoyed were my theater and music classes. And performing. When a friend told me about the auditions for a new touring troupe, I went to Houston on a whim and was thrilled when they accepted me. It was just a place in the chorus, but all I could think of was that I was now a professional actor and being paid to do what I loved."

Piper paused. "Don't get me wrong, Sullivan. I have thoroughly enjoyed performing all these years. Singing and dancing on stage. Bringing joy to others. It's a natural high. At the same time, I wish I would have returned to school after that first tour. Even if I would've gotten my degree in theater, at least it would have been a degree. Now, I feel too old to go back."

"That's not true. You're never too old to learn."

She smiled ruefully. "Maybe I didn't word that the right way. I wouldn't mind going back to school, but I don't have a way to support myself if I did so. I'm not about to ask Mom and Dad to pay for their thirty-year-old daughter to finish college, especially with them on the cusp of retirement. I'm an adult, responsible for myself. I have to live with the consequences of my actions from years ago. I'll find something I enjoy doing right here in the Bay. I just won't be as well compensated as say, an architect with a fancy degree from Yale."

Piper gave him a sad smile, and he hated that her options were so limited, but he knew they were. A degree set job applicants apart. Even though she was bright, not having one would keep her from getting in the door most places.

She looked at him, her eyes soulful. "Do you have any regrets?"

"I've never really thought about that. I would say that I regret not standing up to my parents more. Yes, I rebelled at first and ran away, hitchhiking my way to Maine. They simply brought me back. Actually, they were too busy to come themselves. They sent their driver. I do regret not ever having seen my grandparents alive again, though. We always wrote letters to one another, but I would give anything to spend just one more hour with them.

"After they were gone, it was as if I flipped a switch. I became who my parents insisted I be because it was just easier not to fight about it anymore. I had a lot of pressure on me because I had an older brother who drowned when I was a baby. Mother had a difficult pregnancy with me and couldn't have any more children after I was born, so they pinned all their hopes on me—and I morphed into the perfect son. I earned top grades. Excelled in athletics. Moved through society with ease. They were able to totally disassociate with me, yet they still bragged about all my many accomplishments to their friends."

He swallowed. "I still see them on occasion. I actually went home for Christmas last year. They take no joy in holidays such as that. It's all about setting the table with the right china and having the best caterer serve Christmas dinner to a bunch of people they talk about badly behind their backs but smile to their faces and welcome them to their table. I should've stayed in the Bay and celebrated with my new friends and Neville and Nellie."

"I hate to say this, Sullivan, but it sounds like you lead a really lonely life. At least I made friends on the road with my fellow cast and crew. You don't seem to have anyone in New York."

"I have Zane," he said. "He's like a brother to me. His flesh and blood brother is a real piece of work. They barely speak to one another. You're right, Piper. I meet with other people regarding various Wagner projects, but because of my line of work, I'm left on my own a lot of the time as I research and draw up my plans. I enjoy getting out of New York and traveling to different sites, but that's temporary."

Sullivan came to a halt and gazed across the water. "I've actually stayed in the Bay much longer than I normally do anywhere else. I told Zane I found something good here. Something real and pure. I've lingered on the coast, enjoying the friendships I've made as I've started a new project. I'm thirty-four and have attained professional success and financial security, but I don't really have anything to show for my life beyond that. That's a hard pill to swallow, especially thinking back to what I thought I would be doing by my mid-thirties."

He cupped her cheek. "Maybe you could help me to find myself before I move on."

His thumb stroked her cheek, and Sullivan yearned to kiss her. His gut told him that wouldn't be the right thing to do, though. Piper had returned home to put down roots. To find a man to love and cherish her and share the rest of her life. He let his hand fall away.

"Let's get you home."

They trudged up the unwieldy sand dunes and returned to his car. He opened her door, and she got in. They didn't speak on the short drive to the inn. When they reached the Bay Breeze, he got out and escorted her to the door.

Sullivan brushed a kiss on her cheek. "Thank you for tonight. I haven't bared my soul to anyone like I did to you tonight, Piper. I appreciate you listening to me. For being my friend."

Turning, he trotted down the stairs. He would wait in the car and make certain she got inside okay, and then he would head home. It was time to pack his things and leave Driftwood Bay.

Before his heart hurt so much that it would make leaving unbearable.

"Wait!" she called.

Reluctantly, he turned to face her again. They stared at one another wordlessly, and then she raced down the stairs and threw her arms around him.

"Don't go," she begged. "I don't want you to."

Knowing it was a mistake to stay—and that both of them were going to be badly hurt in the long run—he enveloped her in his arms anyway. His lips came crashing down on hers.

At least for now, everything was right.

Chapter Ten

Piper watched Sullivan as he walked away from her. Something inside her shifted. She knew he had been more honest and vulnerable with her tonight than he ever had previously. Although he was leaving at some unknown date in the near future, she knew she wanted him in her life for as long as possible. Whether that was a day, a week, or a month, it simply didn't matter. What was important was that she live each day to its fullest. Not every friendship or relationship was meant to last a lifetime, but she would be a better person for the time she would spend in Sullivan Shepherd's company.

"Wait!" she cried, seeing him turn.

Their gazes met, and emotions washed through her. He was a good man. She would be a better woman for taking him into her heart—and bed.

Piper flew down the porch steps and ran to him, throwing herself at him, clinging to him in desperation. Her gut told her he had not planned to see her again, and she always trusted it. She wouldn't let him push her way.

"Don't go," she said, pleading with him. "I don't want you to."

Thankfully, his mouth came down hard on hers. The spark which had existed between them ever since they'd met lit, and desire flooded her. She kissed him with everything she had, trying to convey that she was his.

For a little while...

He broke the kiss. His gaze searched hers, his hazel eyes wordlessly asking a thousand questions.

"I don't know how long you have left in the Bay, but I want to spend as much time as I can with you, Sullivan," she said breathlessly. "I want to be with you. In every way."

Before he could reply, she pulled him down to her, kissing him again, her body heating as it pressed against his.

He kissed her back, his tongue plunging deep inside her mouth, searching for answers to his own questions. She reveled in the kiss, realizing it was, without a doubt, the best one of her life.

This time, she ended the kiss. "Would you like to come inside?" she asked hopefully.

"I would," he replied, his voice low and rough.

She could feel every beat of his heart as they remained linked to one another.

"But I'm not sure that's wise, Piper." He added, dashing her hopes. Yet Piper was not the kind of person who ever admitted defeat.

"I disagree. I think inviting you inside is one of the best decisions I've ever made. You accepting my invitation will be one of the best which you've ever made."

She kissed him softly, hoping it would help convince him to choose her. Now. This moment. Piper ran her fingers through his rich, brown, silky hair, sensing the shiver running through him.

"I haven't really had any long-term relationships, Sullivan. Because of constantly being on the road, I could never make any kind of lasting commitment to a man. Honestly, I've never dated a man who made me even consider something permanent. All I know right now is that I would be a fool to ignore the chemistry between us. I'm walking into this with my eyes fully open. I understand there can't be any kind of lasting relationship because of our situation. You have a life and job in New York. I want to build my new life here in the Bay. What I do know is that you are a good man, and I think I could learn something about life—and myself—if I'm with you. If only for a little while," she added softly.

She could see him wrestling with his decision, but she had stated her case and simply waited patiently. Either he would act in a gentlemanly fashion and turn down her request, not wanting to hurt her, or he would see the clarity of her argument. Piper saw the moment he came to a decision, the spark in his eyes giving it away.

"I hope we won't regret this," he said huskily.

"We may down the road," she said matter-of-factly. "But when you leave the Bay? I don't want to be suffering from a case of the What Ifs. What if I had told you how I felt? What if we had made the most of our limited time together? I don't regret many things in my life, but I know I would regret it if we didn't make love."

Suddenly, he swept her off her feet. Just like in one of her romance novels. It caused her to giggle as she entwined her arms about his neck. He carried her up the porch steps. Leaning down, Sullivan scooped up the purse which had fallen from her shoulder. Sullivan handed it to her, and she retrieved the key.

He took it from her and unlocked the door to the inn, a place they had all to themselves tonight. Carrying her inside, he nudged the door closed with his foot. She leaned down and turned the lock.

"It's just you and me tonight, Sullivan. There's no past. No thoughts of the future. Just here and now."

He seized her mouth with his, the kiss both thorough and scalding. Desire raced through her, and Piper kissed him with abandon. She knew she was giving everything she had to him in this moment.

Even her heart.

Especially her heart.

She wouldn't think about the heartache to come when he was gone. She was truthful when she told him that she wanted to have no regrets when he left the Bay.

Easing her to her feet, he continued the kiss, which was full of fire. She molded her body to his, thinking them a perfect fit. Then he startled her, breaking the kiss, swearing under his breath.

"What's wrong?" she asked anxiously, wondering how something so right could go sideways in an instant.

"No condom with me," he said, cursing again.

"I've got that taken care of. Being on the road with no permanent address or gynecologist to see, I checked off handling birth control a long time ago. I've got a long-acting copper IUD." Smiling, she added, "You are free to have your way with me, Mr. Shepherd."

He returned the smile. "I like a planner."

He kissed her again, a slow, delicious kiss which had her toes curling.

"I think we need to take this to the bedroom," she advised.

Piper found herself back in his arms again as he carried her around, turning off lights. She directed him to her bedroom on the bottom floor. One lamp sitting on the end table burned softly.

"We're leaving that on," he said, his voice rumbling low in his chest. "Because I want to see you as I explore every inch of your deliciously tempting skin."

Those words caused shivers to run along her spine.

"Keep talking that way, and I may come right here without you even touching me," she warned playfully.

"I plan for you to come several times tonight."

"Is that a promise?" she asked coyly.

His gaze met hers. "It's a fact, babe. I guarantee it."

He kissed her again, and she thought she could kiss this man for hours. Piper had always enjoyed kissing, but Sullivan took the art of kissing to a new, unexplored level.

Setting on her feet again, he turned away, removing the decorative pillows from the bed and turning back the comforter and sheets. Then he returned to her, slowly unbuttoning her blouse, kissing the exposed flesh with every button that came undone. He pulled it from her shoulders. His mouth went to the column of her throat, his tongue slowly gliding down it and along her shoulder. He slid the strap of her bra away, and his tongue continued, causing her to shiver in anticipation.

His hands moved behind her, unclasping the bra and ridding her of it. He cupped her breasts, kneading them slowly.

"These are perfect," he announced, his mouth going to one, feasting upon it.

Her blood heated, singing in her veins, and her arms went about him, holding him close as he suckled hard. Then his teeth toyed with her nipple, grazing it again and again, causing her core to tighten and throb in anticipation.

"I may come right now," she gasped, causing him to lift his head. "No, don't stop," she begged.

"I've got to," he said, panting. "I'm wearing way too many clothes. So are you."

"Then let me help solve that problem."

She unbuttoned his shirt, parting the material, her lips trailing down his bare chest. When the last button had come undone, he quickly doffed the shirt.

"Time to work on you again," he told her, removing her shoes, socks, and jeans, leaving her in nothing but lacey black panties.

His hand cupped her, and she could feel they were already damp.

"You're definitely getting ready for me," he said, a wicked smile playing about his lips.

She took his face in her hands and kissed him again, needing the taste of him once more.

He clasped her elbows, pushing her away from him so he could quickly remove the rest of what he wore. Her eyes roamed his body, her fingers reaching out to stroke the ridges of his six-pack.

"My, you take working out seriously."

He caught her wrists and brought her hands up, turning them over and kissing the center of each palm.

"I hit the athletic club a couple of times a week. Play handball with Zane if he's in town or swim laps. Lift a few weights. Mostly, though, I run in Central Park." He released her hands and captured her waist, his thumbs stroking her ribcage, causing tremors to run through her.

"You're in top shape yourself," he complimented, admiration in his tone and eyes.

"Actors have to be. You have to build stamina in order to get you through so many rehearsals and hours performing onstage. I've told you that I enjoy moving. Exercising. Dancing."

His eyes darkened with desire. "Babe, you've got all the right moves." His hands slid lower, his fingers tucking inside her panties, ripping the scrap of material away. The sudden move surprised her. Delighted her.

Because it let her know how much he wanted her.

They collapsed onto the bed, their limbs entangling even as their tongues did. She had never had a man kiss her so deeply. So thoroughly. She thrilled at each kiss. With every touch. And there were plenty of both.

He explored her body. Even worshipped it. His hands glided along each curve, his mouth and tongue following. The passion rose between them, and she thought the sheets might catch on fire with the heat generated between them.

Breaking their kiss, his mouth moved down her body. The lower it went, the more her heart fluttered wildly. He moved between her legs, his large hands parting her thighs to give him better access to her. He slowly licked the seam of her sex, causing her hips to rise, even as she whimpered. Wrapping his arms around her thighs, he plunged his tongue deep inside her, making her gasp aloud.

Her fingers tangled in his hair as his tongue moved inside her. Tasting her. Draining her. The orgasm quickly erupted, taking over her body as waves of pleasure rocked her. She writhed on the bed, bursts of white light accompanying the incredible, pulsating sensations rippling through her. She rode the pleasure as it encompassed her and then lay limp when it came to an end.

Sullivan kissed his way back up to her mouth, and she clung to him tightly as his fingers parted her. His cock pressed against her a moment, and then he thrust quickly into her. Another gasp erupted from her. His hands found hers, lacing their fingers together. He lifted them so they rested beside each side of her head. He hadn't moved after that single thrust, and he smiled at her now.

"I want to watch you as I make love to you, Piper," he said, his voice hoarse and ragged.

He began moving slowly inside her, their gazes locked upon one another. With each thrust, she felt not only physically but emotionally close to him, an intimacy building between them. His eyes never left hers as he continued thrusting, his fingers tightening around hers. She didn't bother to keep quiet. She had never been vocal during lovemaking with other partners, usually being in cheap hotels the troupe stayed in, ones with thin walls. They were alone tonight, though, and she let her enthusiasm go unchecked now, encouraging him.

"Yes, yes. There. Hard. Harder. Harder. Yes!"

Her whimpers grew louder, and she finally shouted one final, "Yes!"

The powerful orgasm tore through her. They came at the same time, his own shout escaping his lips, as well as his body's shudder. He collapsed atop her, driving her into the mattress, and she welcomed his weight, her arms going about him, her fingers locking behind his back.

"You," he managed to get out, his breathing ragged as he gazed at her.

"You," she echoed, freezing this moment in her mind, wanting to always remember it.

His lips sought hers, the kiss tender. Piper held him to her, wishing she never had to let go.

A quick roll, and she was now atop him, causing a giggle to escape. His hands framed her face.

"That was incredible," he said. "*You* are incredible."

She was afraid if she told him it had been the best sex of her life, it would frighten him off. Make him think she expected more of a commitment from him.

"You were just this side of spectacular," she said, taking a light, teasing tone.

"Hmm. Shy of spectacular. Guess I'll have to work on my technique. I'm Sullivan Shepherd. I have to be the best at everything I do."

"I'm ready and willing to help you perfect your technique," she flirted.

Sullivan leaned up and kissed her lightly. "I plan to take you up on that generous offer. For now, however, I'm exhausted."

Piper wriggled her way off him, cuddling against his side. He stretched and turned off the lamp and then reached down and brought the sheet up to his waist, covering them both. Usually, she needed more covers than this, but she had a human blanket of heat which would keep her cozy.

"Let's take a nap," he said, "Then we can go another round."

"Okay," she mumbled, tumbling fast into a deep sleep.

Chapter Eleven

Sullivan finished dressing after his shower, thinking about how Piper had offered to go shopping with him for a pair of jeans. It was just one of the sweet things about her, wanting him to fit in the Bay. He decided he would take her up on it. It would be just another excuse to be in her company.

He cut through the diner since he hadn't done so in days, waving to Neville and giving Nellie a kiss on the cheek.

"We haven't seen much of you lately," Nellie said.

Shrugging, he said, "Been busy. Work. Friends."

The old woman smiled at him. "I'm glad to see you making friends in the Bay, Sullivan. I can't wait for Zane to get here so that I can spoil the two of you together. Where are you off to?"

He saw no reason to hide his plans from her and said, "I'm having dinner with Piper Roberts and her parents. I met her through Keaton and Layne, and we've really hit it off."

"Why, that's wonderful, sweetie. The Roberts are such a wonderful couple and have given so much to this community. I haven't seen Piper since she's been back, but I hear she's going to be running the Bay Breeze."

"At least through Labor Day. She's not quite certain what she wants to do after that."

Nellie's brows knitted together. "It was terrible, what happened with Jack and Lark. I'm glad Layne has been able to lean on her friends in such a time of heartache."

Sullivan knew Nellie referred to the murder/suicide of Layne's parents, the reason she had inherited the B&B.

"Well, I'm off," he said, heading to his car.

It had been drilled into him that as a guest, a person always brought a hostess gift. Since he didn't know a thing about Mrs. Roberts, he decided to stop by and pick up some flowers. He didn't know a female who didn't like a pretty bouquet. Then it hit him that he had overheard Piper mentioning him bringing wine to dinner this evening. As he turned into the parking lot where he could buy both, he dialed her number.

"Hey, you. Are you on your way over? You usually text."

"You said something about making sangria tonight, and I was going to be responsible for the wine. I just stopped at the supermarket to pick up a bottle or two."

He entered the doors and headed toward the wine and beer aisle.

"It's a grocery store in Texas, Prepster. Don't worry, I've got you covered. I stopped by and picked up the things I needed to make the guac, plus everything for the sangria. Just head my way instead."

"Will do," he said, changing directions and moving toward the floral section.

His eye was drawn to a beautiful bouquet of what was labeled Mexican petunias and daisies in a vase of water. The mix of purple and white flowers appealed to him, so he claimed it and went to the checkout. It proved tricky balancing the large vase as he drove to the Bay Breeze, though. When he arrived, he rested the vase on the floorboard of the passenger's seat and bounded up the steps, ringing the doorbell.

Piper answered the door, looking beautiful in a lightweight cornflower sweater which brought out the blue of her eyes. What got his attention more, though, was the pair of faded jeans which molded to her hips and legs like a second skin.

"Come on back. I'm just gathering up everything to take in the kitchen."

Sullivan enjoyed walking behind her, the sway of her hips hypnotizing him.

She opened the door to the fridge and removed a glass bowl capped with a lid and a bottle of lemon juice. Setting down both on the island, she retrieved a fork from a drawer and opened the lid, sprinkling a bit of the juice on top of the dip and stirring it briskly with the fork before replacing the lid. She held up the fork to him, and he opened his mouth, tasting the dip, which had a wonderful smoothness to it.

As she placed items into two canvas bags, he said, "You say you didn't know how to cook, but this dip is better than anything I've eaten in a restaurant. You also knew exactly how to make Texas Trash."

She scooped up one bag and handed it to him as she claimed the other for herself, motioning him to leave the kitchen.

"Making dip is not what I'd consider cooking. It's like making popcorn in a microwave. Nothing to it. Although I do think you'd like my Texas caviar dip."

"I'm afraid to ask what's in that because I'm guessing it's not the caviar I know," he joked. "Why did you add the lemon juice?" he asked, curious about that as she locked the front door and they headed toward his car.

"I like to mix up guac a few hours before serving it so the flavors really settle well. Avocados have the tendency to turn slightly brown, though. Lemon juice brightens the color back up and makes the guac look more appetizing."

They reached his car, and he opened the door, saying, "Watch out. I've got flowers on the floorboard. "You'll need to hold those on the way over."

Sullivan took the canvas bag from her and placed both in the backseat of the car as Piper got in and brought the flowers to her lap.

"These are gorgeous. Apparently not for me."

He leaned down and kissed her forehead before closing her door and walking around to the other side of the car.

"They're for your mom. Her hostess gift."

"You must've been a real hit with mothers," she said.

As he started the car, he nodded. "I was. That was fifteen years ago, however. To be honest, I don't think I've met a single parent since my early college years."

She looked pensive. "So, you really haven't seriously dated anyone."

"Nope. I'm pretty much a workaholic. I also saw what a disaster Zane's marriage was, and that has kept me in my single lane."

"Oh, he was married?"

"Briefly. From the time we graduated from college, we lived together before Amanda came along." Shaking his head, he added, "He moved back in three months after their wedding. It took another six months to cut all ties with her."

"What went wrong?" she asked.

"What didn't?" he countered. "It was destined to fail from the start. It's the only time Zane has never listened to me."

"I guess you two are the hot catches on the singles scene in New York."

"We both go out some. Me a little more than he does. Zane travels quite a bit for his job. It's not conducive for a permanent relationship. Since his brief marriage left such a bad taste in his mouth, I don't think he'll ever try marriage again."

Sullivan knew the turns to make from their previous trip to the Roberts' house earlier in the day, and they arrived in minutes. He helped her from the car and collected the two bags and both fishing rods. Since the garage door was open, Piper had them cut through the garage. While he replaced the rods, she hung the boat key back on the wall and then opened the door leading into the kitchen.

Immediately, the aroma of something delicious baking filled his nostrils. He saw an attractive woman standing by the stove, stirring something in a pot.

"Hi, sweetie," Mrs. Roberts said.

Piper set down the flowers and hugged her mother. "Hey, Mom. This is Sullivan Shepherd. He's responsible for your lovely bouquet."

"Why, thank you, Sullivan. That was a very thoughtful gesture on your part."

"Nice to meet you, Mrs. Roberts."

"Oh, please. Call me Ellen. I'm only Mrs. Roberts at school. Unfortunately, I can't break Mila or Layne from calling me that."

"Mom, they've known you since before they could count to five. It's just a sign of respect. Besides, you know you're a second mom to both of them."

Looking pleased, Ellen Roberts said, "Well, it has been nice being able to help plan Layne's wedding, with Lark being gone."

Chief Roberts appeared in the doorway. He crossed the kitchen and offered his hand. "Good to see you again, Sullivan. I see you've met my better half."

"Thanks for having me to dinner, Chief."

Piper began removing things from the bags and set the dip

in the center of the island. She took out a large bowl and dumped a bag of tortilla chips into it.

"Everyone sample the dip and see if I have enough garlic salt in it."

All three willingly obliged, claiming a chip and dipping it into the guacamole. He bit into his and murmured, "Mmm."

"Great job, honey," the chief said. "Don't mess with it. It's fine as it is."

"Anything I can help with dinner, Mom?" Piper asked.

"No, everything's under control. All we need is for the sangria to be whipped up. My mouth is watering for a glass of it."

Piper went to a cabinet and opened it, pulling out a punch bowl. "This is what you and I will use," she told Sullivan. "Have you had sangria while you've been in Texas?"

"No. It'll be a new experience for me."

Together, they prepared the beverage, a new experience for him.

"Open the bottle of wine. It's been chilling," she said. "Corkscrew's in that second drawer on the left."

He opened the wine, noting it was a rioja.

"I like to use a Spanish wine," Piper told him. "A dry red is perfect for sangria. I've used a pinot noir or a malbec before, but I lean toward a rioja." She looked to her dad. "Would you grab some brandy, Dad? I knew you'd have a bottle open."

"I do like a glass of brandy in the evenings," he said, bringing it over and handing it to Sullivan, who looked to Piper for guidance.

"Start pouring slowly. I'll tell you when to stop. There. That's good."

He stirred the spirits and added sugar and orange juice, blending the ingredients in the punchbowl. She had him mix in sugar and let it dissolve before she added the fruit she had cut up. Piper then dropped a cinnamon stick into the bowl and topped the sangria with slices of oranges and lemons.

"That should do it," she said. "Bring the bowl outside for me."

She opened the door leading back to the garage and led him to a second fridge. He placed the sangria inside, seeing the fridge was stocked with everything from beer to soda to bottled waters.

"And you say I'm rich. We didn't have a second fridge reserved for beverages."

She laughed. "It's a thing in the Bay. When your old one is about ten, you move it outside and get a new one. Having a second fridge to stock drinks for football games and parties is practically a requirement in Texas. Plus, it comes in handy during the holidays, to store all the dishes prepared for meals."

They headed back inside to the den, where he enjoyed the conversation with her parents. Sullivan had never been as relaxed with adults as he was now, except for his days with his grandparents in Baker's Cove.

Eventually, Piper and her mother began talking about the upcoming wedding, and Chief Roberts said, "While I enjoy a good wedding, listening to all this planning tuckers me out. How is Tidewater coming along, Sullivan?"

They chatted for several minutes about his design and how the resort would be opening on July first.

"I'm thinking I need to get with their head of security. Just to let them familiarize themselves with me and for me to see their operation."

"I can arrange that for you. Offhand, I can't remember the name of the guy who was hired to be the director of security, but I can put you in touch with Bill Lonsdale. He's Tidewater's manager and is also serving as the head of HR. He's doing all the hiring for each position."

The chief's eyes flicked to his daughter. "I was wondering if Piper might go to work at the resort, but it seems that she's got herself committed to Layne and the Bay Breeze for now." He smiled indulgently. "It's so good to have my little girl home."

Roberts glanced back to Sullivan. "I know you're thinking I'm an old fool because Piper is a grown woman. If you're lucky enough, one day you'll have a little girl of your own. Then you'll see how she rules your roost and has a permanent place in your heart. Piper has always brought us a lot of joy. She's spreads sunshine wherever she goes."

The police chief nailed it. That described Piper in a nutshell.

Studying him, the older man said, "So, are you two keeping company?"

He hated being put on the spot, not knowing exactly what Piper wanted him to say about them, so he replied honestly and yet vaguely.

"We're seeing each other, sir."

"You'll be off to your next project soon, I suppose."

He swallowed. "I will be, but Piper is making my stay in the Bay a lot more enjoyable."

A kitchen timer went off, and Mrs. Roberts said, "The lasagna is ready."

They gathered in the kitchen, with Sullivan being told to bring the sangria back inside. He did so, watching the Roberts work seamlessly, communicating without words as different dishes were placed on the table.

"Would you also like some iced tea along with your sangria?" Ellen asked him.

"Yes, please," he responded.

Minutes later, his plate was full, and he was complimenting his hostess on her culinary skills.

"I don't know anything about cooking, but you may have

to send this recipe with me, Ellen. I would love to be able to eat Mexican lasagna again down the road."

"I'll make sure you take some leftovers with you, honey. You can have Nellie heat it up for you."

"Actually, there's a kitchenette above the diner in the room where I'm staying. I know my way around operating a microwave, so I can do that myself."

Talk turned to some of the shows Piper had performed in over the years, and he learned that the Roberts had gone to see several of those productions in various cities.

"I was never much for vacations before Piper took off across the country," the chief said. "Thanks to her, I've seen places from Atlanta to San Diego."

Ellen added, "We would go in a day or two beforehand to do some sightseeing and then attend Piper's show. Then we'd stay a day or so after and finish up seeing anything we'd missed. We had to work around my school vacations, but it was fun."

She reached for her husband's hand, and Sullivan could see the love she had for the man she had shared her life with.

"Elmo's promised me we're going to keep traveling, even though Piper's back in the Bay now."

"You could always go see Don, wherever he might be," Piper suggested.

"Who's Don?" he asked.

"He's my brother who has a bad case of wanderlust. Don is a travel writer and hasn't set foot inside the US in years. He's ten years older than I am, so we've never been particularly close, but I do follow his blog online. We email some."

"You need to think about how you'll use your talents now that you're back in the Bay," the chief told his daughter. "God gave you a beautiful voice, and you should be using it."

"I've never heard Piper sing a note," he told her parents.

"Why, we can remedy that right now," Ellen declared. "Let's clear the table and save dessert for a little later."

"Mom," Piper protested, sounding like a teenager. "Sullivan doesn't want to hear me sing."

His gaze met hers. "That's exactly what I want to do. I've been eager to hear your voice."

He pitched in with the clean-up, happily pouring what was left of the sangria into the empty wine bottles. As the others scraped plates and filled the dishwasher, Ellen cut a large chunk of the lasagna off and placed it in a dish.

"Don't leave without this," she told him. "This can be lunch or dinner for you tomorrow. Maybe both," she said brightly.

They gathered around an upright piano in the corner of the den. Ellen took a seat on the bench, and said, "We'll act as your chorus, honey. What would you like to sing?"

The moment Piper's rich contralto filled the air, a shiver ran along Sullivan's spine. Her voice had a wonderful range, and she put such emotion into the words she was singing. Her parents chimed in on the chorus, one he had no idea what the words might be. He stood, soaking things in.

Piper switched to songs from other shows, and he actually knew the words to a few. Her parents sang along enthusiastically, Chief Robert slightly off-key, but they were enjoying themselves tremendously. Sullivan found himself joining in when he could, feeling a true part of a family for the first time.

"I'm done," Piper said as the song ended. "We've bored Sullivan enough."

He spoke up quickly. "I wasn't bored at all. Entranced is more like it."

His gaze met and held hers, and a blush spread across her cheeks.

Ellen asked, "Are you ready for dessert?"

Her eyes never leaving his, Piper said, "I think we'll take a rain check on that, Mom."

"Oh, so it's like that?" Ellen observed, amusement in her voice.

They said their goodnights, Ellen pressing the Tupperware dish into Sullivan's hands.

"Enjoy," she said. "The leftovers—and what's left of tonight."

Now, it was his turn to find his cheeks reddening. "Thank you for having me, Ellen. You and the Chief are good company."

As they drove home, he reached over and claimed Piper's hand, lacing their fingers together. Things were growing more complicated. If he were smart, he would cut and run now—before they were in too deep.

When they pulled up in front of the inn, however, Piper asked him if he wanted to come in and stay the night.

"Gladly," Sullivan replied, knowing it was too late to retreat.

Because he had already lost his heart to this ray of sunshine.

Chapter Twelve

Piper thanked Keaton for the ride, telling him that she was going to look for a car.

"No rush on that," the artist told her. "Both Layne and I have cars now. Since we'll be gone a good six weeks, we can leave you the keys. You're free to use either of our cars."

"That's a generous offer," she told him. "I appreciate everything you've done for me." She took his hand and squeezed it. "And thank you for being there for Layne. The two of you go together like peanut butter and jelly."

He laughed heartily. "That's the best compliment you could have given us, Piper. Peanut butter got me through a lot of hard times. I guess I'll think of my sweet wife as the jelly who completes me."

They went inside the house, and Keaton excused himself, going out to his studio to work, leaving her alone with Layne.

"I'm so glad you volunteered to do this," her friend said.

"Layne, honey, you could wear zero makeup on your wedding day and still be the most gorgeous bride. Part of it is your natural beauty, but the biggest thing is the glow you wear all the time. I can just say the name Keaton, and you light up like a Christmas tree."

Layne did that very thing now, causing Piper to laugh. "See? Let's go sit at the kitchen table," she suggested. "The light coming in from the bay window is good. We need to decide the mood we're going for."

"I got online and googled wedding day makeup after we talked," Layne confessed. "There were so many ideas, I finally closed out of all the tabs. You know me, Piper. You've been there practically from the beginning. What do you suggest?"

"We're going to try a few different palettes, but I can tell you that I'm leaning toward a soft palette which plays up your amazing green eyes. I think they're your best feature. Whatever look we go with, I want to emphasize them."

Piper opened the makeup case she had brought, which included a hand mirror. She placed it on the table in front of her friend.

"I don't claim to be an expert. Stage makeup is radically different from what we'll be doing today, but I have learned some tricks about contouring and lip lining."

For the next hour, she applied different kinds of makeup on Layne. They talked as she worked, and Piper was thankful she would be present to celebrate this wedding.

"I hated missing Mila and Carson's ceremony, but it couldn't be helped."

"Oh, honey, Mila understood. They decided to do it so quickly. They didn't expect you to leave your musical and fly back to the Bay. Especially with them getting married right before Thanksgiving, you might not have even been able to get a flight with so many people traveling during that holiday time."

"Well, I'm here now. You're not getting rid of me."

Layne looked in the mirror after each step, and she talked

about what she liked and didn't like. Her friend settled on what Piper had known she would, a soft, romantic look which made Layne's perfect complexion dewy. It played up her eyes, causing them to pop.

Piper said, "We definitely will use this waterproof mascara. I always wear it onstage. The lights can get really hot and melt makeup. Besides, if you do shed a few tears, you don't want rivers of mascara cascading down your cheeks."

Though they had tried a bold mouth, Piper went with a lighter shade which complemented Layne's caramel hair. She handed her friend the mirror one last time, and Layne's pleased smile let her know this was what they would go with for the wedding.

"This is absolutely perfect. I couldn't do this myself. Please say you'll be my makeup artist on my wedding day."

"Just tell me when to be here, and I'll have you ready in no time. How about your hair?"

"Leave that to me," Layne said. "It'll be how I usually wear it. That's Keaton's request."

"I want to leave this makeup on so that Mila and Kylie can see me," her friend said.

"Do you have any idea why Kylie is back in the Bay? I mean, come on. She was homecoming queen and class valedictorian. I never saw her being a full-time resident of the Bay as an adult, working for her parents' charter company."

"I thought that very same thing when you mentioned she was here and wanted to get together. It's not like I've booked anything through Mayfield Charters since I've been home, and I haven't needed to use the ferry, so I haven't run into her. I wonder if Kylie will be open to talking about it."

"She was always so nice to me," Piper said. "Kylie never stayed in that popular girl bubble, ignoring everyone else. She was friendly to everyone."

"Maybe she needs friends now," Layne said. "We can be here for her."

Fifteen minutes later, Mila arrived.

"Layne! You look gorgeous."

"Piper has promised to do my makeup for the wedding. This is what she came up with. Any feedback for her?"

Mila smiled. "Layne Larson, you're going to be the most beautiful bride the Bay has ever seen."

The doorbell rang again, and Layne admitted Kylie into the foyer. She carried a white bakery box.

"Hi, everyone. Thanks for letting me crash the Three Musketeers' dinner. The three of you were so tight in high school. I was a little jealous of how close y'all were. I remember when we studied in history about the formation of NATO. That an attack on one was an attack on all. Immediately, you three came to mind."

"Kylie, you were the most popular girl who's ever graduated from Driftwood Bay High School," Piper said. "You had friends everywhere."

Kylie smiled wistfully. "I had a lot of acquaintances, not really good friends the way the three of you were. I spent most of my time with the cheer squad or the track team. The cheerleaders were really cliquish. I might've been their captain, but if I'm being honest? They excluded me from all their whispering and secrets."

Piper put her arm around Kylie. "They could be a bunch of mean girls. You've got us now, though. It's funny how we've all returned to our hometown. How long have you been back?"

She felt Kylie stiffen slightly. "I think it's been about a year now," she said, a little too casually, causing Piper's gaze to flick to Layne and then Mila. The subtle message hit home, and the three of them knew not to ask Kylie any more intrusive questions. If they were destined to become close friends with her, it would be up to Kylie to open up. For now, they would protect her and make certain she was comfortable in their presence.

"You all look amazing," Kylie told them. "But Layne looks better than she ever did in high school."

"It's the makeup," Layne credited. "Piper came over this afternoon, and we've been playing with the makeup for my wedding. It's in a few days."

"I learned from different stage makeup artists and simply applied that knowledge today," she told the others. "I think it's a fantastic look for Layne."

"Let's move from the foyer," Layne said. "I've got wine breathing, along with cold Dr Peppers and bottled waters. Come into the kitchen. We can get drinks and relax. Kylie, you can put dessert on the island."

As they walked through the house and entered the kitchen, Kylie said, "This house is incredible, Layne."

"It's got a small cottage in the back. Keaton is using as his studio. He draws inspiration from being so close to the water."

The kitchen door opened at that moment, and Keaton appeared. He kissed Layne's cheek.

"I know these two. Who's the newcomer?" he asked.

Kylie offered her hand. "I'm Kylie Mayfield. I grew up in the Bay and was a year ahead of the Three Musketeers."

He cocked one brow. "Oh, is that what they were called? I should've guessed."

"Kylie's going to be our fourth," Layne told him. "You can call her d'Artagnan."

Piper noticed the pleased look on Kylie's face.

"Well, I'll leave you musketeers to it. I'm heading over to your place, Mila."

"Carson said he was ordering from Pizza Perfecto," she said. "Sullivan will be there, too."

At the mention of his name, Piper felt her cheeks grow warm.

Keaton grabbed a six-pack of beer from the fridge and told them goodbye.

Layne said, "King Ranch casserole is in the oven. That gives us time to sit and visit a little before it's ready. Let grab drinks and go gab."

She noticed everyone but Mila opted for a glass of wine, setting off her radar since Mila had always been fond of a glass of wine and often sipped one during their bi-monthly Face-Time chats. She wondered if her friend might already be trying for a baby—or even pregnant. She kept quiet, knowing Mila would share any news she had when the time was right.

Piper sat on a love seat with Kylie, while Layne and Mila settled themselves on a nearby sofa.

"How is it being back in the Bay, Piper? Your mom pretty much let the entire high school know you were returning," Mila revealed. "She was so excited."

"That's Mom for you," she said, chuckling. "We actually had dinner with my parents last night."

"*We*?" Layne asked.

"Sullivan and I took out Dad's fishing boat yesterday. He'd never gone fishing before, and I thought it was something he should do before he left the Bay. Afterwards, Mom had us stay for dinner."

Layne studied her intently. "What are you leaving out?"

She decided to be open with her friends and said, "Sullivan and I are seeing each other. It's...casual. He'll be leaving for New York in the near future, so we're just enjoying one another's company for now."

"I'll bet he's a great kisser," Mila said. "He's got kissable lips."

"Mila!" Piper cried.

"Hey, I'm just making an observation. I may be married to the most gorgeous man on the planet, but I can still appreciate a handsome guy—and that's definitely Sullivan Shepherd."

"You looked good together on the ferry," Kylie noted. "When you went to go see Tidewater."

She thought the resort would be a safe subject and said, "I was really impressed by Tidewater. It's obviously a place none of us will be staying at, but it's a thoughtful design. I enjoyed seeing how Sullivan's dream on paper became a reality. He told me it's the first beach resort he's been commissioned to create."

"Sullivan told Carson that he would put us on the list to give feedback to the Tidewater staff. That we could stay in a room for a night. Eat at a restaurant or two. Test out the pool. Be guinea pig guests."

"I'm going to do the same," Piper said enthusiastically. "It'll be fun to see how the other half lives."

"Keaton hasn't mentioned anything," Layne said.

"Maybe because you'll be on your honeymoon," she said.

"That's true. I'll take being on a romantic honeymoon with my hot husband any day."

"Where are you going?" Kylie asked.

They talked for a few minutes about the cities in Italy and France which the newlyweds would visit before the kitchen timer sounded.

"Time to eat," Layne said brightly, and the three of them followed her into the large kitchen.

Mila worked on refilling glasses and getting everyone iced tea or water, while Kylie opened chips and stirred the Rotel heating in its small crockpot. Piper retrieved plates and set the table. Within minutes, they were seated, talking over old times in high school.

Then Kylie said, "Catch me up on what all of you have been doing. It's been years since I've seen any of you."

"I'll go first," Mila said. "I played volleyball in college and have been coaching it ever since. I came back to the Bay and am really proud of the competitive program I've built at the high school. I fell head over heels for our new basketball coach, who also is the district's athletic district. We got married right before Thanksgiving, and I'm a stepmom to Lily, his daughter."

"Was that hard?" Kylie asked. "Becoming an instant mom?"

"I thought it would be, but Lily is such a sweet girl. Her mom was killed several years ago, and she doesn't really remember her. Carson and I have decided to let her call me Mommy, but we'll always talk about her mom."

"My turn," Layne said. "I worked in Dallas for a small company after graduating from college. I designed an app which put us on the map. It turned the company into an overnight success, and they were bought out by a larger competitor who didn't want me around anymore."

"That's awful," Kylie said.

"I thought so at the time, but I got a sweetheart package to walk away." A shadow darkened Layne's face. "At the same time, I found out about my parents' deaths. I returned to the Bay, my future up in the air. I worked on renovating the Bay Breeze because it needed a complete makeover. Coming back to my hometown gave me the chance to find Keaton." She smiled. "I wasn't looking for a relationship, much less anything permanent, but I now finally believe in the idea of soulmates—because Keaton is definitely mine."

Layne waved her hand around. "Keaton had just bought this house. I moved in, and now we're getting married, as I mentioned. You need to come to the ceremony, Kylie."

"No, I don't want to crash your wedding."

"It's very casual. We're holding it at the house. Actually, the ceremony will be on the beach right outside. You're more than welcomed to come." She named the day, and Kylie shook her head.

"It's a sweet invitation, Layne, but I have a charter that day. I do wish you and Keaton all the best, though." Kylie turned her gaze on Piper. "What's your story?"

"These two earned their college degrees, but I left college after a couple of years to pursue a career in the theater. I've been in touring productions of various musicals for the last decade. Worked my way up from chorus to the lead."

"You definitely had the voice for it. Why would you come back to the Bay if you're so successful?" Kylie asked.

Piper grew thoughtful. "Life on the road gets old, Kylie. You travel to different cities but never see much of them because of the shows you're performing in. You live out of a suitcase. Friends and lovers come and go as one production ends and you wind up in another one with an entirely different group of people."

She shrugged. "I'm thirty now. My two best friends came back to the Bay. I missed them. My parents. A stable, steady kind of life. I'm grateful for all the success I've experienced, but I want to be able to have a permanent address. Go to my own closet and pick out an outfit for the day. Head to the mailbox to get my bills. Sit in front of the TV and watched the new streaming show everyone's talking about."

Piper swallowed. "And I really want to find someone to share my life with," she said quietly. "I really don't know what awaits me here in the Bay. Layne has generously given me a job, and I'll be managing the Bay Breeze Inn at least until Labor Day. After that? I don't know what I want to do—or who I want to do it with."

That was the only statement Piper misspoke. More than anything, she wanted to share her life with Sullivan, but that would be impossible. Tears formed in her eyes, and she quickly brushed them away as they began to fall.

Kylie put an arm around Piper. "What's wrong?"

She began crying. "I may not have found what I want to do —but I have found who I want to do it with—and it'll never happen."

"It's Sullivan, isn't it?" Layne asked quietly.

Piper nodded. "We both went into it knowing he would wrap things up at Tidewater soon and head back to New York and his next project, but the feelings I have for him aren't like anything I've ever experienced."

"Does he feel the same way?" Mila asked, her own eyes misting in tears. "Is there a possibility that you could go back to New York with him?"

She shook her head sadly. "I know he cares for me, but I don't want a life in New York, Mila. I want one right here in Driftwood Bay.

"And that means that things with Sullivan will have to come to an end. Sooner or later."

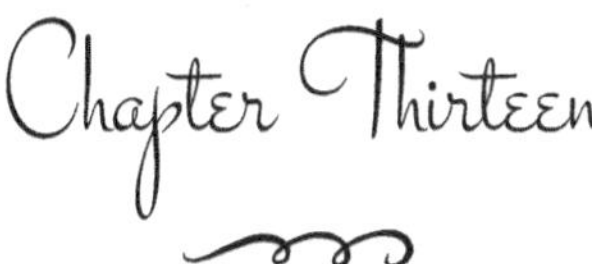

Sullivan slipped into a dark blue sports coat. Looking into the mirror, he ran a hand through his hair, hoping to tame it. It was Keaton and Layne's wedding day.

He'd never attended a wedding with such mixed emotions.

While he was very happy for his friend, thinking Layne was the yin to Keaton's yang, it didn't escape him that a few sparks of jealousy filled him, as well. He had tried pushing it aside, but jealousy stuck to him like shit on a shoe, an expression he'd recently picked up from Neville.

Sullivan wasn't ready to get married. Or was he? Back in New York, he was considered an eligible bachelor, coming into the prime of his life, with good looks and plenty of money to accompany them. He had social status. An apartment in a prime Manhattan location. Worked for one of the most prestigious companies on the planet.

But all that seemed to fade into the woodwork here in Driftwood Bay. What counted in this small Texas town was if you were happy and healthy. If you did something you enjoyed and had someone you loved by your side. You counted your blessings in the number of kids and good friends you had.

Living in the Bay these past few months had definitely messed with his head. The *Don't Mess with Texas* slogan had become more of a *Texas Messed with Me*—at least as far as Sullivan was concerned. He struggled now, believing it was time to return to the old, familiar world he'd grown comfortable in—and wanting to stay in this new one.

With Piper—who held his heart.

He'd be certifiably insane to walk away from his position at Wagner Enterprises. Being an architect was something he enjoyed doing. He created something magnificent out of literally nothing. What began in his head became a solid design on paper, one which he had a great deal of leeway, with a little input from the higher ups at Wagner. His detailed drawings and building specifications became a physical reality, and he enjoyed the site visits he made to ensure the project lived up to his vision. He worked closely with the contractors to make certain they had a clear path through construction and resolved any problems that cropped up. His work was challenging, and he was well compensated for his efforts.

Yet those hours spent in Neville's woodshop had felt incredibly good. Talking with Nellie about what she wanted in a coffee table. Drawing it up and receiving her approval. Choosing the right wood and then physically making the small piece of furniture. Just thinking about how satisfying it had been to use his hands made him itch to do it again.

Impulsively, he raced down the steps to the diner and found Neville.

"Think I might be able to use your workshop again?" Sullivan asked.

"You gonna make those end tables Nellie's been wanting?

If you don't, she'll bug me to do it, and my work can't hold a candle to yours."

He hadn't had any ideas in mind, but he ran with it. "Yes. Nellie will get her end tables. Just don't tell her. It may be one or two."

"Depending upon how much time you keep in Piper Roberts' company?" Neville asked, a knowing look in his eyes.

He shrugged, not willing to bare his soul to the old man.

"I'll slide the key under your door," the diner's cook and owner said.

"Thanks, Neville."

Sullivan left the diner, glad Nellie was engaged with a customer, and got in his car. He texted Piper he was on his way.

It was little things like that which had him thinking about how his relationship was different with her than anyone preceding her. He'd only dated casually over the years, never interested in any woman beyond a few dates. A courtesy text like this had never been on his radar before, yet it seemed the right thing to do. While he'd always opened car doors for his date or held her chair at a restaurant, he did those things for Piper because he wanted to, not because it was the polite task a gentleman performed for a lady.

She waited for him on the porch, as she usually did, and pushed herself from the chair, picking up a black case beside her feet. Her raven hair was pulled away from her face, showing off her high cheekbones. Those blue eyes sparkled at him, full of life as they always were. She wore what his mother called a sheath dress, sleeveless, striking her just above the knees and hugging her hips. His mouth grew dry as he got out.

"Let me take that for you," he said, and she handed over the case. "I know it's not a purse because you're carrying a clutch."

"No, it's a makeup case. I'm going to help Layne get ready for the wedding by doing her makeup."

Sullivan opened the car door, watching her slide in gracefully. He placed the black case on the floorboard by her feet and then returned to the driver's seat.

"Did you get them anything?" he asked. "Keaton told me not to, but I'm thinking I should have."

"Not yet. I plan to, but everything's unfolded pretty quickly since I've come home. At least Keaton is going to let me drive one of their cars while they're gone, so you won't have to chauffeur me around anymore."

"I don't mind," he said quickly. "We still need to go car shopping."

"I'll have to figure out when to squeeze it in. With the inn opening on Friday, I'm going to be really tied up."

"Do you have anything left to get ready? Like swish toilets?" he asked, grinning.

She laughed. He loved the sound of her rich laugh. It wasn't a weak, half-hearted sound. Instead, it was full of gusto, just like Piper herself.

"All toilets are sparkling clean. Really, everything is done. I'm just waiting for the first guests to check in."

"Then we should go car shopping tomorrow," he told her. "If you're going to be tied up, tomorrow would be perfect. Think of it as the lull before the storm."

"Why not?" she said. "Let's talk about it after the wedding."

By now, they had arrived at the house, and they got out of the car and headed to the porch.

"I think it's romantic, being married on the beach," Piper said.

"It's outside?" he asked.

"Yes." She looked at him, smiling wryly. "You and Dad

didn't listen to a word Mom and I said about the wedding the other night, did you?"

"Guilty as charged," he freely admitted, looking down at his Gucci loafers.

Her eyes followed his. "Don't worry. The bride and groom are going barefoot on the sand. I'm sure the guests will be encouraged to do the same. Your luxury loafers won't have to suffer the sand. And you're already halfway there, Mr. Sockless," she teased.

They went inside, and Piper told him she would see him at the ceremony. He found Carson, who wore flip-flops.

"I see you were apprised of the appropriate footwear. I was just informed the ceremony is outside on the beach."

Carson chuckled. "Welcome to the Bay, where casual rules the day."

"You aren't kidding. I'd never been to a wedding in a school gym before, much less a potluck reception in a school cafeteria," he quipped, reminiscing about Carson and Mila's informal wedding, where half of the Bay's residents turned out.

Laura Perry appeared. "You boys need anything? We've got some Dr Peppers and iced tea in the kitchen if you're thirsty."

"We're good," he told Mila's mom.

They talked about how Carson's basketball season had ended and what he thought about the talent on next year's team. That led to more sports talk, attracting a few other men present. While Sullivan followed a few pro teams, these Texans took their sports seriously, football most of all. He wondered what it would be like to go to Driftwood Bay Pirates' games on Friday nights, hitting the tailgate beforehand and then sitting with his friends, cheering on the home team. He'd attended a few of Carson's basketball games in the local high school gym and been amazed at the turnout, as well as how passionate fans were.

What would it be like, being a part of daily life in the Bay?

Laura came by again. "Enough sports talk, fellows. We'll be starting in a few minutes. Everyone head outside. Bill, you stay for Layne," she instructed her husband.

Sullivan followed everyone to the beach. He slipped off his loafers, leaving them beside the flip-flops Carson had discarded, and went to stand in the sand. The scent of the salt water wafted over him, and he closed his eyes, deeply inhaling, as the cry of seagulls swirled overhead.

Piper slipped her arm through his. "Hey, handsome. Ready for a wedding?"

They watched as Layne appeared on Bill Perry's arm. Sullivan glanced from the bride to the groom, who looked spellbound. Dr. Perry led Layne to Keaton, and they joined hands.

It surprised him to see Piper's dad standing before the couple. She leaned over and whispered, "Dad only performs a handful of weddings. Layne is like one of his own kids, though, so he was happy to accommodate her request."

He thought it was decent of both Dr. Perry and Chief Roberts to step up and make this day as joyful as they could for Layne since she had lost both her parents last year.

"Piper?" the chief asked, and she released Sullivan, moving to stand close by the couple.

Sullivan realized that she was going to sing a cappella as she cleared her throat. Anticipation filled him.

Hearing the first few words, he immediately recognized the song as Elvis Presley's *I Can't Help Falling in Love With You.* Memaw had been a huge Elvis fan, and Sullivan had heard this particular song played many times during his visits to Baker's Cove. He closed his eyes as Piper sang, seeing Pawpaw pull Memaw to her feet and dance around the small living room, holding her close as he sang along with Elvis in her ear.

When Piper finished, Sullivan opened his eyes, blinking back tears. She rejoined him.

Leaning over, he slipped his arm about her waist and whispered in her ear. "You sang it better than Elvis ever did."

She beamed at him, resting her head against his shoulder.

Chief Roberts oversaw the couple's vows and pronounced them man and wife. The small group of guests returned inside, leaving their shoes behind. The food was delicious, and the cake from Seaside Sweets Bakery was moist and just the right amount of sweet. Piper and Mila placed scoops of vanilla Blue Bell on the plate to accompany it.

Then the party really started.

Piper had been put in charge of the playlist. Furniture in the great room was pushed back, leaving a large space, and everyone danced with enthusiasm. He'd never done the Cotton-Eyed Joe before and quickly caught on to the steps. The sounds of Motown took over after that, and Sullivan let his inhibitions fly far away.

Dancing the night away with Piper was simply magical.

Then the beginning of *Marry Me Before Sundown* sounded, a song which had special meaning for Keaton and Layne. Everyone stepped back as the newlyweds danced to the song alone.

When the last note ended, Piper told the group, "I think it's time to tell the newlyweds goodnight."

Flurries of kisses and goodbyes were exchanged. Keaton handed over his car fob to Piper, telling her to take the car home with her tonight.

"We've already got a ride to the airport," he told her.

Layne added, "If anything comes up with the B&B, then—"

"Don't call us," Keaton said, kissing his wife.

"I'll help if a crisis arises," Sullivan told the happy couple. "But I think Piper has everything under control."

He caught her hand and led them back to where they'd left their shoes. Slipping on his loafers, Sullivan said, "I think dancing barefoot is an aphrodisiac."

"I suppose that means you'd like to stay with me tonight."

Damn. He wanted to stay with this woman every night.

"If you'll have me," he said instead.

Piper stopped and looped her arms around his neck. "I'll take as much as you're willing to give—for as long as you're here, Sullivan."

Chapter Fourteen

It was hard waking up in an empty bed.

Piper had gotten used to having Sullivan next to her, but she had sent him home last night after they had made love. She wanted to be focused on the first group of guests which had arrived yesterday.

Check-in was from three until six each afternoon, and Sullivan had brought by a beautiful bouquet to place on the desk to greet guests. Piper had gone shopping for groceries, stocking the pantry and fridge. She had picked up fresh cookies at Seaside Sweets and set them out, along with cucumber water. She told each guest at check-in that cookies would be available each day at three, along with a flavored water. It would be interesting to see which guests availed themselves of the treat, and she would need to adjust the amount she set out daily based upon their preferences.

She had spent Thursday in Corpus with Sullivan, looking at cars. She had seen a few models she liked but wasn't willing to commit so quickly on such a major purchase. Having the luxury of driving either Keaton or Layne's car gave her time to make an informed decision. Since Layne's car was brand-new, Piper opted to take Keaton's keys and use his vehicle until she had one of her own.

Getting out of bed, she did a series of stretches before dressing. She decided to get in an exercise session after she cleaned the rooms each day, then she would shower.

Piper had been determined to make the Bay Breeze as green as possible and had set up recycling bins, as well as trash cans, in each guest suite. She placed cards in the center of the beds, saying the sheets would be changed every third day as long as guests left the card on the pillow. If not, a fresh set of sheets would be placed upon the beds. The card also said that guests could choose to reuse towels if they so desired. Towels still hanging on a bar or the hook on the bathroom door would be neatly folded, while those on the floor would be washed and replaced. Sullivan warned her that most people would want fresh sheets each night, along with clean towels. He said people might be more conscious of those things at home, but on vacation, they would take advantage of someone doing laundry for them. She would have to see if he were right or not.

Entering the kitchen, she set out plates and silverware for the breakfast buffet. She heated water and poured it into the chafing dishes, lighting them to keep items warm. She would serve a hot breakfast from seven until nine each weekday morning and until ten on weekends. Layne had told her that most people would eat by eight-thirty, wanting to get a jump on the day's activities, whether that meant a day at the beach or shopping. Piper would need to keep track of who came down for breakfast so that once everyone had eaten, she could clean the dining room and kitchen.

The same would be true of guestrooms. At check-in yesterday, she had asked each guest to place the hangtag on their outer door handle to indicate whether they wanted privacy or the room cleaned. Check-out each morning was at eleven, and she wanted to be near the desk for that.

She realized because she was on her own, unlike the Larsons who had shared duties, she wouldn't have as much free time as she'd anticipated. Mornings would be busy with cooking breakfast, cleaning rooms, and checkout. Then she would need to be back at the front desk from three until six. At least each guest had been issued a key not only to their room, but one to the front door. Piper wouldn't need to remain on duty every evening as people came and went from the B&B.

She also would have no days off between now and Labor Day. While Piper didn't mind hard work and was used to long hours in the theater, she hadn't anticipated being involved with Sullivan when she agreed to manage the inn. He still hadn't informed her of his last day in the Bay, and she already missed the carefree days she had spent in his company.

Heating two pans on the stovetop, she began scrambling eggs and frying up bacon, which would be this morning's main offerings. She also cut up fresh fruit and placed it in a large bowl, taking it to the dining room. A loaf of bread and sleeve of English muffins sat next to the toaster, and Piper added butter and jams to the table. The small fridge in the corner was already stocked with yogurts and bottles of orange juice and water, along with small cartons of milk. She had moved the coffeemaker from the kitchen into the dining room and had a tree pod which made it easy for guests to see available flavors.

As she placed eggs into the chafing dish, the first two guests appeared in the dining room.

"Good morning, Mr. and Mrs. Anderson," she said brightly to the couple who had been the first to check-in yesterday. They were annual visitors to the Bay Breeze and came several times a year. "How did you sleep?"

Mrs. Anderson smiled. "Best night I've had in months. I

must say that George and I really think you've done a wonderful job with the Bay Breeze, Piper."

"I can't take credit for the renovations, ma'am. That was all Layne Larson. When she inherited the inn, she decided to do several updates."

"Well, everything looks marvelous," Mr. Anderson said.

"I'm just setting out eggs and bacon. Drinks are in the fridge here, along with some yogurts. If you prefer coffee, you can make your own."

"Thank you, dear," Mrs. Anderson said.

Piper returned to the kitchen, nerves flitting through her. She knew what she had prepared this morning was good. She just didn't know how often she would need to replenish items. She danced a fine line between checking on her visitors and intruding on their privacy.

The next time she returned to the dining room, a second couple had arrived. The Batemans had told her they lived in Corpus and liked to drive up and down the coast, trying out different B&Bs and rating them online. She saw they had availed themselves of the buffet, both of them toasting English muffins for themselves.

Mrs. Bateman said, "Piper, I didn't see any tea set out."

She hadn't thought about tea for breakfast. "Let me remedy that for you, Mrs. Bateman."

Hurrying to the kitchen, she found a tea caddy, bringing it to the coffee bar. Hot water could be brewed in the coffeemaker.

"May I brew you a cup?" she asked, thinking she would need to add tea pods to her shopping list.

The woman stepped to the coffee bar and glanced at the selections in the tea caddy. "I don't see any herbal teas. Or even decaf." She sniffed in disapproval.

"I'm sorry we don't have that available for you, ma'am. I'll make sure that we have some for you tomorrow morning. In the meantime, could I interest you in a cup of decaf coffee?"

Mrs. Bateman's nose wrinkled. "I don't think so. I'll just have orange juice."

When the older woman returned to her seat, Piper retrieved an orange juice from the fridge and brought it to her, pouring it into a glass. Apparently, the Batemans expected her to wait on them. She glanced to the buffet and found she needed to add more eggs and bacon and returned to the kitchen. It worried her, thinking Mrs. Bateman would give the Bay Breeze a low rating for a minor inconvenience.

After half an hour, both couples had left, and the Doyles didn't appear until eight-thirty. She made certain they had everything they needed. Once they had eaten, Piper began cleaning up. Since no one would be checking out today, she had a little bit of a breather.

Once the kitchen was clean, she went upstairs and checked the three occupied rooms. Two, the Doyles and Andersons, had indicated for their rooms to be cleaned, and she got to work on those. As Sullivan had predicted, both wanted their sheets changed and new towels. She decided that would mostly likely be the norm and would plan accordingly. Layne had bought beautiful linens for each room, as well as plenty of extra towels, so restocking wouldn't be a problem. It would simply be more time consuming, doing more laundry than she had anticipated.

She took all the sheets and towels to the laundry room and put the first load on to wash. By the time she had finished servicing the two guestrooms, the Batemans' hangtag also notified her that the room was available for cleaning, so she tackled it. While the Andersons and Doyles had been fairly neat, the Batemans were very messy. Somehow, that didn't surprise her after this morning's encounter at breakfast. Piper decided she would make a game out of predicting which guests would be high maintenance and messy and which would be what she would consider thoughtful guests.

As she worked she wore her earbuds, singing along with the music, but she decided that wouldn't be wise in the future. The earbuds were of good quality, blocking out all external noises. If someone called her name, she wouldn't be able to hear them, much less the bell which sat on the registration desk downstairs. She would have to clean without music in the future, or at least hum quietly to herself to help pass the time.

Sullivan texted her, asking if she could talk, and she replied she could. Immediately, her phone rang with a FaceTime call. She drank him in as she answered, thinking of all they had done last night before he had left her for his room at the diner.

"How was the first breakfast shift?" he asked.

"I would give myself an A for the eggs and bacon. I screwed up, though. I didn't have any herbal or decaf teas available."

"I didn't even think of that."

"I've just finished cleaning all the rooms, so I'll head out to the grocery store and pick up some. I promised Mrs. Bateman that a variety would be available by tomorrow morning."

"Don't let that get you down. Layne didn't mention it."

"She probably didn't know herself," Piper said. "She never really had any involvement in running the inn. Yes, back in high school, she would help her mom clean some of the rooms, but she never did any of the cooking or shopping. I'll make a note of it so that whoever eventually takes over, he or she will know it's something to provide."

"Were the cookies a hit yesterday?" he asked.

She chuckled. "Oh, they scarfed those down. Drank most of the cucumber water, too. I'm going to go with a different flavored water each afternoon. I think it's a nice touch,"

"How many people checked in total?"

"Three of the four rooms were occupied last night. All those couples are staying another night. I'll have a new check-in this afternoon, and they're staying an entire week. Going back through the previous records, they've stayed at the Bay Breeze multiple times over the years."

"I wish we could grab some lunch now, but I'm over at Tidewater."

"That's okay. I've got laundry going now, and I need to pick up the tea."

"I know you're on desk duty until six tonight."

"Actually, I'll I only need to stay until the Millers check in. Since they're the only guests coming today, I'll be done for the night when they check in. Of course, I have no idea when they'll arrive."

"How about we eat dinner in tonight?" Sullivan suggested.

"I think I may be too tired to cook by tonight. Not that I know how to make anything other than breakfast."

"Leave dinner to me," he said. "I'll be over at six."

"Thank you," she said, glad she would be able to see him tonight.

Piper wondered how long she had with Sullivan. A part of her wanted him to give her the date he would be leaving the Bay so that she would be able to prepare herself for his departure. Yet at the same time, it almost might be better not knowing. Not having that countdown clock hanging over her. If Sullivan left abruptly, it would be like pulling a Band-Aid off with one, swift move. It would still hurt—but maybe not as much.

Her eyes welled with tears. Who was she fooling? Sullivan leaving Driftwood Bay would be the worst thing that had ever happened to her. At least she would have her parents and friends to lean on once he was gone.

She collected towels from the dryer and put another load of

them on to dry before doing a thirty-minute Zumba routine. Having worked up a good sweat, she jumped into the shower, feeling more energized now. She dressed in jeans and a short-sleeved shirt and picked up her purse in order to head to the store.

Her phone chimed, and she saw it was a text from Layne. It was a good seven or eight hours later in Italy.

> Aren't you glad I waited so long to check in? I didn't want you to think I was hovering over you, but I do hope everything went smoothly yesterday and that breakfast was fine this morning. Rome is everything I thought it could be—and more! I've already eaten my weight in gelato today, but we're doing a lot of walking when we're not in our room, and I know you know what that means.

She typed a reply, telling her friend everything was perfectly fine and to enjoy her honeymoon. Piper then sent a second text, telling Layne not to check in daily and concentrate on her new, handsome husband and exercising in bed. Layne sent back three heart emojis.

Going back to the laundry room, she pulled out the last load from the dryer. After folding those sheets, she placed them on the shelf in the supply room and headed downstairs to Keaton's car. She went to the grocery store, picking up a variety of teas, both individual teabags and pods to use in the coffee maker. While there, she added hot chocolate, just in case anyone got a hankering for it.

Then she stopped by the bakery and chatted a few minutes with Denise, telling the bakery owner the cookies she had purchased yesterday disappeared quickly.

"I saw two guests munching on them, while they carried

more on napkins back to their rooms. I found cookie crumbs in the bedsheets in one room." She didn't mention it was the Batemans.

Denise laughed. "There's nothing like a good cookie to close out the day. What can I get you today, Piper?"

She had gone with sugar cookies and oatmeal raisin ones yesterday, so she said, "Let me have chocolate chip and peanut butter. A dozen of each."

Piper hoped some might be left over for her and Sullivan to nibble on in bed and decided she would set a couple aside before she placed them out for the guests so they would have a sweet treat themselves after dinner—or sex—tonight.

She returned to the inn and made herself a quick sandwich and grabbed an apple to go with it. The rest of the afternoon she sat at the desk, scrolling through the Driftwood Bay Chamber of Commerce site. It connected to all members, and she perused those business websites carefully, hoping she might find an idea of what she wanted to do in the future beyond caring for the B&B.

At a quarter after five, the Millers arrived. She greeted them warmly, going through her spiel and giving them their keys.

"We are delighted the Bay Breeze underwent a facelift," Mr. Miller said. "We've come here for many years, and it was beginning to look a little sad."

"I think you'll be happy with all the changes you find," she told the pair. "You'll be staying in the Daffodil Room. It's the third on the left."

"It was so clever to decorate the rooms and name them after flowers," Mrs. Miller said.

"You can credit Layne Larson with that. She inherited the inn from her parents after their deaths. Actually, she's Layne Maxwell now—and on her honeymoon."

"Oh, I remember Layne as a teenager," Mrs. Miller said. "A

lovely girl. Please pass along our best wishes to her on her marriage."

"I'll do that," Piper promised.

She texted Sullivan, letting him know that the Millers had checked in and she was free for the rest of the evening. Piper went to her room to freshen up, spritzing on a bit of perfume.

When he arrived, he had a large, brown sack in hand. She recognized the logo of Ming Dynasty stamped in bright red on the side.

"You mentioned you liked Chinese," he said as he followed her into the kitchen. "Since I didn't know exactly what you preferred, I brought several things."

"I adore Chinese. I could eat it every day. Thanks for picking up dinner tonight. I'm more hungry than I thought I would be."

"You're in the people pleasing business now. That's what Zane calls it—and people can be high maintenance. Even the nicest ones."

"When will he be arriving in the Bay?"

"I need to touch base with him about that. He's been in Asia for a couple of months now, so we haven't talked much."

She claimed plates from the cupboard while Sullivan set the various cartons on the table and opened them.

"Shrimp fried rice. Orange chicken. Moo Goo Gai Pan. Pepper steak. And chow mein. A couple of eggrolls in case you want one of those. Huh. They only put in one fortune cookie with all this food?" he complained.

"You can keep it."

"No, it's yours. Open it."

Piper yanked apart the cellophane and removed the cookie. Halving it, she gave him his share, which he immediately popped into his mouth. She removed the slip of paper and read her fortune.

Your future holds a big decision. Be sure you make the right one.

"What does it say?" he asked.

She passed the slip to him and sat, picking up a carton of the orange chicken and placing some on her plate.

Sullivan set the fortune aside and filled his own plate. He told her a little about what he'd been doing at Tidewater today and then said, "I've got to head up to Vancouver tomorrow. It's the next place I'll be designing for, and I always go in person to see where the resort will stand. That helps me generate ideas, plus I take a ton of pictures to refer to in order to incorporate the surrounding area into my design."

Piper's appetite disappeared in an instant. Dully, she said, "I didn't realize tonight would be our last night."

Chapter Fifteen

The minute his words left his mouth, Sullivan realized he should have better prepared Piper for this upcoming trip. Then looking at her face, it hit him.

She thought this would be the last time they saw one another. She confirmed that thought when she said, "I didn't realize tonight would be our last night."

The light had gone out of her eyes.

"It's not," he quickly assured her, seeing relief sweep across her face.

She had a beautiful face, one full of energy and liveliness, but she would be the worst poker player in the world because she telegraphed her every emotion on it.

He captured her wrist and pulled her from her chair, tugging so that she landed in his lap.

"I wouldn't do that to you," he assured her. "This is just the exploratory trip for my new project. I'll be coming back in a few days. Tuesday."

"Oh," she said quietly, but he could still feel the tension filling her body.

"I'll still be around when Zane comes," he added. "I can't wait for you to meet him."

Mustering some of her usual spirit, Piper said, "I wonder if I can get stories out of him about what the two of you were up to as kids."

"Nah. Zane would never break. Our code of silence is powerful. Besides, the statute of limitations ran out years ago on the mischief we created."

His teasing words seemed to mollify her some, but then she said, "We both know you'll be leaving soon. Even though you haven't told me exactly when."

"I'm not quite sure myself," he said, not wanting to commit to an end date for his time in the Bay.

And with her...

"Why don't we just walk away now?" she asked. "Make a clean break. We've enjoyed one another's company."

"Why sit around and be miserable with both of us still in the same place?" he countered. "I like being around you, Piper. I think it would be foolish for us to both be in the Bay and not see one another for as long as we can."

Her gaze held his, and he saw tears shimmering her eyes.

"I need to protect myself, Sullivan," she said quietly.

He threaded his fingers through hers. "Don't say this is over," he pleaded. "Not yet."

She sat silent for a long moment, and he held his breath, waiting for the verdict. It was true. He wasn't ready to be done with her. Already, he couldn't think of returning to his life before he had come to this small, idyllic, seaside town. He couldn't imagine sleeping in a bed without Piper's warmth next to him.

"All right. We can continue to see each other, but you need to give me fair warning when you're leaving. Not a day or two. At least a week."

"Deal," he said, his hand wrapping around her nape to pull her down for a long kiss.

When he broke it, he said, "You still hungry?"

She shrugged. "Not really."

"Then let's put the cartons in the fridge. I want to make love to you before I go to Vancouver. I need to take a little piece of you with me."

It didn't take long to clean the kitchen. Sullivan took her hand in his and led her back to her bedroom. Slowly, he undressed her, marveling at every sweet curve on her body. He made love to her tenderly, savoring each moment, committing it to memory.

Afterward, she lay in his arms. He stroked her hair absently, wishing this night could go on forever. He needed to leave, though.

Pressing a kiss against her temple, he said, "I better go home and pack. I have an early flight in the morning."

"I guess that means I can't take you to the airport since I'll be busy with the breakfast service."

"My flight is at seven. I'll connect in Dallas and then fly nonstop to Vancouver."

"What will this resort be like?" she asked.

He was relieved, hearing her curiosity returning. Sullivan gave her what details had been provided to him and then said, "I'll be sure to share the pictures I take with you. Vancouver is a beautiful place. I wish you could go with me and see it."

She snorted. "You do remember that I have a job, cleaning shower stalls and feeding guests."

"You do more than that and you know it," he insisted, hating how she devalued herself.

"Even if I weren't tied to the Bay Breeze, I wouldn't be able to go with you."

"Why not?"

"I don't have a passport, Sullivan."

Her admission threw him for a moment. A passport was just something he assumed everyone held. Then he realized she came from a very small town and a middle-class family, one where both her parents earned public servant salaries. Even he knew policemen and teachers were severely underpaid. The kind of vacations her family had taken would be far different from the ones he had gone on with his parents and as a bachelor. He had traveled to five different continents, both for work and pleasure.

"Maybe you need to put that on your bucket list," he said lightly. "Once your time is done at the B&B, we could plan a trip abroad together."

She drew away from him. "I'm not interested in making plans which we'll never keep," she said flatly.

"Who knows what's in the future for us, Piper?"

"What's in my future is not a part of yours," she said, her tone sharp. "You'll go back to New York and all these projects you participate in, while I'll be here in the Bay. Even if I do find a job beyond managing the B&B, I wouldn't have vacation time coming for another year. I sure wouldn't be pulling in the income to share expenses on some exotic trip to Europe or Asia. Face it, Sullivan. We come from different worlds. You're sharing a little time with me in mine, but it's impossible for me to ever become a part of yours."

"You wouldn't have to worry about the cost. It would be on me," he told her.

Her eyes grew wintry, and he knew he'd made a mistake saying he would pick up the tab. Piper was an independent, proud woman, and his words had definitely angered her.

"If you can't understand why I couldn't allow you to pay for a trip, then you really don't know me as well as I thought you did, Sullivan. I think you better leave now."

He longed to reach out. Touch her. Kiss away her fears and feelings of inadequacy. The look on her face told him not to dare attempt that.

"All right," he said, climbing from the bed and quickly dressing.

She had pulled the sheet up, covering herself. Usually, Piper was so carefree, but her crossed arms and stubborn countenance told him not to push her at this point.

"I'll text you when I get to Vancouver. Better yet, I'll call you once I get settled in. When would be a good time to talk?" he asked, putting the ball into her court.

"I don't know," she said stiffly. "Maybe you should just concentrate on what you're supposed to be doing in Vancouver and let me work on running the Bay Breeze."

She was shutting down fast.

And he didn't like it one bit.

Sullivan came around to her side of the bed and brushed a quick kiss against her soft lips. "Text or call me when you have a chance," he told her.

She tossed back the covers and slipped into her robe, following him to the front door. Opening it, she waited for him to leave so she could lock up. He felt like it was a mistake, leaving on such a bad note, but he had no idea how to solve the problem between them.

"Goodnight, Piper."

He stepped onto the porch and turned to look at her. She didn't meet his eyes as she closed the door and locked it. The sound of the lock being thrown struck him hard. It seemed a metaphor for her locking him out of her life.

As he walked to his car, he thought he shouldn't expect any more from her. They had both gone into this relationship knowing it would be temporary. Hell, he went into every relationship knowing it wouldn't last. Yet Piper Roberts was tugging heavily on his heartstrings. Sullivan decided this break of a few days would be good for both of them. It would help him clear his head and turn his focus back to his career. When he returned to Driftwood Bay, he would do so, keeping in mind that he wouldn't be in the small town much longer.

PIPER REMOVED her phone from her pocket, pulling up her text messages. She touched Sullivan's name and read the last one he had sent. It was from Saturday and told her that he'd landed in Vancouver on time. That was the last contact between them. She hadn't even responded to it, feeling guilty about that now.

The last few days, she'd no longer been Piper Roberts. Instead, she was playing the role of a small-town innkeeper. She greeted guests. Efficiently cleaned their rooms and cooked for them. Everything was done with a smile on her face as she went through these tasks.

Because being Piper meant that she'd have to live with the hurt filling her heart.

Today was Wednesday. Sullivan had said he was coming back on Tuesday. She had replayed their conversation numerous times in her head and waffled back and forth on how she wanted to handle his remaining time in the Bay. The smart half of her advised that she keep him out of her bed and life, only seeing him if he were present with one of her friends. Her heart protested that decision, though, telling her she would be crazy not to soak up every moment she could with him before he stepped out of her life.

She fretted about him not contacting her to let her know he had returned from Canada. Maybe he'd gotten in so late last night that he thought she might already be asleep. Or worse—that he didn't contact her because she hadn't been responding.

She finished cleaning the Millers' room. They were the only current guests mid-week. That would change once summer came. According to the bookings, from Memorial Day on, the Bay Breeze would be full every day through Labor Day weekend. The Millers had proved to be very friendly and had even asked her to join them for breakfast the last two mornings. She had done so this morning simply because she was so lonely.

Frustration filled her, not knowing what she was meant to do with her life. She couldn't help but dwell on the fact that Mila would have a baby come October. By then, surely Layne would also be expecting. As much as Piper wanted to stay in her hometown, she didn't think she could build a life for herself here. She felt completely unqualified for any kind of job. She could see the months and years stretching aimlessly in front of her, her friends trying to set her up on blind dates that never worked out because her heart belonged to a man who had left years earlier.

Piper realized she had made a huge mistake leaving the theater world. If there were one thing she was good at, it was performing for an audience. She had never tried her chance in New York on Broadway. At thirty, she had a good deal of professional experience under her belt and the confidence to go into auditions which she would have lacked half a dozen years ago.

She decided as much as she would like to remain in the Bay and try to find a fulfilling job and someone to share her life—even start a family with—that wasn't in the cards for her. Determination filled her. She had already saved a good deal of money while living on the road. Her expenses had been minimal, with her hotel rooms paid for and a meal stipend awarded daily. While she would remain as manager of the Bay Breeze until Layne found someone reliable to take her spot, Piper would head straight for New York once that obligation was done. She would give herself a year of auditioning to see if she could land a show. In the meantime, she could wait tables for additional income.

If after a year she hadn't been hired for at least a supporting role in a musical or play, she would begin auditioning again for traveling companies. She had a sterling reputation in the industry and a solid work ethic, along with an excellent voice. She would need to keep training her voice, though, to be ready. It was like a muscle, use it or lose it. Piper couldn't count on a future with Sullivan, much less one in the Bay. It was time she looked out for herself. The theater world was familiar to her, and she was wasting her time and talent not pursuing a career in it. Who's to say she wouldn't fall in love with a fellow actor or crew member and actually marry and have children?

The thought of being with a man other than Sullivan, though, left a bad taste in her mouth. The handsome architect had spoiled her for any other man. Piper decided it would take time and distance to get over him, but she could do it. She wouldn't think about the fact that he lived in New York part of the year because if she did, she would never stand on her own two feet. No, when he left the Bay, it needed to be a clean break between them. He would go his way, and she would head hers, no further contact taking place.

Piper spent the afternoon singing, beginning with scales and then moving to songs. She didn't try anything which stretched her range too much since she was sorely out of practice. Gradually, she would need to rebuild her vocal stamina. What she could do besides that is keep up her physical training. Exercise had always invigorated her, and she did a long Zumba session now, enjoying building a sweat.

After she showered, she went into town and picked up

cookies at the bakery, setting them out, along with lemon water. She snagged a cookie for herself and then retreated to the common room, opening her Kindle and losing herself in one of her beloved Regency romances. They had never let her down, always providing a happy ending, no matter what obstacles the leads faced.

She was into a scene at the last ball of the Season, hoping the hero would wise up in time to realize the heroine was the best thing for him, when banging sounded on the front door. Startled, she closed her Kindle and moved from the comfortable sofa, going to answer it.

When Piper opened the door, her heart slammed against her ribs.

Sullivan stood there, a huge bouquet of flowers in his hand. He yanked her to him, his mouth coming down hard on hers for a kiss driven by need. She felt herself responding, wanting to push him away, yet desperately drinking him in.

When he ended the kiss, he immediately began apologizing.

"My flight had mechanical issues. We sat on the tarmac for almost three hours before they had us deplane. I was going to scramble and find another flight, but I left my stupid phone on the plane."

She saw how upset he was, his usual, steady demeanor gone.

"Piper, I didn't know your number. I didn't know anyone's number. My life was in my phone, and I couldn't get back on the plane to get it."

"You could've called the Bay Breeze," she said, sounding calm though her heart was beating wildly, his intoxicating, masculine scent causing her to grow as dizzy as any besotted Regency heroine ever had been.

"I should have. I wound up taking three different flights, and they were a bitch to schedule without a phone. Wouldn't you know, two of them also had problems. One came in so late that a new flight crew was needed. By the time they called them in and I landed in Houston, I'd missed the last flight to Corpus for the night. I almost rented a car and drove from there to here. Just to see you."

She made a decision in that moment. She wouldn't continue to push this man away. Instead, she would keep her plans to go to New York to herself and simply enjoy every moment with him while it lasted.

"Come inside, Prepster. Let me make you some breakfast for dinner and hear all about your trip."

Chapter Sixteen

Sullivan looked on with pride at the two end tables he had crafted for Nellie over the past ten days. She had requested that the coffee table be mid-century modern, and he had matched these end tables to his previous design. Yesterday, he had sanded and stained them. Today, he had applied a final finish of polyurethane, sanding between each coat to allow for a smooth, durable finish, which highlighted the wood grain. Nellie would appreciate the drawer in each, along with the storage space below the drawer. Like most women her age, she had a ton of knickknacks she could display atop each table and in the space below the drawers. She could even put books in that lower space.

A sense of accomplishment filled him, more than when he finished drawing up plans for a new Wagner property or even seeing it brought to life. It was hard to explain, how a single piece of furniture brought more satisfaction than a hotel twenty stories high—but it did.

Tidewater had come in ahead of schedule. He'd worked closely with the project manager to make certain they were in full compliance, from local codes to anticipating client needs throughout the property. Sullivan had documented every step, adding written reports to the detailed drawings and specifications which had been the beginning of this project. All quality control checks had been made. A majority of the staff had been hired. It was now the first week in June.

And he should be leaving for New York—but he wasn't going to just yet.

His phone rang, and he saw Zane's picture filling the screen. Answering it, he said, "Hey, buddy. Where are you?"

"I'm in the air, heading your way. My flight lands in Houston, and then I have another short leg to Corpus."

"Then tell me the time you land, and I'll pick you up. Do your grandparents know you're coming?"

"Just talked to Gran and Gramps. They're thrilled."

"I guess I need to give up the room over the diner so you can have it."

"Keep it. I can stay with them a couple of days, then the rest of the time, I'll be at Tidewater, testing everything out. You're welcome to do so, too. I'm surprised you haven't moved to the resort already. It's way better than where you're staying now." He chuckled. "I've slept on that lumpy bed."

Sullivan thought of how the ferry ride to Tidewater put too much distance between Piper and him. "I'm good where I am."

Zane looked at his watch. "We'll be landing in Houston in a few minutes. I've got an hour before my connection to Corpus. That leg is about an hour long."

"I'll meet you. It'll be good to see you, Zane."

"Maybe you'll finally explain to me why you've spent so much time in Driftwood Bay."

Sullivan had gone to Zane months ago when he decided he

wanted to work from the Bay, cleaning up details on other projects and working closely with the construction crew here.

"Sure. We'll talk about that and whatever's going on in your life. See you soon."

He cleaned up Neville's workspace, leaving the end tables to finish drying. Locking the woodshop's door, he returned to the diner. Nellie stood at the hostess stand, scribbling on a pad.

"I finished the tables," he told her. "I think you're going to be pleased."

She gave him a smile. "I'd hug you, but you're filthy, Sullivan."

"I hear you'll have Zane to hug in a couple of hours."

The old woman lit up like a Fourth of July fireworks display. "I'm so excited to see him again. It's been almost eighteen months since his last visit. He's good about calling us, but nothing replaces a hug in person. I'm making a list of what to feed him. He loves my sweet potato pie and mac and cheese. My stuffed green peppers and baked squash."

"I'm sure he'll bring his appetite. Do you think I might steal him for dinner tonight, though? A group will be at a cookout at the Maxwells' house, and I'd like Zane to meet everyone."

Nellie smiled fondly at him. "Zane will like that, honey. Just be sure I get to see him beforehand."

"I'm picking him up at the airport and will bring him straight to the diner. Cookout's at six."

"I'll be sure he's ready to go." She paused. "Even though I haven't seen them yet, thank you for my beautiful tables, Sullivan. You have a true craftsman's heart. Your grandfather would be proud of the work you do and the man you've become."

Her words touched him. While he knew Pawpaw would appreciate his talent with wood, Sullivan wasn't as sure if he would approve of his grandson's choice to remain an architect.

"You can look at them but don't touch. They need a good twenty-four hours to dry."

"I'll take a little peek. Even show Zane," she told him.

Sullivan moved through the diner, waving at a few people he knew. He went upstairs and took a long, hot shower before shaving and dressing. Then he called Piper.

"Hey. Zane's on his way to the Bay. I'm leaving now to pick him up at the airport."

"I know how eager you are to see him. Just skip the cookout tonight. I can go by myself."

"No, I'm going to see if I can bring him. I want him to meet everybody." He paused. "I want him to meet you."

"That won't be a problem. Layne will be happy to have one more tonight. I'm actually bringing potato salad. I had a few of the guests taste it this week. I believe I have it down."

"Good for you, Miss Roberts. We'll be there at five-thirty. I want him to get a tour of the Bay Breeze."

"See you then."

He hung up and went to his car, still wondering why Piper hadn't made a decision about buying a car. She'd driven Keaton's the six weeks he and Layne had been gone on their honeymoon. Every time he asked her about it, she put him off, saying she wasn't ready to commit. When they went to pick up the newlyweds at the airport, though, she surprised him by asking him to drop her at the car rental desk. She'd rented a car and had been driving it for the entire month of May. He learned not to press her, though. Piper had a stubborn streak and could really dig in her heels.

On the way out of the Bay, he called Layne.

"Hey, can I bring my friend Zane to the cookout tonight? He's coming in from New York, and I'd like him to meet my friends here in the Bay."

"Definitely. I'd love to meet him, especially since you said he'd added our names to the test list. Keaton and I are really looking forward to staying at Tidewater next weekend."

"Okay. I'll bring him and the wine I promised."

He arrived in Corpus ahead of schedule and stopped at a wine store to pick up his contribution to tonight's gathering before arriving at the airport. Zane texted him that he'd just gotten to baggage, and Sullivan told him he'd loop around and be waiting outside.

Zane came sailing through the doors, oozing his usual confidence. Sullivan tooted the horn and pulled next to the sidewalk, popping the trunk as he got out. Zane put his suitcase and backpack into the trunk, and they gave one another a bear hug.

"So, where did you come from? I know you've been to several cities in Asia recently."

"I took a redeye from Singapore to LAX and then from there to JFK. Dumped clothes at the apartment and repacked. Went into the office yesterday to catch up on a few things before flying here today. You know I live out of a suitcase these days."

They got into the car, and he pulled back into traffic, saying, "I'm supposed to deliver you to the diner, where Nellie is creating a list of all the things she wants to feed you before you head over to Tidewater."

Zane smacked loudly. "Gran's sweet potato pie better be at the top of that list."

"It was. I cleared it with her. You're going to a barbeque with me tonight. I want you to meet a few friends." He paused. "And Piper."

Zane grunted. "I suppose she's what kept you in Texas this long."

"Yes and no. Piper wasn't in the Bay when I cleared it with you to work from here. I don't know if I can explain it, Zane.

There's something magical about Driftwood Bay. The people. The water. The slower pace of life. I feel I've gotten more done and been way more creative by working here. I made a couple of friends. I've mentioned them to you, Keaton and Carson."

Zane thought a moment. "Artist and basketball coach, right?"

"Right. Then Piper showed up. She's a Driftwood Bay native and part of the Three Musketeers. The other two are the wives of Carson and Keaton." He ran a hand through his hair. "She's really special, Zane. We've hit it off in a way I can't really explain."

His friend stared at him. "You've never been serious about any woman. I've known you since we were in diapers. You go through women faster than someone with allergies does a tissue box."

"I like her, Zane. I more than like her."

Sullivan could feel Zane's intense gaze trained upon him. "Are you going to leave Wagner Enterprises?"

"No," he said quickly. "You know I have my dream job. You and your dad have been fantastic to me. It's just that...it'll be hard to leave Piper behind."

"Ask her to come to New York," Zane suggested. "See if you can make a go of things. You'd have to do a better job than I did with Amanda."

"Hey, Amanda wasn't your fault. Okay, well, some of it was your fault. I'd put her at ninety percent to your ten." He swallowed. "Even if I asked, though, Piper wouldn't come."

Sullivan explained how Piper had lived on the road for her entire twenties and that she was ready to settle down in her hometown and build a new life there.

"I can tell she wants kids. I don't know that I do. I'd probably be terrible with them."

"You would not," Zane insisted. "You'd be a great dad. But

I can't see you being happy in a place as small as the Bay, Sullivan. You live an exciting life. You travel quite a bit. As much as I enjoyed spending some of my summers in the Bay, as an adult? I'd be bored stiff."

"You really would," he agreed. "I'm not so sure about me, though."

Zane's stare pierced him. "Think really hard before you make a major change in your life, Sullivan. You know how fast we move at Wagner Enterprises. If you stepped away, I'm not certain Dad would have you back if you changed your mind and wanted to return. He's all about loyalty to the company."

"I know. I'm not saying I'd do that. It's just going to be hard to leave Piper, that's all."

"I'm looking forward to meeting her. She must be very special to tempt you to walk away from a thriving career."

Sullivan knew he was going to choose New York and his career over Piper.

And knowing that left him feeling totally depressed.

They arrived in the Bay, and he drove around the square. Zane pointed out things excitedly.

"That's where Gramps would take me for ice cream. That's where I'd go buy comic books."

He pulled up at the diner, and Zane hopped out of the car. "Pop the trunk. I'll get my stuff. Gran will take me home after she feeds me. What time are you picking me up for this barbeque?"

"Five-fifteen. We'll go over to the Bay Breeze Inn then. I want Piper to walk you through it. She's acting as the B&B's manager for a few months. You need to see it. And lose the coat and tie for the cookout. Everyone will be very casually dressed."

"Got it."

Zane lifted his bags from the trunk and closed it. "Later. Thanks for the ride."

Sullivan watched him enter the diner and then called Piper. "Hey, you busy?"

"Just doing a little paperwork," she replied. "Did Zane's plane get in on time?"

"Yes. I just dropped him at the diner. Nellie's ready to stuff him like a Thanksgiving turkey. Do you have time to come see something now?"

"It's almost two. I was going to run by the bakery and grab cookies before check-in starts at three."

"How about I pick up cookies and bring them to you? Then I want you to come see something. We don't have to stay long."

"See what?"

"It's a surprise."

"Okay." She gave him her cookie order.

He got out of the car and went into the bakery, waving at Denise, who was with a customer. Sullivan had a clerk ring up the cookies Piper requested and then drove straight to the inn.

She came down the porch stairs and got into the car. She sniffed. "Not your cologne. Must be Zane's."

"I'm sure it is."

"Are you going to give me an idea where we're going?"

He gave her a silly grin. "Nope."

A few minutes later, he pulled up at Neville and Nellie's house, and she asked, "Is Zane here now? Am I going to meet him?"

"No, I'm sure he's still at the diner. I wanted to show you something."

Her eyes lit up. "You finished the end tables?"

"I did."

Sullivan had shown Piper a picture of the coffee table he'd made for Nellie. She had raved over it. He wanted her to see his work in person, however. Escorting her to the backyard, he unlocked the woodshop, and they entered. He warned her not to touch the tables since they were still drying.

"Oh! Wow! These are gorgeous, Sullivan." Piper dropped to her knees, moving close to inspect the pair of tables. "Mid-century modern, just like the coffee table. Oh, look at the legs on these. They're beauties. And the storage is incredible. Nellie's going to go crazy over them."

She beamed up at him, and all he wanted to do was kiss her senseless.

"You have a true gift. Just like my voice is my talent, you can not only draw furniture and buildings, but you can craft something lasting with your hands."

Piper rose, taking his hands in hers. "I'm so glad you brought me to see your work."

In that moment, Sullivan decided that he would design and craft a goodbye present to Piper, one which would last her a lifetime.

Chapter Seventeen

"There's nothing to be nervous about," Piper said aloud as she looked into the mirror. "Just because you're about to meet a zillionaire and Sullivan's best friend, it's no big deal."

She worried that Zane Wagner wouldn't like her. It really didn't matter, though. It wasn't as if she were marrying Sullivan and Zane would be the best man at the ceremony and in their lives until she took her last breath. No, the Wagner exec and Sullivan's best friend would only be in the Bay for a short while. Piper would be around him a few times. Then Zane would return to New York—along with Sullivan. Unless Sullivan went first. She had a feeling that was how things rolled. No matter how many times she thought she could prepare herself, she knew Sullivan's departure from Texas would gut her.

She swept her hair into a high ponytail. She already wore a T-shirt and shorts, and Piper added a pair of sandals to the mix. Tonight's cookout was one she had been looking forward to as it was the first time Layne and Keaton had hosted a large gathering at their house since they returned from their honeymoon. She and Sullivan had gone over for dinner, joined by Mila and Carson, but the cookout would have even more people present. Kylie would be there, along with her older brother Danny and his wife, Denise. Mila's older brother would also be coming. Michael Perry was a local firefighter, and he would be bringing Cecily, his wife, and Mila's good friend.

Piper went downstairs, seeing all but one cookie had been claimed. It took willpower not to eat it herself, but she knew there would be plenty of sweets to choose from at dinner this evening. With it being a Saturday, all guests at the B&B were staying over, so she didn't have to man the desk and wait for anyone who was checking in.

She went to the common room and picked up a magazine, leafing through it, waiting for the doorbell to sound. When it did, she came to her feet and went to answer it, taking a calming breath before she opened the door.

Standing on the porch were Sullivan and Zane, and she promptly asked them to come in. Once inside, Sullivan said, "Piper Roberts, I'd like you to meet Zane Wagner, my best friend."

Zane's hypnotic, amethyst eyes drew her in. He was less than an inch shorter than Sullivan and had jet-black hair and cheekbones which could cut glass. He possessed an easy grace, as if he wore his millions well. Naturally, he was dressed in a Polo shirt and a pair of tailored shorts, looking as if he stepped from the pages of an ad in *GQ*.

"Nice to meet you, Piper," Zane said, his voice low as he shook her hand.

"I'm happy to meet you, as well," she replied, her mouth dry, nerves still zipping through her. This man was important to Sullivan, and she desperately wanted to make a good impression on him.

"I actually came to the Bay Breeze years ago," Zane told her. "Probably when I was twelve or thirteen. Gran had a friend who was staying in the Bay, and she and I came over and picked up the woman." He glanced around. "This is really nice."

"My friend, Layne, inherited the inn from her parents and did a complete makeover from top to bottom. Would you like to see it?"

"I would," Zane replied.

Piper led him around, showing him all the rooms downstairs and describing the renovations Layne had undertaken.

"She has a good eye," Zane said. "The place has lost none of its charm."

"Her husband helped her with the remodeling. Keaton used to be in construction before he became a painter." She laughed nervously. "He transitioned from painting walls to painting on canvas."

"I'm eager to see his work," Zane said. "Sullivan has raved about his use of color."

"Keaton has a few of his paintings on the walls of their house," Sullivan said. "I'll bet he'll show you his studio if you ask." He looked to her. "Any way we can see a few of the guestrooms?"

"The Porters said we could go into their suite. I told them Zane Wagner was coming by and wanted to see the inn. Mr. Porter is in finance and knew exactly who Zane was. Let's go upstairs."

Once they arrived, Piper unlocked the door and ushered them inside, saying, "This is the Bluebonnet Room. Those are flowers native to Texas."

"I'm familiar with them," Zane said, his eyes roaming the room. He stepped into the ensuite briefly and then appeared again.

"This is first-rate," he complimented.

"Tell Layne and Keaton," Piper encouraged. "She'll be thrilled to hear that."

"You ready?" Sullivan asked after she locked the room again.

"I need to grab the potato salad. Meet you in the foyer."

She went to the kitchen, calming herself. Zane Wagner was as scary as she'd built him up to be in her head. At the same time, he was Sullivan's longtime friend. She needed to give him a chance.

Piper brought the covered bowl from the kitchen, and Sullivan took it—and then her hand. She knew that didn't escape Zane's notice.

As they approached the car, she said, "You sit in the front, Zane. There isn't much leg room in the back of this sedan. I'll be fine."

She listened as Sullivan prepped Zane on who would be at the cookout tonight, explaining how everyone was connected.

"So, Sullivan tells me you and your friends were known as the Three Musketeers in school."

"Yes. We've been friends for a long time, probably even longer than you and Sullivan."

"I doubt it. My dad and Sullivan's met in college and became best friends. We played together since we were in diapers. Went to the same private schools and then changed to boarding school when we were twelve," Zane said. "From the time we were young, Sullivan was as quiet as a dormouse and the smartest person I've met—and that includes my dad. I was almost as smart and pretty wild. We've always balanced each other."

"Mila and Layne are like sisters to me," Piper said. "I have an older brother. He went away to college when I was going into third grade, so we've never really been close. He's a travel writer."

"Has he ever stayed at a Wagner property?" Zane asked. "If not, give me his address. I'll comp a week for him."

"That's very generous, Zane."

He shrugged. Piper still didn't have a good read on him, and she was used to figuring out people pretty quickly.

They arrived at Layne and Keaton's, and Zane was introduced to who was already there and then others as they arrived. Michael and Cecily came in, with Cecily saying that Bobby and Gina were spending the night at their neighbor's house, so she was ready to enjoy the night. Danny and Denise showed up next, Denise's baby bump larger than Mila's since she was due in August. Zane asked if they had any other children, and Danny whipped out his phone, showing pictures of Amber, their three-year-old. Piper watched Zane's face, but he smiled and seemed perfectly at ease looking at the pictures. After they talked some, Zane remembered playing pickup basketball at the park with both Danny and Michael. They'd been the same age.

"I do remember that now," Michael said. "You were here to spend some of the summer with your grandparents. You had a mean bank shot."

Then Kylie was the last to arrive. Piper watched Zane eye Kylie with interest. She introduced her friend to him and then led her away.

"He's filthy rich. Like millionaire—or even billionaire—rich, and he won't be staying in the Bay long," she warned. "He's watching you now. I'd stay away if I were you."

"Thanks for the heads up," Kylie said. "I don't see myself getting involved with him. Right now, he's the one who'll be negotiating regarding the new ferry. Just because he's super-hot doesn't mean I'll fall at his feet and capitulate. I'm the one who'll be handling the business talks." Kylie grinned. "Zane Wagner has no idea who he's up against."

Not only had Kylie been her class valedictorian, she'd also been on the debate team with Layne and had smoked every opponent she'd ever gone up against. If Piper were a betting woman, every last dime she had would be placed on Kylie Mayfield.

Layne made certain everyone had drinks, while Keaton manned the grill. People began breaking off into smaller groups, and Piper found herself standing with Zane.

"You seem pretty close with Sullivan," he said, holding a beer in his hand and taking a swig of it.

Her cheeks heated. "We've spent a fair amount of time together."

"Playing it close to the vest, I see."

"Not really," she challenged. "Sullivan and I met through our mutual friends. We hit it off. We've enjoyed hanging out."

"He seems to be reluctant to go back to New York."

Her heart sped up hearing this, but she shook her head. "We've grown on each other, but we're from very different worlds. Sullivan is creative and has an important job back in New York. That's home to him. He travels internationally and has an apartment overlooking Central Park. I'm a homebody who never finished college, looking for a job. We know there's never going to be anything permanent between us. We're just having fun, Zane. I'm sure you can relate to that."

"I've never seen him this way. He cares for you, Piper."

"I care for him, too," she replied evenly.

Inside her, she was screaming at the top of her lungs, though.

I LOVE HIM!!!!

She'd never uttered the L-word to anyone, especially not

Sullivan. He was so kind and gentlemanly, he'd probably say it right back, just so she wouldn't feel so awkward.

And that would destroy her.

"Don't worry, Zane," she assured him. "Sullivan and I know we'll be going our separate ways soon." She brightened, using every bit of the acting skills she possessed. "But first, we're going to kick up our heels next weekend and enjoy our stay at Tidewater. I'm looking forward to dining on delicacies. Taking advantage of the swim-up bar. Luxuriating in sheets with an obscenely high tread count."

Piper smiled. "I really appreciate you allowing me to accompany Sullivan to Tidewater. It's not the kind of place I've ever stayed before. I know I'll enjoy it. Our friends, too." She glanced around. "Cecily is a nurse, and Michael is a firefighter. Mila and Carson teach at the high school. Danny runs the ferry, while Denise owns the local bakery. It'll be nice for all of us to be spoiled by staying at Tidewater."

He shrugged. "Sullivan is the one who is in charge of the list. He's added who he wants. What I will need is honest feedback."

Now, she laughed. "After running the Bay Breeze and cooking and cleaning for guests, you can be sure I'll be very frank in whatever feedback I provide."

Zane smiled. "Being in the people business is tough." He glanced up. "I think Keaton is taking things off the grill. Shall we grab something to eat?"

They headed back to the patio, and Sullivan joined them, slipping an arm about her waist.

"Enjoying yourself?" he asked. "Getting to know Zane some?"

She didn't tell him that his friend had moderately grilled her over their relationship.

"Yes. He's a really nice guy. Protective of you."

"Yeah. That's how brothers are. You're like that with Layne and Mila."

"I am," she said softly, finding her two friends. Mila had a glow about her these days, and she would make for a fantastic mother. She already was to Lily. Layne had come back from Italy, showing all the pictures she had taken, and she had told Piper that she thought she wanted to pursue something to do with photography. She loved these two women more than she could express.

And she would miss them terribly once she left the Bay.

They enjoyed eating burgers and chicken. Baked beans and coleslaw. Her potato salad was a huge hit. She had Sullivan and Zane sample the Texas caviar Kylie had brought. Keaton had picked up several pies at the bakery, along with cartons of Blue Bell ice cream, and Denise had brought several dozen cookies.

"This has been so peaceful," Cecily said, sipping on her wine. "And as much as we would love to stay and visit longer, our house has no kids right now. A rare occurrence."

Michael's eyes lit with mischief. "That's my lovely wife's way of saying I better get my rear in gear and politely tell all you people goodnight—because I'm getting some when we get home." He kissed Cecily lightly. "Time's a-wasting, babe. Let's go."

Everyone laughed and started to stand, offering to help clean up.

"There's not much to do," Layne protested. "Go home. Enjoy yourselves. Thanks for coming tonight."

People did help bring plates and glasses to the kitchen, then Layne shooed everyone off.

Zane said, "I'll get a ride from someone."

"No," Sullivan said. "It'll be easy to drop you at your grandparents' house. It's on the way to the B&B."

The three of them said their goodnights and returned to

Sullivan's car. They drove in silence to the Wagner house, and Zane got out, telling Piper to move to the front seat.

"I like the friends you've made," he told Sullivan, eyeing her. "I'm glad you've enjoyed your time in the Bay."

Zane closed the car door for her, and Sullivan drove to the inn.

"Can I stay tonight?" he asked huskily, leaning in and nuzzling her neck.

"I'm glad you want to."

Once they were in her bedroom, he made tender love to her. Piper hadn't bothered to close the blinds, and moonlight streamed in the window, making their bodies glow.

Holding her close, Sullivan said, "You told me to give you a heads up when it was time for me to leave." He paused. "I booked a flight to New York for next Monday morning."

Her throat grew thick as she mustered a smile. "At least we'll go out with a bang, getting to spend time together at Tidewater."

Piper buried her face against his chest, snuggling close.

She would make the most of every minute left—and deal with her broken heart after he was gone.

Chapter Eighteen

"Mom, I can't thank you enough for doing this," Piper said.

"Why, honey, I'm happy to help out. Besides, you haven't had a day off in over three months. Even we overworked teachers get a little time to ourselves."

"You can no longer count yourself in that category," she teased. "You're retired."

Ellen Rogers beamed, looking happy and relaxed. "I think retirement is going to be everything I thought it was—and more," her mom confided. "Your dad thinks so, too. He was looking forward to his fishing trip with Bill this weekend. Not having to take a radio with him. He'll never be on call again, and I'll never have to write a lesson plan or sit in a boring meeting."

"I'm afraid it's going to be too much for you."

"Don't worry. Laura is going to come over and help me out at the Bay Breeze since Bill is gone."

"Good, you won't have to do everything yourself then."

"I hope you and Sullivan will enjoy your stay at Tidewater."

"I'm sure we will," she said quietly, not wanting to think how this was going to be the end of them.

They had spent every night together this past week, as well as in-between times when she had a couple of free hours in her day. Piper had put out of her mind that he would be leaving because she didn't want to be overwhelmed by sadness while he was still in the Bay. She wanted them both to remember this last week together as a good one.

Sullivan had gone home early this morning to pack for their weekend getaway at Tidewater and would return soon to pick her up. They would take the eight o'clock ferry over to the resort, along with Layne, Keaton, Mila, and Carson. She was glad it was easy for Layne and Keaton to work out their schedules to go this weekend. Mila and Carson would be starting their sports camps soon, and so this was the last opportunity they would have to take advantage of Sullivan's offer to come test the amenities at Tidewater. Cecily and Michael's nursing and firefighter schedules had them tied up this weekend, so they would be staying at the resort mid-week, along with Danny and Denise.

Her mom interrupted Piper's thoughts. "Your dad and I are going to head over to Tidewater next Wednesday."

"You are?" she asked, surprised to hear that.

Mom nodded. "Sullivan said that Zane likes feedback from people of all ages because they observe different things. Especially since we're retired now, it's easy to accommodate a getaway. Laura and Bill are also going with us." She paused. "I only wish Lark and Jack could be here."

Just as the Three Musketeers had been close for years, their parents had also been good friends during that time. Piper had only thought of how Layne had been affected by her parents' deaths and now realized her mom and dad had also lost close friends. She embraced Mom, holding tight, knowing she would be leaving in the fall. She'd miss her parents dreadfully.

Her phone dinged with a text, and she checked it. "Sullivan's on his way. Let me check the buffet again to see if I need to put out anything fresh."

"No, that's my job this weekend," Mom insisted. "You go wait for your man."

Tears swam in her eyes as she turned away and left the kitchen. Her suitcase stood next to the front door, and she picked it up, going outside to wait for Sullivan as she had on so many other occasions.

He pulled up moments later, popping the trunk and bounding out of the car. Hurrying up the porch steps to claim a kiss from her before picking up her suitcase. He placed it in the trunk of his car.

As they drove to the ferry landing, he asked, "Everything go okay with breakfast service this morning?"

"So far, only one couple had come downstairs before you showed up. Mom says she has everything under control. Mila's mom is coming over to help out and keep her company this weekend."

"You don't need to worry about anything. They'll take care of everything."

"I know they will. I just need to push work away as far as possible and focus on this weekend with you."

His fingers found hers. "I think we're going to have a wonderful time, Piper."

"I think so, too," she said softly.

He parked the car and took their luggage from the trunk, bringing it down to the dock. Carson and Mila already stood waiting, and she waved to them as Layne and Keaton pulled up. She met them at their car, asking Keaton, "Did you finish?"

"I did. Be sure you get his address so that I can ship it to New York."

"Thank you for taking on the commission, Keaton. I still insist I'm going to pay you for it."

"I don't want you to do that, Piper. I painted it at a friend's request, and it's going to a friend I've grown to love like a brother. It was a project of the heart. No payment necessary."

Keaton took his and Layne's luggage to the dock, and Layne slid her arm through Piper's. They walked slowly toward the others.

"How are you doing?" her friend asked.

"A little shaky," she admitted. "I'm going to enjoy this weekend, however. I'll never stay at a luxury resort again, so I want to make the most of it and my remaining time with Sullivan."

They reached the others, and Piper spied the ferry approaching. Kylie wasn't on it. She said she rarely worked ferry shifts on weekends because she was too busy running the deep sea charters, especially during the high season. Piper's dad and Dr. Perry were two of those customers this weekend. Kylie and her dad would sail down toward South Padre and the tip of Texas before bringing the charter home. Piper was sad that Kylie couldn't be a part of their group this weekend.

Danny tooted the horn as he grew near. They were the only people waiting for this ferry. In the past, it would have been the first ferry of the day, but with so many employees from Tidewater now living in town, she knew the Mayfields were running one at six and seven each morning from the mainland to the resort.

"How's everyone doing?" Danny called. "Looks like it'll be a quick turnaround for your group."

While the men loaded the luggage on board, Danny helped the women. Piper pulled her sunglasses from her purse and slipped them on since the light was reflecting so brightly off the water.

Sullivan came and took a seat beside her, lacing his fingers through hers. She swallowed the lump forming in her throat. This weekend was not going to be about sadness. Rather, she wanted it to be a celebration of this man she had come to know.

And love.

Piper had not admitted this to anyone, even herself. Until now. She knew not every love lasted, but she had a feeling that decades from now, she would still harbor love in her heart for the man who sat next to her.

He smiled at her. "I want to hang out with these guys a little, but I want to reserve most of my time to be with you."

"I'll follow your lead," she said lightly.

On the way over, Sullivan told them what was available at Tidewater, as well as describing the three different specialty restaurants and the outdoor, casual one.

"If any of you play golf, Zane definitely wants feedback on the condition of the course. Otherwise, it's up to you to do whatever you want. There's snorkeling, stand-up paddleboarding, kayaks, and canoes for the water. Tennis courts, and you can book a lesson with the pro there. Spa services. At some point, Zane wants you to order room service to see how that goes."

Carson and Keaton decided they would hit the links after they arrived and then meet their wives for a late lunch. Mila and Layne said they wanted to try out the spa.

Zane met them at the dock, saying, "Welcome to Tidewater. You are true guinea pigs, but your opinions matter a great deal. Keep your eyes and ears open and let me know if there's anything that doesn't run smoothly or is off in any way. You'll be rating everything from how the pillows feel to how long it took your server to appear with your dinner. I want to know if the drinks are too strong or too weak. How easy it is to book water sports equipment or bikes. Everything you share with me will go to improving other guests' experiences when Tidewater officially opens for business. Thank you for agreeing to come and help us make this the premiere Wagner Enterprises resort yet to be."

Zane had golf carts for them all. Employees placed their luggage into different carts, taking it to the lobby for them.

After they decamped in front of the hotel, Zane said, "Even though you probably wanted to be placed closed together, I put you on different floors. I want to see how fast it takes for you to receive anything you request from the front desk, housekeeping, or the kitchens. How long you have to wait for an elevator." He smiled. "You'll find a bucket of champagne in your room, with some chocolates."

The check-in process was streamlined, and they agreed to meet as a group for dinner at the restaurant where Tyler Chastain was head chef.

Sullivan led them to the concierge desk, where he made their dinner reservations.

"Not that we need reservations, since there's only a smattering of people staying this weekend, but I want to make certain our request went into the system properly to test it out."

They would be dining together at seven this evening. It was a little before nine now. Sullivan suggested they take separate elevators to their different floors, conscious of how Zane wanted them testing everything.

Sullivan unlocked the door to their room, and Piper saw it wasn't a room at all. It was a suite.

"You've got to be kidding me!" she said, entering and gazing about.

In front of her was a wall of glass which looked out over Driftwood Bay. She could see the town nestled on the other side of the water.

"Check off spectacular view," she murmured approvingly, and then she turned and began inspecting the room.

It was a large living room, bigger than the one she'd grown up with, with two plush sofas and end tables. A giant TV screen was mounted on one wall. The living room flowed into the dining space, with a table which seated six. Off to the side, she saw a small kitchenette.

Sullivan followed her into it.

"A handful of suites have a full kitchen because there are a few people who want to entertain with a catered dinner while they're here. Others will merely order from one of the restaurants and have that meal brought up so they can eat in privacy. Let's go check out the bedroom."

They entered it. Their luggage stood in a corner, waiting for them, and he frowned.

"They should've placed these on the luggage stands." He took out his phone and jotted a note.

She wandered over to the windows, which ran floor to ceiling and saw the same terrific view of the cove. Then Piper went to the bathroom, which seemed larger than her shared Brooklyn apartment had been. It had a shower big enough to host a party and a soaking tub which would easily fit Sullivan and her. She began thinking of the things they could do in that tub.

He stepped behind her, wrapping his arms around her, nuzzling her neck. "What do you want to do first?"

Although she would be happy to stay in bed with him the entire weekend, that wasn't going to give Zane much feedback.

"I think we should get bikes and explore the island," she told him. "Then come back here and soak in this marvelous tub."

"You're on."

They didn't need to change since they both already wore shorts. Sullivan had on a Driftwood Bay Pirates basketball shirt he must have gotten from Carson. Piper wore a white tank top and pink sports bra.

"Let's unpack before we leave," she suggested. "I didn't bring much, but I don't want the dresses I brought for nice dinners to wrinkle."

Afterward, they headed downstairs to the bike stand. They pedaled around the island for almost ninety minutes, seeing bits of the golf course and even waving to Keaton and Carson as they passed by the pair. After they returned their bikes, they cut through one of the pool areas, where Sullivan asked her if she might want a drink.

"I'll take a pina colada," she said spontaneously.

He looked at the bartender. "Make it two."

They sipped on their drinks as they returned to their suite, and then Sullivan said he would start the water for the bath. Ten minutes later, he climbed in first, setting what was left of his drink on the edge of the tub. Piper followed suit, leaning back against his hard, muscled chest. His arms went around her, and she closed her eyes, blissfully soaking in this moment.

They finally left the tub, drying off one another, and then retreated to the massive bed. Sullivan made love to her with a fierce passion, and she lay nestled in his arms afterward, committing this moment to memory. When lonely times came —and she knew they would—she would close her eyes and transport herself back to this bed, this man's strong arms encircling her.

Then her stomach growled, causing them both to laugh.

"I guess it's time to check out room service," Sullivan said, climbing from the bed and going to the closet to slip into one of the luxurious robes provided by Tidewater.

Handing her the menu, he said, "Look over that and see what you might want."

Her eyes skimmed it, and she passed it back to him. "I'll do the chicken fajita salad, with an order of queso and chips. And iced tea."

He called room service and relayed their order while she climbed from the bed and slipped into the remaining robe.

Their order was delivered in a timely fashion, the salad greens crisp and the fajita meat tender.

"If there's anything missing from the salad, make a note," Sullivan reminded.

She did so, noting the guac had been slightly oversalted and that she would have liked a dollop of sour cream to accompany the salad.

"I haven't ridden a bike in forever. I'm probably going to be sore tomorrow," he told her.

"Then let's see if we can book a couples' massage. I've never done that before."

"Good idea."

He called the spa and arranged for the service. They went downstairs, and Piper's eyes roamed the beautiful setting, the faint scent of eucalyptus present and soft, instrumental background music playing.

Two employees appeared and introduced themselves. They each had a tablet and asked for Piper and Sullivan to mark any areas which might need special attention before leading them to a room with two tables. Once the masseuses had left, they disrobed and climbed under the sheet. The table was warm, surprising her, and Piper almost fell asleep before the massage even began.

She forced herself to stay awake, though, and was glad she did so because she enjoyed every stroke. When they dressed again, they were met in the meditation room with tall, cold glasses of water flavored with raspberries.

"Stay here a few minutes and unwind before you hurry back to the real world," the massage therapist who had worked on her told them.

They idly chatted for a few minutes before they were joined by a woman with beautiful auburn hair and green eyes.

"I hate to intrude. I'm Quinn Walker, the manager of the spa. I just wanted to check and see how your experience was."

"It was my first massage ever," Piper shared. "I don't have anything to compare it to. Does it help to say that I feel boneless now?"

Quinn smiled appreciatively. "A first massage is always a landmark. Did your masseuse listen to any instructions you gave on the amount of pressure or places which needed to be worked on?"

Both of them agreed that their masseuses had been knowledgeable and listened well to their requests. Piper even said that her mother was coming to Tidewater next week and that she would definitely recommend she have a massage during her stay.

"I'm so glad to hear that," Quinn said. "I know you'll also be with us tomorrow, so if you want to partake in any other service, please let us know." Looking to Piper, she added, "If you've never had a facial before, Miss Roberts, I highly recommend you try one. The HydraFacial would be a good start."

"Why don't you do that now, honey?" Sullivan said.

His use of the Southern endearment made her heart speed up. "I'd like to if someone is available to take me now, Quinn."

"I'll take care of you personally," the spa manager said.

Sullivan leaned over and kissed her brow. "See you back in the room."

Quinn led her to another treatment room, just as inviting. For the next hour, Piper was spoiled. When the facial ended, she took the mirror Quinn offered, seeing that she was glowing.

"My skin has never looked better. I could get used to being pampered like this. Unfortunately, I probably won't be back at Tidewater. I'm simply a local helping give feedback on the resort."

Quinn smiled knowingly. "I hear you. I may work at Tidewater, but I could never afford to partake in the services in the spa, and I'm paid very well. I give myself home facials, though. I'm renting an apartment in town. Maybe we could get together for a girls' night of pampering. I'd be happy to share a few tips with you."

"That would be a lot of fun," she agreed. "Could I ask a few friends?"

"The more, the merrier," Quinn replied.

Quinn took one of her cards and scribbled something on the back. "That's my cell. Text me sometime."

"Maybe we could do dinner and then enjoy a night of pampering," Piper said. "I manage the Bay Breeze Inn. We could meet there. Or actually, my friend Layne's house is really large. We'll work it out."

"Thanks, Piper. It's nice to meet a local," Quinn said. "I've been so busy setting up the spa, I haven't really met anyone in town."

"I'll text you once this weekend is over. Gotta enjoy all the luxury I can while it's available."

Though she would only be in the Bay a limited time, Piper decided it would be good to get together with Quinn, as well as introduce Quinn to her friends.

She returned to their suite and knocked on the door since Sullivan had been the only one to bring a keycard when they left. He opened the door, his hair still damp from the shower he had taken. He was freshly-shaved and the most handsome man she had ever seen.

And he was all hers for the next two days.

Chapter Nineteen

Sullivan had them gather outside Le Point Idéal, waiting for Keaton and Layne, and Mila said, "I can't believe Ty is the chef here."

Zane joined them, looking dashing in a dark suit. "We're incredibly lucky to have landed Tyler Chastain, not only to act as head chef for our most important restaurant, but to head our food and beverage program."

"You eating with us tonight?" Sullivan asked.

"I thought I would if you don't mind. Gran has been stuffing me like one of her green peppers. I need to lay off the Southern cooking for a few days."

"Are you staying here?" Piper asked. "Or with your grandparents?"

"I stayed in town for a few days and then started spending nights here. I'm trying out different types of rooms, plus the bungalows. I still make time to go into town every day, though, and stop by the diner."

"They've missed you," he said. "My advice? See them as

often as you can. You never know when the day will come that they aren't here any longer."

He felt Piper's fingers close about his, squeezing lightly.

"Sorry we're late," Layne said. "My zipper got stuck. Wouldn't go up or down."

"I zipped too fast," Keaton admitted. "It got off-track." He looked to Zane. "But thanks to your staff, they sent a seamstress right up. I stepped aside, so I don't know what magic she worked, but the zipper is fine—and my gorgeous wife looks amazing in this dress."

Layne gave a little twirl. "It's one I got at a little boutique in Paris. Not a name place, just a Parisien mom-and-pop type shop. And look—it's got pockets!"

As Piper and Mila exclaimed over that fact, the men simply shook their heads, with Carson saying, "Every female teacher at school raves over anything with pockets. And if they have a dress on sale with pockets, watch out."

"Let's go inside," Zane suggested.

They entered, and Sullivan saw that half a dozen tables had guests at them.

"Who are all these people?" Piper whispered as the maître d' seated them, handing each of them menus. "I don't recognize anyone."

"Wagner Enterprises brings in others in the industry, as well as locals," he replied. "Some of these people might be travel writers. Restaurant critics. That kind of thing."

"Maybe I should see if Zane will put Don on his list," she said.

"Don? Don Roberts is your brother?" Zane said, apparently overhearing their conversation.

"Yes, I mentioned him to you before."

"But not by name," Zane said. "Don Roberts is one of the best in the business. Highly respected. I follow his travel blog."

"So do I," Piper said. "When he posts an article I enjoy, I email him about it. We haven't seen each other in years and years, though. He's always traveling for work, and I was on the road for ten years."

"I know he specializes in reviewing Asian properties. Maybe you should fly out and see him when one of our new properties opens," Zane said. "We're launching a hotel and resort in Bangkok in late October. If you agreed to come, I'm sure he'd meet you there and give us one of his famous critiques."

"You mean scathing critiques?" Piper said, biting back a smile. "My brother has always been opinionated. He doesn't hold back."

"That's why his input would be so valuable. Even earlier than the opening would be nice. If you'd like, I can get you a seat on the corporate jet."

Sullivan saw her flush. "No, thanks, Zane. By then, I'm hoping to be gainfully employed, working somewhere other than the Bay Breeze. I can't just drop everything and take off for a week in Thailand."

His friend frowned, Piper's reply obviously surprising him. "If you change your mind, let Sullivan know."

He wanted to say that he doubted Piper and he would be in touch once he left Texas, but Sullivan kept quiet.

A staff member appeared and asked if they would like still or sparkling water, pouring everyone at the table their preference. Then the sommelier arrived, introducing himself and made suggestions regarding the wine list. He remained while the server came and explained the day's specials.

"Give us a few minutes," Zane said, and like magic, everyone disappeared.

Sullivan perused the menu, trying to decide what to order.

"Good evening, friends," a voice said, and he looked up, seeing Tyler Chastain at the table in his chef's whites.

"Ty!" both Layne and Mila cried, standing and giving the chef hugs, making Sullivan ashamed at how he'd been jealous of Piper doing the same.

The pair introduced their husbands to the chef.

"Obviously, you're someone from the Bay," Carson said.

"I am. Tyler Chastain. I was a year ahead of these three gals. Left the US for cooking school in Paris, but I've finally made my way home. I wanted to see if you had any questions about the menu at Le Point Idéal."

"Exactly what is continental cuisine?" Piper asked.

"It's a pretty broad term," the chef said. "Encompassing culinary traditions from mostly Northern and Western Europe, especially Spain, France, Italy, Germany, and Greece. A heavy focus on herbs and sauces and proteins—chicken, pork, beef, and seafood. Instead of spicy, think more refined. More subtle flavors, especially layers of herbs." He chuckled. "And it leans into rich ingredients. Butter. Cream. Cheese. Olive oils. I won't get into the structure because I don't want to sound like I'm teaching a class. Just look at the menu and go with your gut. If you don't like what you order, we'll replace it with something you will."

"That was helpful," Mila said. She looked to Layne. "I'm sure you ate continental in Dallas all the time."

"I did enjoy fine dining," Layne agreed. She smiled at her husband. "These days, I appreciate whatever my husband decides to cook for dinner."

Tyler brightened. "You cook?"

"The basics. Nothing fancy. Carson here grills a mean steak."

"Oh, Ty, you'll have to come to one of our cookouts," Mila said. "Where are you living?"

"I've got an apartment not far from the ferry. I'm pretty tied up here, though. People need their three meals, plus all kinds of snacks and goodies spaced throughout the day."

Mila frowned. "Don't you get days off?" She looked to Zane.

"I do," Tyler replied. "But weekends will be our busiest time, and that's when most of you are off."

"I'm not letting you off the hook," Mila said, looking stubborn.

"We'll work something out. For now, let me cook for you."

"Do you recommend anything special, Ty?" Piper asked.

The chef grinned. "I make a mean coq au vin and ratatouille, but order what you want. I'll be waiting for those orders in the kitchen."

They each studied the menu and made their selections, the server returning to record them and forward their choices to the kitchen. Sullivan went with a seafood risotto.

"What are you getting for your main course?" he asked Piper.

"The coq au vin. Not just because Ty suggested it. I mean, reading this description makes my mouth water. Chicken slowly braised in red wine, cooked with onions, mushrooms, and bacon. What's not to like?"

When their salads and soups arrived, an amazing assortment of breads accompanied them. Sullivan had a weakness for bread, but thanks to running, he usually could eat whatever he wanted.

"Maybe I need to learn how to bake bread," Piper said, slathering butter on a slice of sourdough bread and biting into it. "This is heavenly."

"Wagner hotels and resorts are known for their food," Zane said proudly.

"Well, I'm certainly giving them high marks for this meal," Keaton said.

Everyone raved once their entrées arrived, with plates being passed around so others could taste things they hadn't ordered. He exchanged glances with Zane and shrugged.

"The Bay has their way of doing things," he told his friend. "Everyone here is very relaxed. It's one of the things I liked about the place and why I wanted to stay a while. Don't you get tired of the rat race in New York? All the traveling you do?" he pressed.

"I'm usually too busy to think about it," Zane told him. "When are you leaving? Dad was asking me when you'd be back in the office. He wants to see your early drawings for the Vancouver job."

"I fly out Monday morning," Sullivan replied, the pit of his stomach heavy at the thought. "I'll be back in the office on Tuesday. I want a day just to acclimate myself again. Send out laundry. Order some groceries."

"I'll stay just past the opening here. Fourth of July is a big thing in the Bay. I promised Gran I'd stay through it, then I'll join you in New York." Zane paused. "How is Piper taking things?"

"We're totally ignoring that elephant in the room. Haven't mentioned it at all. We're going to enjoy Tidewater together. I need to get back to the conversation." Sullivan turned, looking at Piper sampling a bite of something. Her eyes lit up.

"This is incredible. I should've ordered it instead."

"You can get it here tomorrow," he told her.

"No, we need to try out the other restaurants. But I'm definitely going to ask Ty for the recipe—to give to Keaton." She grinned, causing everyone to laugh.

Their chef returned to the table as they were finishing. "I

know you're going to be providing formal feedback, but any tips for me now?"

"Yes," Piper said. "Leave Tidewater and open a restaurant in the Bay. I doubt any of us will ever be able to come here again, Ty, and I know how proud the residents of the Bay are of you, especially your parents." She looked at Zane apologetically. "Sorry, Zane. I don't mean to be putting ideas into your head guy's mind."

"If Tyler tries to leave, I'll just have to pay him more to stay," Zane said smoothly.

Even though he knew his friend was only teasing, what Zane said didn't sit well with Sullivan. Money didn't solve everything. Well, maybe it did in the world Zane and he inhabited, but Sullivan had been exposed to a different world during his time on the Texas coast.

"Shall we order desserts?" Zane asked, which quickly got the women's attention.

He and Piper wound up splitting some tiramisu since they both were getting full. Just a few bites of the sweet was enough for him. By now, Sullivan was ready to go back to their suite and make love to Piper.

Zane had other ideas. "Why don't we all go for a nightcap to the club? We've hired the talent, but they haven't reported yet. We can at least check out the drink selection, and I can ask for opinions regarding the décor."

"Piper could sing for us," he said.

"No, Sullivan," she immediately responded. "No way."

"Why not?" Mila asked, her hands resting atop her bump. "I haven't heard you sing in years, and I know Carson would like to hear you."

"I second that," Layne said. "Come on, Piper, it'll be fun."

"Maybe we all should just karaoke," Piper said.

"*After* you sing for us," Sullivan said. "Please? I'd like to hear you one last time."

He could tell his words got to her. "All right."

They left the table, the last in the restaurant to do so, and headed up a floor to the club which would be a hive of activity every night. While everyone settled themselves at several of the small tables, Piper went to the piano. Zane followed her, asking her to use the microphone so he could hear the acoustics in the club.

Sullivan wondered what she would sing for them, and it didn't surprise him when she began playing one of the songs they had all sung at her parents' house that night he'd gone to dinner there.

The room filled with her rich contralto as she sang a poignant version of *Over the Rainbow*, giving him chills.

"She's...really good," Zane said, looking surprised.

"No. She's fucking great," he responded.

Piper sang numbers from *A Chorus Line. Phantom of the Opera. Rent.* Then she did an electrifying version of *Defying Gravity*, causing the hairs to stand up on the back of his neck.

As their friends applauded, Zane asked, "Why on earth is Piper wasting her time in Driftwood Bay? She could be starring on Broadway."

"Thank you, everyone," Piper said. "Now, let's do a sing-along. A favorite of everyone."

She hit a few notes on the piano and then sang the first line from the Backstreet Boys' *I Want it That Way*. It was a song they all knew, and they became her backup singers, letting Piper be the star of the song.

When she finished, she stood and came straight to him. Sullivan took her in his arms and gave her a long kiss, listening to the catcalls from their friends. He broke the kiss and looked at them.

"This talented lady and I have a date," he declared. "We're leaving the party now."

"Wait a sec," Zane said. "Piper, I've heard you'll only be managing the Bay Breeze until the end of summer. If you're interested, you can be the headliner at Tidewater—or any other Wagner property you want."

Chapter Twenty

Zane's offer stunned Piper.

And for a brief moment, she was tempted to say yes.

If she did so, she could remain in the Bay. Be with her family and friends. Yet she had too many memories now of herself with Sullivan here. Each day would be a painful reminder of the time they had shared together. It would be better to make a clean break with her hometown and the memories. Start a new life, hopefully in New York and if not, return to life on the road.

"Thank you, Zane. That's a lovely offer, but I think I'm going to have to pass."

"Why?" Layne demanded. "You have more talent in your pinky than most singers do in their entire bodies, Piper Roberts. This is the opportunity you've been looking for."

She would never be able to explain why she couldn't accept the offer to entertain at Tidewater, much less why she would be leaving the Bay.

Looking to Zane again, she asked, "What about the other performers who are scheduled to work here?"

He shrugged. "No one holds a candle to your voice, Piper. I can always find another place for them. Or if you'd like to work somewhere else, Wagner Enterprises has places all over the world. Name where you want to go. I'll make that happen."

"I appreciate you wishing to give me a job, Zane, but my answer is no. I have plans of my own, but thank you again for the offer."

Before Layne—or anyone else could argue with her—she looked to Sullivan. "Come on, Prepster. Let's go."

Piper didn't try to decipher the enigmatic look on his face. She just needed to get out of here.

They left the club and went to the bank of elevators, riding to their floor in silence. As they stepped from the elevator, however, Sullivan stopped her in the corridor.

"Why wouldn't you accept Zane's offer?" he asked. "It's a great one. To sing here or anywhere else around the world? You could do a lot worse, Piper."

"Well, I would have to get a passport to take advantage of that, and I hear it takes a long time for the application to go through these days," she said lightly. Seeing the questioning look in his eyes, she grew more serious. "I have plans for myself, Sullivan. Singing at Tidewater isn't the direction I want to take."

He didn't question her answer. He merely took her hand in his and led her back to their suite, for which she was grateful.

Once they were safely inside, he yanked her to him, kissing her hard. Passion flared between them, a white-hot heat pouring through her. She tore at his shirt, not wanting to take time unbuttoning each button. Instead, she jerked it wide open, buttons flying everywhere. Her lips went to that hard chest, and she drank her fill of him, her hands gliding across it and around to his back, stroking the sleek muscles there.

Hunger gleamed in his eyes, and he made quick work of

her clothing, and soon they stumbled to the bed, tumbling onto it. The next hour was defined by passion and frenzy. They couldn't seem to get enough of one another. He brought her to orgasm, first with his fingers and then his mouth and tongue, and Piper was soaring on waves of adrenaline and pleasure.

When he finally thrust inside her, she relished the feel of him deep within her. He pumped harder and harder, and she raked her nails against his back, wanting to claim him as hers for all time. Just as her orgasm erupted, he gave a hoarse cry of his own, their bodies shuddering together, melded as one, the feeling part pleasure and part pain. He collapsed against her, and she welcomed his weight, thinking she might never have a man in her bed again after this perfect coupling.

At least not one she loved as she did Sullivan Shepherd.

Piper kept those words of love to herself, burying them deep into her heart.

Sullivan rolled to his side, turning her so that he could spoon with her. This was a night memories had been made, and she enjoyed the feel of him against the length of her, his strong arms possessively holding her close to him. She fell asleep, basking in his warmth, knowing this was the best man she had ever known

And the best night of her life.

When she awoke, it was to find his lips nibbling her nape. Piper turned and kissed him, long and deep, and Sullivan made slow, tender love to her. Afterward, they showered, and she remarked on how fluffy the towels were.

"Zane will want to know that detail," he said, seeming quieter than usual.

Piper thought he was already withdrawing, protecting himself, the same as she was trying to do.

They dressed in shorts and T-shirts and went to breakfast, joining their friends. Layne eyed her speculatively, but Piper shook her head slightly, not wanting to get into anything right now. Layne could be like a dog with a bone, and she wasn't going to easily let go of this idea of Piper performing at Tidewater. She would have to discuss this with both her friends because eventually she would need to inform them of her plans to leave the Bay and head to New York.

"What's on the agenda for you two today?" Keaton asked. "Layne and I might try out the bikes."

Carson said, "If you don't mind, Mila and I will join you. It would be a great way to see all the island."

Sullivan looked to her. "I think we're going to go have a tennis lesson," he told the others.

They finished eating, and he took her hand in his, leading her down to the courts.

"You think I need to take up a preppy sport?" she asked teasingly, ready to infuse less seriousness into their remaining time at Tidewater.

"Tennis isn't just for the rich. Besides, you look athletic to me. Must be all that Zumba-ing you do."

Barry Blaise, the tennis pro, greeted them, and Sullivan told him they were here for a lesson.

"For Piper," he clarified. "I already play tennis."

"I know nothing about tennis. Or pickleball," she said.

"You look to be in great shape, Miss Roberts," the tennis pro said. "Tennis won't be too taxing for you."

"I do regular workouts, but I've never picked up a racket before."

"Then I'll go over a few basics with you. Not so many that it seems as if you're in school, but I want to give you a good handle on how you can use your forehand and backhand. If I turned you loose without any instruction, you might already have some bad habits that I'd have to break."

Sullivan took a seat while Barry walked her through how to hold and handle her racket. He demonstrated how to serve and then had Piper do so.

After a few dozen serves, he said, "You're a natural at this."

"It actually is pretty fun," she admitted. "Then again, I'm a competitive person."

"Let's do some volleying together," Barry suggested, going to the other side of the net.

He indicated for Piper to serve to him and returned it, coaching her as she hit each shot.

"Okay, we've done enough back and forth, keeping the ball bouncing. Let's see if you can start aiming your shots toward the lines so that I have to really work for it."

After a few more volleys, she found she could place shots fairly well, causing the tennis pro to gallop across the court to different spots. Then he started testing her, doing the same, and Piper found she responded well.

Barry called a halt. "You have a good grasp of play, and I can see you have the strategy down. Why don't we let you and Mr. Shepherd play some now?"

"Go easy on me, Prepster," she said, grinning at her new opponent.

They played several games, with Piper actually winning two of them. She was beginning to tire, though, after so much running around, and Sullivan picked up on that, motioning for her to meet him at the net.

When she did, he awarded her with a kiss.

"You did really well, Miss Roberts. I hope this is something you'll keep up. And maybe think of me whenever you play."

The happiness in the moment fled, much as a balloon quickly deflating.

They returned their rackets and balls to Barry, who had sat watching them, calling out advice to Piper as they played.

"For a rookie, you did very well, Miss Roberts."

"Piper, please."

The tennis pro shook his head. "If I see you in town, you'll be Piper. Here at Tidewater, I'm conditioned to show guests respect."

"I hope we do run into one another, Barry. Are you living in the Bay?"

"Actually, my wife and I are living with her parents, along with our two small kids. She grew up in the Bay. Cindy Kelly. I don't know if you remember her."

Piper smiled. "I think Cindy was in my brother Don's graduating class."

"We came to her high school reunion two years ago."

"Yep. That was Don's class. He never comes back for stuff like that, though."

"Cindy was hoping one day we could actually live in the Bay. According to her, it's the only place to raise kids. We're saving up to buy a house, but there's not much local inventory right now."

"I might be able to help you," Sullivan interacted. "I drew up some house plans for Carson Andrews, the basketball coach at the high school, and his wife. If you can find a piece of land to buy, I'd be happy to draft blueprints for you."

"That would be great, Mr. Shepherd."

"Sullivan." He took out his wallet and handed Barry a card. "Just email me. Give me an idea of some of things you'd like to see in a house. The number of bedrooms and bathrooms. That kind of thing."

Barry accepted the card and slipped it into his pocket. "How much will this cost?"

"Not a thing," Sullivan said, making Piper's heart swell at the generous offer, knowing Sullivan's time was very valuable. "I'm heading back to New York on Monday, but I'll squeeze in a design around my workload once I hear from you. We can even FaceTime about it. In fact, that might be better. Get you and Cindy on a call before I start work. Women always seem to know exactly what they want when it comes to a house."

"This is fantastic!" Barry said. "Cindy is going to go crazy when I tell her. I can't thank you enough."

Sullivan asked for the card back and wrote his cell number on it, then the two men arranged a time when Barry would be home and Sullivan was free so they could FaceTime.

As they left the tennis courts, Piper said, "That was very sweet of you."

"I met him before on the ferry when he was coming to interview for the job. He seemed like a truly nice guy and said his wife would be happy if they could come to live in the Bay and be close to her parents."

They spent of the rest of the day being lazy, trying out the three pools, arranging to meet the others at the Asian fusion restaurant at five o'clock. The last ferry to the mainland was at seven, and they needed to be on it.

They both showered when they returned to their room, washing off their sunscreen and then packing. Dinner was a boisterous affair. Zane joined them and collected their email addresses, saying they would each receive an in-depth survey tomorrow regarding their stay at Tidewater.

"Remember, don't sugarcoat anything. I want to know the nitty-gritty details of what we did right or wrong. If you have any ideas on how to improve something, I'd love to hear them."

Everyone thanked him for the opportunity to visit Tidewater free of charge, and then they were taken back to the ferry in golf carts. Once they got into Sullivan's car, they were both subdued. Piper did ask him for his mailing address, though.

"Not that I'm some great letter writer, but I just wanted to add you to my address book."

He gave her the address, and she couldn't help but wonder how expensive his New York apartment was, especially knowing it overlooked Central Park.

When they pulled up to the Bay Breeze, he lifted her suitcase from the trunk and escorted her up the porch stairs.

"Want to come in? she asked, already knowing what his response would be.

He looked at her a long moment before responding. "I think ending things at Tidewater was a high note, Piper. I have an early flight tomorrow. I'm going to just go home now. Say goodbye to Neville and Nellie. Finish packing."

"I understand," she said quietly, her throat growing thick with unshed tears.

Sullivan leaned in and brushed his lips softly against hers in a sweet, farewell kiss. Then she watched him return to his car and drive out of sight—and out of her life.

She unlocked the front door and found her mom sitting in the common room, reading.

"Hey, sweetie. How was your weekend?"

"Spectacular. I'll tell you all about it tomorrow. Maybe I could come over and have dinner with you and Dad."

"We'd like that. I'll make chicken spaghetti. I know it's a favorite of yours."

"Thanks. How did things go here at the Bay Breeze?"

"Thanks to your very specific notes, everything went swimmingly."

Mom briefed her on who'd checked in and out and kissed Piper's cheek. "Okay, I'll see you tomorrow night then, honey. What time do you want dinner?"

"I'll text you when the last guest checks in. Two different parties are due to arrive. Let's just aim to eat at six-thirty."

"Will do," Mom said. "Goodnight."

Piper rolled her suitcase to the bedroom and flipped on the light. Immediately, she noticed a new piece of furniture in the room. It was a bookcase.

She knew exactly who had made it.

Moving to the other side of the room, she ran her fingers along the spines of the different titles gracing the shelves, seeing all of them were romances. Some she recognized as the biggest names in the industry. Others were names she was unfamiliar with. An envelope with her name scrawled across it sat on top of the bookcase, and she opened it, her heart in her throat.

Piper –

I wanted to do something for you that would have meaning as we parted ways. The only thing I could think of was making this bookcase for you. I know how much you like to read romance. Since I know nothing about it, I got online and ordered a bunch of books which are popular, including several of those Regencies you love. I also read blurbs from authors not on the bestseller list, so I threw in a few authors who haven't quite been discovered yet, hoping you might enjoy the stories they told.

I crafted this bookcase with love for you, Piper. Meeting you has been the highlight of my life. If you ever need anything, please reach out to me.

Sullivan

Tears poured down her cheeks now, and Piper sobbed audibly as she ran her hands along the smooth wood. This was the most thoughtful gift she had ever received. What hurt the most—beyond Sullivan leaving her—was that she would have to leave it behind when she left the Bay.

Chapter Twenty-One

Piper heard the four, soft chimes sound and knew they would be landing at LaGuardia in about ten minutes. Mentally, she needed to shift her focus from the Bay to New York. Thankfully, Layne had been able to find a capable couple to take Piper's spot at the Bay Breeze. She had recommended to her friend that Layne hire two people for the job. While Piper hadn't minded putting in long hours of hard work the past few months, it would be easier for two people to share the load of running the B&B.

Becca and Chase Compton seemed to be the perfect team. Becca had retired from teaching after thirty-five years, while Chase had left his electrical engineering job at the same time. Both enjoyed water sports and were looking forward to small-town life in Driftwood Bay. Since they had been available, Layne had asked them to start immediately, allowing Piper the opportunity to head to New York three weeks before Labor Day so she could begin the auditioning process.

It had been hard breaking the news to her friends and family that she was leaving the Bay. She told them that she was eager to see if she could make it on Broadway, a longtime dream, and that's why she'd turned down Zane Wagner's offer to perform at Tidewater. Layne and Mila had supported her decision, though, knowing she had career ambitions but that she needed a change of scenery after her whirlwind romance with Sullivan. Mila had pointed out that she would be in the same town as Sullivan, but Piper had no intentions of contacting him.

She had only heard from him once, when he texted her a thanks for the painting which had been delivered to him. Piper had asked Keaton to paint Driftwood Bay, with all its brilliant hues. In turn, Piper had texted a thanks to Sullivan for the bookcase he had crafted for her, as well as the books filling it. That had been the only communication between them.

If Sullivan were in contact with anyone from the Bay, Piper didn't know. It seemed an almost unspoken rule in their friend group not to bring up his name. For that, she had been grateful.

It had also hurt saying goodbye to her parents. She had only seen them sporadically when they attended one of her musicals on the road, but she had frequently stopped by for dinner or simply a chat during her months home. She encouraged them to come to New York at some point, whether she was in a show or not. Mom had assured Piper that her talent would land her in a production, and those words had instilled confidence within her. She left with their blessings, insisting that she would play tour guide when they came to the Big Apple.

She wasn't arriving in New York at the optimum time, however. Though it was mid-August, a flurry of new productions always started in September each year. She had missed out on the casting of those roles. Thankfully, a new group of shows would be cast in the next couple of weeks for the next round of musicals and plays, which would open just before Thanksgiving, when tourism really picked up. If she didn't get hired for one of those November shows, though, she would have to wait for the next rounds of auditions in January. Another slate of productions would begin in March. Hopefully, she would be cast and performing by the time winter arrived. If not, she would place her hopes on the spring shows and landing a job then.

In the meantime, she had updated her résumé and had scanned both the *Playbill* and *Backstage* websites, where postings for casting calls for union and non-union members were advertised, as well as becoming familiar with Actors Access, an online submission site, which she would definitely use to begin her audition process.

The plane landed and taxied to the gate, and Piper headed to baggage claim. She'd only brought one of her two suitcases with her, along with her backpack. She was fortunate to be returning to the same Brooklyn apartment she'd shared with other actors. Chloe and Claire were sisters and the current occupants of the apartment. Chloe couldn't sing to save her soul, but she had great comedic timing and would be playing the second lead in an Off-Broadway comedy this fall.

Claire, on the other hand, sang like an angel, and Piper had been in two different touring productions with her, even being Pink Ladies together in *Grease* years ago. Claire had returned to New York after that production and had spent most of her time in the chorus of various musicals. To her credit, she had finally been cast in a featured role of a new Broadway musical which would open the second week of September.

Piper didn't know if they would look for a fourth roommate or not. The other two wouldn't be at the apartment often, while she would see if she could find a job as a server as she made the rounds of auditions. If she were cast in a musical set to premiere in November, rehearsals would begin in earnest soon, so she, too, would spend little time at the Brooklyn apartment.

She saw her suitcase coming down the conveyor belt and grabbed it, slinging her backpack over one shoulder as she moved to catch a train. A rideshare would be faster, but she was already economizing, wanting to save as much money as possible in case lean times were ahead.

After she left the Brooklyn subway station, she rolled her suitcase along the two blocks to her destination, seeing how familiar the neighborhood still seemed to her after several years of being gone. A random thought of Sullivan struck her, and she wondered if he might be in town now. If she weren't feeling so raw, she would text him to get together for a friendly drink to catch up, but her emotions were ragged. Seeing him would make her want to be with him again, and sex had to be off the table. A huge hole remained in her heart, an empty space he used to fill. Piper still loved him.

And that was the biggest reason she could never contact him again.

As she turned the corner and the apartment building came into sight, she texted both Chloe and Claire to see if either might be home. Chloe responded immediately, saying she was about to walk out the door for rehearsals. Piper texted back she was entering the building now, and she spied Chloe step outside into the hallway.

They exchanged a brief hug, and Chloe said, "Your key is on the kitchen counter. Put yourself wherever you can find room. Edie's looking for a server. Hope you've been scanning the trades. Gotta run!"

"I have," she called out as Chloe hurried away. "Going to set up some auditions now. Thanks for the tip about Edie's."

Chloe waved and went through the front door.

The apartment was even smaller than Piper recalled. It didn't have a closet, so occupants hung their clothes on two racks which Claire had brought home a few years ago. Empty hangers hung on the rack, and Piper unpacked, hanging what she could. Her suitcase would function as a drawer, and she had packing cubes filled with underwear, bras, and socks.

She found her key and when she logged in, she noticed the Wi-Fi password hadn't changed. Superstition had kept her from booking an audition until she arrived in New York. She hadn't wanted the plane to have mechanical problems or some other delay, causing her to miss an audition. Now that she was actually here, she was ready to hit the ground rolling.

Fortunately, she was able to sign up for slots with two different musicals being cast. One was a revival of a classic, an old familiar shoe to her, while the other was an off-Broadway production with music and lyrics written by a new team on the New York scene. That meant sight-reading, going in cold. At least she had continued to sing a lot this summer, and she felt her voice had never been in better shape.

Since Piper didn't have any obligations until tomorrow, she decided to do two things. Stop by Edie's and apply for a job and do a little food shopping. While she lived on takeout for the most part when in New York, she decided she wanted to have breakfast items available. She had gotten used to eating a large breakfast and thought she'd keep with that habit.

Edie's was only three blocks away, a typical Brooklyn diner opened twenty-four hours a day. Edie herself greeted Piper by name.

"I wasn't sure you'd remember me," she told the owner. "It's been several years since I've been in."

"I don't forget a face. You back with Claire and Chloe? I heard that they had a vacancy."

Piper nodded. "I'm also going to be auditioning. I figure it's time to try my hand at Broadway. Or Off-Broadway."

"Don't get stars in your eyes," Edie warned. "You may have the sweetest set of pipes on the planet, but unless you're at the right place and the perfect time, it ain't gonna happen for you, girl."

She had forgotten how frank New Yorkers could be, especially a former singer and actor such as Edie, who had languished in the chorus for two decades before deciding to find permanent employment at her aunt's diner. The aunt had also been an Edie, and she'd left the restaurant to her niece when she passed away a decade ago.

"Chloe said you need some help at the diner. I'd like to apply. My days of waiting tables are pretty far in the past, but I've been managing a B&B for a friend recently. I cooked breakfast daily. Cleaned the rooms. Handled check-ins for the guests. I figure I can do whatever you need me to do, Edie."

"You cook. Hmm." Edie thought a moment. "I may have a place for you in the kitchen, Piper. Then again, the tips are better serving."

"I can do either—or both," she said.

"Come back to the kitchen. Make me breakfast. We'll see if you have what it takes."

Confidence brimmed through Piper as she followed the diner owner to the kitchen and asked, "What's it going to be? Eggs and bacon? French toast and sausage?"

"All those," Edie said.

"How do you want those eggs?"

"Sunny side up."

"Bacon crispy or greasy?"

The older woman's eyes lit up. "Now, that's something I haven't heard in a long time. Greasy bacon."

"I had a friend teach me about it. His grandmother in Maine made it greasy. It's grown on me."

"Fry up some of both kinds. I'll try each."

Piper washed her hands and pulled an apron from hanging on its hook, tying it around her. She took the hair tie on her wrist and secured her hair in a ponytail and then went to work, her movements efficient after months of cooking breakfast daily in the Bay. Edie watched every move Piper made like a hawk, and she saw the older woman nod in satisfaction as she plated the items.

"You're quick. That's a plus." Edie took a bite of the French toast. "I like that you put a dash of cinnamon in it. Nice touch."

"Thanks."

She watched Edie sample everything on the two plates. She only ate a couple of bites of everything except the greasy bacon, finishing both strips of those, a smile playing about her lips.

"You'd be wasted as a server. You've got this breakfast thing down. How about we go with line cook, and you can fill in at server if someone doesn't show."

"I can do that," Piper said. "I will be auditioning, though, so I'll need to work my schedule around that."

She told Edie the times she would be unavailable tomorrow, and Edie said, "Come in at five tomorrow afternoon."

"Edie, I only know how to cook breakfast."

"That's okay. People come in and eat breakfast all hours of the day and night. We'll keep you plenty busy when you're not cooking. There's always dishes to wash. Floors to be scrubbed."

"Then I'll see you at five," she said, taking the papers Edie gave to her fill out. "I'll return these completed when I clock in tomorrow."

"Ain't no clocking in, kid. Just be here when you're expected. And don't be late."

She folded the sheets and slipped them into her purse and then walked down to Sal's Market and Deli, where she picked up some groceries. She also purchased a pastrami on rye from the deli side and took it home, eating the sandwich while she put away her purchases.

Glancing at her watch, she decided to call her mom next.

"Hey, baby. You make it in okay?"

"I did. I'm in Brooklyn now. Unpacked. Have two auditions booked for tomorrow, plus I'm a line cook at a diner a few blocks from here."

"Wow, you've been busy."

"It's what I need, Mom."

She had confided in her mom how she'd had feelings for Sullivan, and Mom had commiserated with her.

"Staying busy will be the best medicine possible, Piper. Just focus on your career."

They chatted for a few more minutes, and then Mom put Dad on the phone. She told him all she'd accomplished.

"I'm so proud of you, Piper. It takes guts to do what you're doing."

"I figured if I don't try now, I may never do it. We'll see how auditioning goes."

"You'll get a part, hon. My gut tells me you will. And you know we'll come to see you perform."

"Even if I don't find work in a musical or even a play, there's lots to see in New York."

"Don't be a negative thinker," Dad cautioned. "Go into those auditions tomorrow and *know* you're going to kill it."

"Okay. Thanks for the pep talk, Dad."

They said goodbye, and she sent a long email to Mila, Layne, and Kylie, updating them on everything. Then she went and stood, looking out the window.

Trying not to think of Sullivan being so close.

Chapter Twenty-Two

Sullivan's watch beeped, reminding him of his upcoming FaceTime with Barry and Cindy. He had called it. Cindy Blaise knew exactly what she had wanted in a house, and Sullivan had gone back to the drawing board a few times after each conversation with the couple. He hoped his latest tweaks pleased the Blaises, and they could move forward with the project.

Getting up, he closed the door to his office. Not that anyone was left at this time. Alexander Wagner didn't push his people to work ungodly hours, as so many other New York firms did. Most employees were at their desks by nine at the latest, with many arriving by eight. Usually, the office emptied out at six. Right now, it was six-thirty. He would have plenty of time to take the call and still meet his parents for dinner at seven-thirty since the restaurant was nearby.

He had seen them last month when he arrived back in Manhattan, but it had been uncomfortable for him. His mother peppered him with questions he didn't feel like answering. Thankfully, his father had rescued him, talking about nothing but business. At least that was something they had in common.

His cell rang, and he touched the screen, seeing Barry and Cindy smiling at him.

"You did it, Sullivan," Cindy declared. "The latest plans you sent nailed everything I could possibly want in a house."

"You gave me good directions," he told her. "It's great when a client knows what they want, and I can marry their vision with blueprints in hand. Are you ready to look for a builder?"

The couple had already purchased a lot, which wasn't that far from where Carson and Mila's house stood, which he had also designed.

"Not a traditional builder," Barry replied. "Keaton recommended we talk with Joey Jordan. He did some work on the Bay Breeze. We went over to see it and also met with him in person. He shared pictures on his website and had files on other projects he's worked on over the years."

"He has a small crew—only two guys—but we're not in too big a rush," Cindy added. "They'll continue to complete renovations they've signed up for, and they'll work on our house in-between those jobs."

Sullivan smiled. "I'm glad it's all coming together."

"Are you sure you shouldn't be doing this for a living?" Cindy pressed. "I was invited to Mila and Carson's, and I love what you designed for them. I know you were responsible for creating Tidewater's layout and you create all kinds of big, fancy things, but you could easily open your own place and design homes for people. I hear you even build furniture."

In that moment, it was as if lightning struck him.

Why he hadn't seen this light before puzzled him—but he was seeing everything clearly now.

He *liked* working on small-scale projects. He *enjoyed*

listening to a couple and then creating a livable, comfortable, affordable space for them. More importantly, he missed working with his hands. The hours he had spent crafting Nellie's tables and Piper's bookcase had taken him back to those happy times in childhood, sitting next to Pawpaw in the shop, magically creating something beautiful and useful from a block of wood.

For too long, he'd pushed aside what he wanted to do with his life. He'd stopped fighting his parents years ago and simply gave in, becoming what they envisioned for him. He liked the money he made, working for a prestigious company. He certainly enjoyed the freedom of being able to design large projects. But Cindy's words had jostled loose something buried deep within him.

And it was time to be his own man. The man he now knew he should be.

"I'm happy you're happy," he told the Blaises. "Pass along my cell number to Joey. Tell him to call me if he has any questions regarding the blueprints."

"Will do," Barry said. "We'd love to have you over once the house is complete. Will you be coming back to the Bay?"

Sullivan nodded. "A whole lot sooner than I anticipated."

When he got off the phone, he sat, shaking his head. It was hard for him to understand why he'd left the Bay.

And Piper.

He loved her. Loved her desperately. In the time he'd been back in New York, an emptiness had gnawed at him. He'd shoved it aside, burying himself in work.

Why hadn't he realized that he'd foolishly walked away from a life of happiness with the woman he loved? Yes, he loved Piper. He'd never said it. Never thought it. But his gut told him she was the one who made him complete.

And he was going back to her. As soon as he could.

Sullivan left the office and took a cab to the mid-town restaurant where he was meeting his parents. The hostess recognized his name when he gave it to her and led him to a table. While his watch told him that he was on time, his parents were already seated, his dad thinking on time was late.

The trouble was, someone else was also at their table.

His gut clenched uncomfortably.

Taking a seat, he looked directly at his mother, who beamed at him.

"Oh, Sullivan. I want you to meet Anastacia Morrow. Her father is in banking and—"

Interrupting, he looked at the pretty stranger, who appeared to be in her late twenties, and said, "I didn't know you would be at dinner, Anastacia."

She gave him a coy look. "I didn't know I'd be here either, Sullivan. Your mother and I were at a Junior League meeting this afternoon, however, and she insisted I come and meet you." Anastacia paused, looking at him like a hungry wolf. "But I'm so glad I did."

"I'm afraid this isn't a good time," he said, seeing the startled look on her face at his blunt words. "I have some very personal business to discuss with my parents. I'm sure you understand. I can call you a cab if you'd like."

Anastacia's face went from flirtatious to angry. "You'll what?" she asked sharply.

At the same time, his mother said, "What in the world are you doing, Sullivan?"

"Trying not to air our dirty linen in public, Mother. Unless you'd prefer Anastacia stay, that is. I'm sure she'll be able to give a full, blow-by-blow account of what I'm going to say to her friends. Her family. Other Junior Leaguers."

"Listen here, son," Father began.

He shook his head. "No, I'm done with listening. I've been

the one listening to you for fifteen years. You're going to be the ones listening to me for the next few minutes. I'm sure you'll disown me, and I'll be all right with that."

Her face now bright red, Anastacia rose from the table, glaring at him. She looked as if she wanted to say something to him but thought better of it. He had to hand it to her. She walked away from their table with her dignity intact, her head held high.

"What is the matter with you?" Mother hissed. "Have you lost your mind? She is one of the most eligible women in Manhattan. Beautiful. Poised. Educated. It's time you settled down, Sullivan."

"I agree completely," he said easily, taking a sip of his water.

The sommelier came toward them, but Sullivan subtly shook his head, and the man turned and headed in the opposite direction, stopping the server who also was approaching.

"Quit being cryptic," Father admonished.

He looked at the both of them, seeing their outrage, and thought it was only going to get worse. Then again, he'd most likely never see them again after tonight. He would have the Roberts in his corner, though. He thought how comfortable he'd been with Piper's parents and knew he would grow to love them. They wouldn't judge him as his own parents did, and they would be adoring, attentive grandparents to the grandchildren Piper and he would create. That thought calmed him.

Clearing his throat, he said, "I'm going to leave Wagner Enterprises and do what I wanted to do with my life years ago, but I was too brainwashed by then and decided to please the two of you."

His mother's look of horror told him she knew exactly what he was talking about.

"You can't mean it, Sullivan. You want...to become...a carpenter? Spend your days in a dirty workshop?"

"Part of my days," he said cheerfully, the heavy burden which had been pressing on him ever since he'd left Piper suddenly easing. "I do plan to craft furniture. Custom furniture. I'm damned good at it, and I will command excellent prices. I also plan to keep using my architecture degree, however. I've drawn up plans for two different friends' houses in Driftwood Bay, and I plan to open Sullivan Design Studio."

It was the name he had once shared with Keaton and Carson. Just saying it aloud sounded right.

"My studio will offer architectural designs, as well as handcrafted wood projects. I'll create furniture. Wall art. Picture frames. Custom signs for homes and offices. The sky's the limit in what I'll design and craft and I'm going to be very happy doing it."

His mother appeared flummoxed, but he actually saw a glimmer of admiration in his father's eyes.

"I also plan to get married," he continued, matter-of-factly. "Her name is Piper Roberts, and she's smart, beautiful, and talented."

"Where will you have this life?" his father asked.

"In Driftwood Bay," he replied. "It's a place which feels like home in a way New York never has."

Mother looked as if she'd bit into something sour. "That place you've been living in Texas? Sullivan, how can you consider it? Your life is here. Your career. Your family."

"My life is where Piper is, and that's in Driftwood Bay. I also have made great friends there, Mother. People who are my chosen family. They don't judge me. They are open and honest and friendly. They'll be supportive of this decision."

His mother started to speak again, but his father said, "Hush, Jacqueline. Listen to him." He looked to Sullivan. "Does she make you happy?"

"Not only that, but Piper makes me a better man," he responded.

"Then go to her. Make a life with her," Father encouraged.

"Oliver!" his mother said. "How can you encourage such insane behavior?"

Though his father spoke to his mother, Oliver Shepherd's gaze locked on his son's. "Because if we don't support Sullivan, we'll lose him, Jacqueline."

"No son of mine would do this," she said, her voice shaking.

"Then I guess I'm no longer your son," he said evenly. "I'm my own man, and this is the life I want. The life which will bring me happiness."

"But you'll be poor," she said, looking at him dismally.

"I'll make enough to be comfortable. Besides, I'll be rich in love."

"I refuse to come to this wedding," Mother announced, her jaw tightening.

He looked to his father. "How do you feel?"

"I will be happy to attend, son."

"Thanks, Dad." It was the first time he had addressed his father that way, and Sullivan could tell his dad looked pleased.

"Have you spoken to Alexander yet?"

"No. I'll tell Zane tonight when I get home. Since Mr. Wagner arrives so early every morning, I'll go in around seven and tell him about my decision."

"This is so wrong, on every level imaginable," Mother complained bitterly.

Sullivan rose, and his father did the same. They shook hands.

"Let me know when the wedding is, son," his father said.

"Will do."

He left the restaurant, his step light, buoyed by happiness

which was bursting from him. He loved Piper. He loved the idea of working for himself. He couldn't wait to get back to the Bay.

Stopping at a vendor's cart, he grabbed at Nathan's and a soda, heading over to Central Park and taking a seat on a bench. It was nice to sit and relax as he ate the frank. His life would be radically changing, but his gut told him he was pursuing what was important to him.

And that was a life with Piper.

He wanted to call her, but what he had to say definitely warranted an in-person meeting. With plenty of kissing. Deciding it would be better to surprise her, he began making plans. He googled and found the Bay had one real estate agent. He skimmed through the property listings, finding one which might serve as his office. It was a small, two-bedroom frame house, but more importantly, it had a large, detached workshop in back. It would take some time to fix it up, but he was on his own time now, not someone else's. Or at least he would be as soon as he wrapped up his time at Wagner Enterprises. He decided to fly to Texas tomorrow and look at the property. If he liked it, he would put in a bid on it.

As far as a house for Piper and himself, he would definitely draw up the plans so they could build their dream home from scratch. He wanted her input regarding every room. Every feature both inside and outside. The kind of brick they would use and the various plants and trees for landscaping. How large the kitchen would be and if either of them would need an office. It would be a labor of love. Their together, forever home.

Sullivan left a message with the realtor, asking for a late afternoon appointment to see the house. He booked a flight to Houston and then one to Corpus. He reserved a car at the Corpus airport. He began looking at websites on how to incorporate a business in Texas and decided he would need an attorney to cut through the legalese in order to establish Sullivan Design Studio.

He itched to call and let Piper know he'd be in the Bay tomorrow, but it had been so long since they'd spoken. He stuck with the thought of making it a surprise. Telling her he was coming back to Texas permanently would only be part of the conversation. He definitely would ask her to marry him, and that definitely needed to be something he did face-to-face. He wanted to drop to one knee and see the look of astonishment on her face. Hear her say yes. Taste the kiss celebrating their love and foreverness. If he called her now, he would ruin everything by blurting out all his plans. Instead, he wanted things in place.

Then he would beg her forgiveness for having left in the first place—and pray she would say yes to his proposal.

Chapter Twenty-Three

Sullivan left his bench and walked the rest of the way home, adrenaline surging through him. He arrived at his apartment building and greeted the doorman. His life in the Bay would be very different from that of Manhattan.

And he could hardly wait to begin it with Piper.

He rode the elevator upstairs and braced himself for how Zane would react. They had been close for so many years, and it would be hard leaving his friend, but a new life awaited him. Thankfully, Zane was actually in New York. He'd been gone much of the summer after Tidewater's opening and would be leaving again in the morning for Canada.

Zane was standing in the kitchen, leaning against the counter, holding a carton of Chinese takeout in one hand and chopsticks in the other.

"How was dinner with your parents?" his friend asked.

Sullivan motioned for Zane to come and sit. Once he did, Sullivan said, "I told them that I'm leaving my position at Wagner Enterprises. Now, I'm informing you. I'll let your dad know in the morning."

Zane looked at him intently. "This is all about Piper, isn't it?"

"In a way, it is," he confirmed. "My life is with her, Zane. But I'm not chucking everything in New York simply because of Piper. It's something which has been inside me for a long time. Something that I pushed down so far inside me, that I forgot who I truly was and what I really wanted out of life. Yes, I may be the son of blue-blooded Jacqueline Shepherd, but I'm also Oliver Shepherd's son, as well. And that means I come from pretty humble stock."

He raked his hands through his hair. "I was always happiest when I was in Baker's Cove with my grandparents, working side-by-side with Pawpaw in his woodshop. I rebelled a little after I wasn't allowed to see them anymore, but with their deaths, I put aside the dreams I had for myself and toed the line. I absorbed the dreams my parents had for me and never looked back."

His gaze met that of his oldest and dearest friend's. "Do I regret going to college and earning my architectural degree? Of course not. I enjoyed every minute at Yale. I had a great time, being with you and our fraternity brothers, and taking classes I loved."

Sullivan sighed. "But deep in my heart, I knew I wanted to make things with my hands. Be my own man. I let the flash of money and prestige and position get to me. Sweep me away. The glamour of working at Wagner Enterprises, one of the top companies in the world. I did go to work there willingly, thankful for the opportunity to build things. Huge things. Spending time in Driftwood Bay, though, helped me get back to my roots. I like a small town, Zane. I like the slower pace. I like walking into the local diner and knowing most of the people I see sitting there.

"Most of all, I love Piper."

"You tried to warn me off Amanda," Zane said. "I was too stubborn to listen to you. What you have with Piper is nothing what I like shared with my ex-wife. I see that now. I saw how you were with Piper. I can understand how you want to move mountains to get back to Piper, so I won't stand in your way. I hope this isn't the end of us, Sullivan."

"Never," he said firmly. "You and I are brothers of the heart until the end. We may have to work a little harder to get to see one another. Then again, we've been ships passing in the night for years now. We may have shared an apartment, but we hardly ever saw one another. I'm going to make a concerted effort to stay in your life, Zane. I expect the same from you."

"I'll make time to come to the Bay a few times a year," Zane promised. "Gran and Gramps aren't going to be around forever. It's time I made them—and you—a priority. So, when are you leaving?"

"I'm flying to Texas tomorrow. I have a lead on a small property which could house Sullivan Design Studio."

Zane's brows arched. "Already have a name for your firm. Impressive. I assume it's a one-man shop."

"It will be. I'm going to build custom furniture. My side gig will be drawing up plans for individual homes. You know I already did that for Carson and Mila, and I also created blueprints for the tennis pro at Tidewater and his family. I don't know how much that side hustle will involve, but I'm going to devote the bulk of my time to building things with my own two hands."

"I admire you, Sullivan. I don't think I could give up the life I lead and move to the Bay, but I can really see you there. You have a woman you love. A circle of friends. And now, you have your life's purpose."

"Thanks for understanding, buddy. I want to keep you in my life."

"Well, I'm not going anywhere." Zane paused, his eyes gleaming with mischief. "But I'd love to be a fly on the wall when you tell Dad that you're walking away."

SULLIVAN TOOK the bag he'd packed and rolled the suitcase to the elevator. He left his apartment building and walked the short distance to work, asking if he could leave his suitcase at the security desk, something he often did before leaving town for a work trip.

"Of course, Mr. Shepherd," the guard on duty said, coming around and taking the handle and rolling it behind the desk. "It'll be waiting for you when you leave. Where are you off to this time?"

"Home," he said simply, turning and heading to the bank of elevators.

He entered the corporate offices of Wagner Enterprises and heard the sound of silence. It was just now seven o'clock, and the office wouldn't come to life for a while, but Mr. Wagner would be in. Sullivan approached his boss' door with a little trepidation. Still, he knew in his heart that he was making the right decision, both for his personal and professional life.

Pausing at the open door, he knocked on the frame, seeing the founder and CEO of the company glance up and then smile.

"Come in, Sullivan. You're here early this morning. Have a seat."

He did so and said, "I wanted to catch you when we had time to speak in private."

Wagner's brows knit together. "Go on," he encouraged.

Sullivan withdrew a sealed envelope from inside his jacket's pocket and placed it on the desk in front of him. "This is my resignation letter, Mr. Wagner. While I am beyond grateful for the opportunities you've given me over the years, the time has come for me to strike out on my own. It'll be called Sullivan Design Studio. Part of the time, I'll serve as an architect. The bulk of my time, I'll be crafting furniture as my paternal grandfather did."

The older man steepled his fingers, studying Sullivan with intensity. "This design studio will be in Texas, won't it?"

"Yes, sir."

"Zane told me you were involved with a woman in the Bay. My son warned me weeks ago that we'd probably lose you to her."

Surprise filled him since Zane hadn't mentioned this conversation to him.

"Her name is Piper Roberts. I love her. I've never loved a woman before. Hell, I've never even told Piper I loved her."

"So, you're giving everything up for a woman who doesn't even know you're returning?" Wagner asked, clearly surprised.

"Yes, sir, that just about sums up the situation. My resignation letter is in that envelope. I'll give you two weeks' notice, but I'll make myself available over the next year if whoever replaces me needs a consultation regarding the Vancouver project. Or even the one in Chicago."

"That's generous of you, Sullivan. You're a bright guy. I never had any qualms about hiring you. You're usually the smartest person in the room, and that includes your father and me."

Wagner leaned back in his chair, a contemplative look on his face. "I never really loved a woman myself," he admitted. "I was attracted to my wife. To her beauty and character. Especially to her family's reputation and wealth. But I never truly loved her the way a man should love his wife. I never gave my heart to her. In the end, she knew it—and that's why she left."

His gaze met Sullivan's. "If you have a chance at happiness, you should take it. Don't worry about owing the company two weeks. Go be with Piper. We'll figure everything out here."

He stood. "Thank you, Mr. Wagner. For all the opportunities you've given me. For your belief in me. If not for the confidence you instilled in me, I doubt I would have the guts to be making such a bold move."

The older man offered his hand, and Sullivan shook it.

"I expect to be invited to the wedding. Do you think your parents will come to it?"

"I've got Dad's support in this. Whether Mother comes around or not remains to be seen. If she doesn't, she'll be the one missing out."

"Good luck to you, son."

He went to his office for the last time and sent an email to his assistant, letting her know he had tendered his resignation, effective immediately. He asked her to box up anything personal. Looking around, it only included a few pictures hanging on the wall and his diploma from Yale. Nothing of real value was found in his desk drawers. He instructed her to give the box to Zane.

Then he left the building and took a cab to the airport. His flight to Houston was uneventful, and he easily made his connection, landing in Corpus ahead of schedule. Claiming his rental car at the airport, he drove to the Bay, his spirits soaring. While he knew he'd make another trip home to New York to pack up his personal items in the apartment and ship them to Texas, he knew this place was now home.

He stopped at Dorothy Ridley's real estate office, and the realtor greeted him enthusiastically.

"Ready to go see the property you're interested in, Mr. Shepherd?" she asked.

"It's Sullivan. And I'm more than ready."

On the short ride over, he told her that he was an architect and furniture designer. That the house would serve as his office and studio.

"I was mostly interested in it because of the shop in back. Not only do I design furniture, but I also build it."

"A true craftsman," she said admiringly. "I'd love to see your work sometime."

She pulled next to the curb in front of the house as he brought up the picture of Piper's bookcase on his phone. Turning the screen toward her, he said, "I built this for my future wife."

"My goodness, that's gorgeous," Dorothy said. "You will find yourself quite busy, Sullivan."

The house had great curb appeal and a large porch, something he was drawn to because of the large one at the Bay Breeze. The structure had good bones, but he would want to do some work to the inside. The wooden floors were scarred and needed refinishing. The entire interior needed to be painted. He decided he would knock out a wall so he would have a larger space to conference with clients. He thought he might also remove the wall between the two bedrooms and make it into a small showroom which displayed some of his furniture.

They went outside to the shop, which was the crown jewel as far as he was concerned. It was large and roomy and still contained several pieces of equipment.

"Does the shop come with this machinery?" he asked.

"Yes, it's included in the sale of the house. The owner was retired for many years and hadn't really used the shop for the last few, so you might need to check and see if the machines are running or need to be oiled. He recently went to a nursing home and passed away two weeks ago. No one in the family has any need for this type of equipment or a small house. They are very motivated sellers."

This would definitely give him a head start. While it would take time to see if the machinery were in good condition, he saw much of what he would need already here. A jointer to flatten and square wood pieces. A lathe to turn wood into different shapes. A drill press for drilling holes. Even a decent sander for smoothing finishes. In addition, a good variety of tools hung along the walls, including both band and table saws, which were instrumental in building furniture.

"I'll take the place," he said, glowing with pride at what would soon become Sullivan Design Studio.

Dorothy beamed. "Well, that's probably the quickest sale I've ever made."

"How long will it take to close?" he asked eagerly.

"We shouldn't have any bumps along the road. It will need to be inspected, of course, but I don't foresee any roadblocks there. Everything is in good working order."

"At a later date, I want to talk to you about rentals available, for myself and my fiancée. Since I'm an architect, I'll be drawing up the blueprints for our house, which will take time to build, but we'll need a place to live in the meantime."

"I'd be happy to show you the handful of rentals which I have available. Let's go back to the office now," she suggested.

Once there, Dorothy called the owners, and they accepted Sullivan's offer. He signed the paperwork, and Dorothy said she would expedite it.

"If you'd like, we can at least look at the home rentals on my website while you're here."

"No, I'll make an appointment with you regarding that. I want both of us here to make that decision."

He stood, shaking her hand, and then left the real estate office. His heart began slamming violently against his ribs the closer he got to the Bay Breeze. With Labor Day in just a couple of weeks, Piper should be leaving her position as manager of the inn—unless Layne hadn't found anyone to replace her yet. That meant Piper would soon be homeless. He wanted them to move in together while they took their time finding some land to build on. He also wanted to marry her as soon as possible.

When he pulled up at the Bay Breeze, it was five-thirty. Piper would be on desk duty until six, unless today's guests had already checked in.

He regretted not stopping to buy flowers for her, but he pushed that thought aside. All he needed was to see his woman.

And tell her he loved her.

Bounding up the steps, he opened the front door, only to find a stranger sitting behind the desk. He stepped toward her now, frowning.

"Hello," she greeted. "I'm afraid if you're looking to rent a room, we're all booked up. I can direct you to a couple of other places around town, however," the woman said brightly.

"Is Piper here?"

The woman smiled. "Oh, Piper is such a lovely young lady. She was so helpful in walking my husband and me through how to run the inn efficiently. We've taken over for her now. Do you have her number? Perhaps you could call her because I'm not sure where she's living now."

He didn't think she would move in with her parents. Maybe she was staying with Keaton and Layne since they had such a large house.

"Thank you," he said, returning to his car, not wanting to text her just yet.

Sullivan drove straight to Keaton's to regroup and knocked on the door, hoping he would find Piper there.

Keaton opened the door. "What a great surprise. Come on in, Sullivan."

He stepped into the foyer and said, "I just stopped at the Bay Breeze. Piper wasn't there. I was hoping she might be here."

"Piper's gone."

He turned, seeing Layne had joined them. "Gone? What do you mean, gone?"

Sympathy filled Layne's eyes. "She's left the Bay, Sullivan. Piper is in New York right now. Auditioning for Broadway shows."

Chapter Twenty-Four

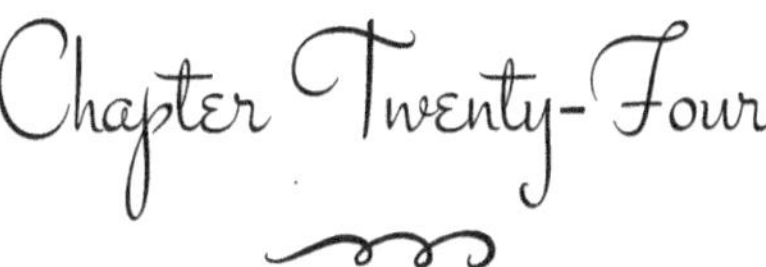

Piper checked her phone again, reading the casting call information to confirm she was at the correct venue for this first audition. It looked to be a regular Manhattan office building. She knew auditions for Broadway didn't occur in theaters, since they most likely had a show running, but it seemed odd to enter an office building.

Her directions told her to check in at the front desk in the lobby. When she did so, she was given a visitor pass and instructed which bank of elevators to take to the thirty-ninth floor. She thanked the person at the desk and peeled the back from the pass, placing it just above her heart. Tamping down her nerves, she rode the elevator upstairs and disembarked.

She found herself in a waiting room, dozens of actors present. Some scrolled through their phones. Others had closed eyes, probably running lines in their heads or thinking about the lyrics to the song they would sing as part of the process.

Going to the new desk, she gave her name and audition time. A woman checked her off as having arrived and told her to listen for her name.

"They're running a little behind, so you've got a bit of a wait."

"That's fine. Thank you."

Piper seated herself and looked about the room, trying to decide who was there for what part. For all she knew, there might be a dozen casting offices and those around her were auditioning for not only the musical she was here for but other productions, as well.

Forty-five minutes later, a guy in his late twenties appeared, tablet in hand, and called her name.

"I'm here," she said, standing and moving toward him.

"Follow me."

They went through a door and down a long hallway. She could hear people singing in different rooms as she passed.

The man stopped at a door. "Piano in there. You've got five minutes to warm up, and then I'll be back."

"Thanks," she said, but he was already racing down the hall.

She opened the door and entered, closing it behind her. Sitting at the piano, she ran through a few vocal scales and then sang a verse and chorus from *Chicago*, the last musical she'd appeared in.

The door opened. "They're ready for you."

Piper accompanied the new person down the corridor. They turned and went into a room where three people sat at a rectangular table. They introduced themselves as the casting director, her associate, and one of the producers of the revival she was auditioning for. She thought this prescreen audition would be a little less low-key, but she wasn't complaining about who was present.

"Have a seat, Miss Roberts," the producer said. "Even though you lack an agent, you've skipped ahead in the audition process, thanks to your stellar résumé. You've been on the road for quite a while. Tell me about that experience."

She elaborated on how she'd gone from chorus roles to meatier ones to finally landing the lead in several touring productions.

The casting director asked her favorite role and why she liked it so much. The producer asked her range, and she provided the lowest and highest notes she sang.

"As you know, this is a revival of a much-beloved musical," the producer explained. "You would be playing the second lead female, with the chance to serve as understudy to the lead." He paused. "I think that's enough background. Let's hear your scene, and then you can sing for us."

The casting call had come with a one-page scene between her and another character.

"I'll be reading with you," a voice said, and she turned, seeing a man seated at the piano. He must have slipped into the room while she was being interviewed.

Piper walked over to him and stood, waiting for her cue to begin. The casting director pointed a finger, and she spoke her first line.

Once they had run through the page of dialogue, the pianist asked what she'd be singing for her audition.

"*Rainbow High* from *Evita*," she replied, calling the music up on her tablet and handing it to him to use. The casting instructions had said she could select whatever song she wanted, but it specifically said not to choose one from the revival, which she found odd.

He looked at her. "Interesting choice."

She faced the committee of three as the pianist's fingers went into action. She got through half the song when the producer said, "Okay. Stop."

She wondered if this were a good or bad stop. A good one

meant they liked her voice. A bad stop meant they were tired of listening to her and would move on.

"Can you try some Sondheim for us?" the casting director asked politely.

The request may have seemed off-hand, but Stephen Sondheim was known for writing some of the most musically challenging numbers with complex rhythms and dissonant harmonies.

"I'd be happy to. Would you like to hear something from *Follies*? *Into the Woods*? *Company*?"

She was thrilled they wanted to hear more but had hoped they would select a song from the revival. She was familiar and comfortable with the entire musical. Piper decided this was a test, and she was determined to pass it with flying colors.

The producer asked for the song he wished to hear, and Piper attacked it with gusto. Again, they stopped her mid-song. This time, she saw pleased looks, and they finally asked her to sing a song from the show itself. She was allowed to complete the entire number this time, which she took as a good sign.

Looking to the pianist, she thanked him. In turn, he nodded encouragingly, handing her tablet back to her.

"We'd like to see you again," the casting director said. "Next week. I'll text you the callback info. Nice job, Miss Roberts."

"Thank you," she said, smiling politely, even as her insides exploded with joy.

She left the casting offices and went to the New York Library at Fifth and Forty-Second. Patience and Fortitude, the two marble lions, graced the entrance. Piper went inside, wanting a quiet place to reflect on her audition while still allowing her to remain close enough to make the next audition ninety minutes from now. She felt good about what she had done. Her voice sounded strong.

Her reading was spot on. She thought her chances were good at the callback. Of course, she had no idea how many callbacks would be scheduled, must less who she might be up against.

Tapping into the Wi-Fi, she checked her email. She had no text messages. Part of her wanted to text Layne and Mila to let them know how she had done, but the superstitious part of her refused to give in to that impulse. Instead, she went to a quiet section of the library and opened her phone's Kindle app, reading a romance for forty-five minutes before going to the restroom and freshening up. Then she set out on foot for her next audition.

This second one was inside a rehearsal studio. Those were dedicated places for different phases of a production. She checked in and was directed to the third floor, where she was met by an assistant and sent to an empty room with a table, four chairs, and a piano. Nerves began flitting through her again. This call had not sent a scene she could prepare for. She had no idea what the musical was about. Piper told herself to merely concentrate on what she did well. She was talented. Flexible.

And she wanted to see if she could make it in New York.

She'd read online that the odds of landing in a Broadway show were slim. Only ten percent of the top talent was hired. She told herself she had a lot of experience and that they would want her.

Two boyish-looking men entered the room, followed by a harried assistant.

"We're the Pearson brothers," one of them said. "I'm Ted. I write the music."

"I'm Tad. I'm the lyricist."

"Nice to meet you. I'm Piper Roberts."

"Yes, we have your info here." Ted turned and snapped his

fingers, and the assistant passed over a tablet, which he then studied, Tad leaning over his shoulder.

"You've done a good number of shows the past ten years," Tad said, turning and eyeing her with interest. "A true working stage actor. That's rare."

"I was fortunate to land a part in a musical which a new touring company was taking on the road when I was only twenty. I haven't looked back since."

Except for my time in the Bay...

"I like that you have touring experience," Tad said. "You've also got looks. But I need to hear you sing."

The lyricist named a song. Since no one was there to accompany her, Piper went to the piano and played for herself. She met the eyes of both brothers during the song and saw they were impressed with her vocal range.

Ted signaled the assistant, who brought Piper a tablet, sheet music loaded onto it.

"Look that over," he said. "We want to hear it."

"I assume this is from your musical," she said, skimming the first page.

"Yes."

"Give me five minutes," she asked.

Piper looked intently at each line, first forming the notes in her head. Then she went back a second time and put the words to the tune. A third time, and she had it down, especially how she would interpret the lyrics for these two men.

"Don't judge my piano playing," she said lightly. "I haven't played in a good while. I can do enough to get through the song, though."

She kept to basic chords, with no flourishes. She would allow her voice to sell herself.

The tune was a ballad, powerful and vocally challenging. She would have preferred it one key lower, but she was out of practice and didn't want to try to transfer the notes in front of her to a different key as she sang a song she had just glanced at a few times.

In the end, though, it didn't matter. She hit the high notes with emotion and depth.

Piper thought she had done enough to receive a callback—if not actually land the role itself. What that role was still eluded her, though. Everything seemed wrapped in mystery.

As she held the last note, she saw Ted and Tad exchange glances, and her gut told her that was a very good thing. She finished and stood, returning the tablet to the assistant.

"How do you think you did?" Ted asked.

"I believe I performed very well for just having seen the song," she replied. "I'm a good sight-reader. I'm even better once I'm familiar with the music. May I ask what role I'm being considered for? I know this is a new musical and the two of you are making your Broadway debut, but if I'm going to receive a callback, I'd like to be more prepared. Know something about my character."

"No callback," Tad said brusquely, causing her spirits to sink. Then he added, "You have the lead role of Evelyn in *The Second Time Around*. If you want it, that is."

Piper grew flustered, feeling her cheeks redden. Still, she wasn't ready to accept without knowing more.

"Before I commit, I'd like to know what this musical is about. While it's an honor to be offered the lead in a new Broadway production, I won't go blindly into anything."

"Have a seat, Piper," Ted said.

She did so, and the brothers spent the next twenty minutes telling her about the production. The theme and overall arc. Particulars about her character and what made Evelyn tick. The other roles which had been written in support of the star.

"I'd like to read the book. Hear all the other numbers," she said, still not wanting to commit to something which might be poorly written. While she liked the song she had sung in her audition, it might be the only good number from the musical.

"Come back tomorrow," Tad said. "Nine o'clock. We'll make available all the songs, which we've recorded, as well as the book."

He referred to the musical's script, which would have the overall story and character development, along with the dialogue which was spoken between songs, linking each musical number together.

"I'll be here," she promised, her spirits now soaring.

The assistant led Piper out and said, "Those two don't impress easily. You should count yourself lucky. They'll be hard to work for, though, because they're such perfectionists."

"I'll keep that in mind," Piper said, not minding the warning because she, too, was a perfectionist.

She rode the subway home to Brooklyn. Neither Claire nor Chloe were home. In a way, she was glad because she didn't want to share this news with anyone yet. Everything was still too new and unknown. She would keep things to herself until she saw the book and decided whether or not it was a project she wanted to be involved in.

Then she realized she needed to get to the diner before she was late. Piper literally ran the few blocks there, hurrying inside. Edie looked up from the register.

"Head to the back. Hairnet on."

"Got it," Piper said, pulling a hair tie from her purse and putting her hair into a ponytail. She claimed an apron from the wall and tied it before reaching in and pulling a disposable hairnet from the box sitting on the table below the aprons.

One cook was already in the kitchen, and they introduced themselves to one another. The orders were slow at first, and he took anything which wasn't breakfast. When six o'clock hit, they grew much busier. Piper cooked for a solid fours, sending out orders of pancakes, eggs, and bacon, along with toasted English muffins and hash browns. She was rather proud of the hash browns, something she had picked up this summer from her mom, who had come over one morning to watch her daughter at work and suggested she add hash browns to her repertoire.

When things slowed to a crawl, Edie appeared. "Good job, Piper. Got some nice compliments from customers. When are you available tomorrow?'

Thinking she'd be tied up most of the day with the brothers, she said, "How about five again?"

"You're on," Edie said. "Go home."

She did as ordered, brushing her teeth and washing her face before putting on an oversized T-shirt and falling onto the couch. She woke up in the middle of the night, setting her phone's alarm and plugging it in to charge. It went off the next morning at seven, and she quickly showered and dressed and made herself a quick breakfast before heading to the subway station. Piper grabbed a cup of coffee along the way from a street vendor, needing the jolt of caffeine.

The brothers were waiting for her. Tad handed her the book, telling her, "You'll need to stay here while you read it. The room is yours, so feel free to try out any songs on the piano."

"Thank you."

"We'll be back around noon to see how you're doing."

When they returned three hours later, Piper had to screw up her courage to tell them she would be passing on the role of Evelyn.

"Why?" Ted asked, frowning deeply, his displeasure obvious.

Wondering how frank she should be, she said, "The storyline is too pedestrian, even for off-Broadway. The song you gave me to sing yesterday is the best in the entire book, but too many of the others are weak. They drag. Sound like fillers."

She looked at the brothers apologetically. "As much as I would like to perform as the lead in a musical here in New York, this isn't the one for me."

"Could you make it better?" Tad asked hopefully. "I'm sure you have some ideas how we rewrite the storyline. Or even what we need to do to jazz up the songs."

"I'm afraid that's not my job. That's yours. I've never written music before. I'm really sorry."

Ted shrugged. "We'll work on it. Could we call you when we've improved it?"

"Sure," she said, not sure at all that would be possible. Hopefully, she would have been cast in another production by then, and that would be her excuse not to work on *The Second Time Around*.

Piper thanked them for their time and left the offices, feeling down in the dumps. The other callback wasn't until next week, so she would be able to put in some good hours at Edie's diner. She returned home and changed clothes before going for a long walk. She wanted to clear her head and hoped the disappointment at having to turn down the role would disappear.

Still feeling down, she turned the corner, humming as she walked. She reached her apartment building.

And saw Sullivan sitting on the stoop.

Chapter Twenty-Five

Sullivan had been stunned to learn that Piper had left Driftwood Bay. Then anger had poured through him when he discovered she had moved to New York and hadn't bothered to contact him. After he calmed down, though, he understood why she wouldn't want to risk her heart anymore. He had made it clear to her that nothing more would come from their relationship, something that had him kicking himself now.

He had obtained her address from Layne and immediately made plans to return to New York. He'd spent the night with Keaton and Layne, driving back to Corpus the next morning and flying back to the East Coast. He hadn't even bothered to bring his suitcase home, getting off the plane and taking a cab straight to her Brooklyn apartment.

A pretty blond had answered his knock and informed him that Piper wasn't home and she had no idea when she might return. The blond closed the door, and Sullivan left the building, taking a seat on the stoop. He would wait there as long as it took until Piper came home.

He'd sat for less than ten minutes when the back of his neck prickled with awareness. Immediately, his eyes scanned the area surrounding him, and he saw Piper had turned the corner and was coming his way. Sullivan shot to his feet and moved to the sidewalk, seeing the wariness in her eyes as she approached him.

"What are you doing here?" she asked guardedly.

"You weren't in the Bay when I came home. To you."

Her eyes widened, his words apparently startling her.

"You…came to Texas. For me?"

"I had to. I was foolish to walk away from you and what we had, Piper. Because you're my everything. I quit my job. I even bought a place in the Bay which will serve as my new place of work." He grinned. "Sullivan Design Studio. It sounds friendly, yet professional. Besides, Shepherd is too hard for people to spell."

Stop babbling, he told himself. *Get to the point.*

"Sullivan Design Studio?" she echoed, her gaze searching his face.

"I'm ready to make a change, Piper. A commitment to you. I want to be with you. Always. I want to do work which fulfills me. Live life in a place which has come to be home to me. I want to have kids with you and raise them in the Bay, alongside the kids all our friends are having."

Sullivan took a step toward her, taking her hands in his. "I got lost along the way after my grandparents died, but living in the Bay—and loving you—helped me to see who I am and what I truly want to make out of my life."

"Loving?" she squeaked.

He squeezed her fingers, his gaze warm on her as he said, "I love you, Piper. I loved you and was stupid enough to think I could walk away and forget you. But you're in every breath I take. Every thought I have. I've been miserable without you."

Suddenly, she flung herself at him. His arms came about her, and he was kissing her, over and over.

"Get a room!" a voice called from a passing cab, and they broke apart, laughing.

"We have so much we need to talk about," she told him, glancing at her building.

"Not there. I think your roommate is still in there."

"Then let's walk and talk," she said, threading her fingers through his and leading him down the street.

"Quitting your job is a huge deal, Sullivan. What do you think you'll do in the Bay?"

"I told you. I'm opening my own studio. You know I drew up plans for Carson and Mila's house. I did the same for Barry and Cindy Blaise, the tennis pro and his wife."

She looked doubtful. "That's all well and good, but I can't see a huge demand for your architecture skills in the Bay."

He squeezed her fingers. "I know. That's going to be a part-time job. My main focus will be on crafting custom furniture."

"Like my bookcase," she whispered.

Piper brought them to a stop and faced him. "I love that bookcase so much," she said earnestly. "It's the most beautiful piece of furniture I've ever seen. Plus, the fact that you filled it with the romances I love. It meant so much to me, Sullivan, but I was too proud to let you know all of this. I'm ashamed at how at how unenthusiastic my thank you to you was."

"Don't be, sweetheart," he said, cradling her cheek in his palm, feeling her lean into it as she closed her eyes.

They stood silently, both savoring the moment, then Piper opened her eyes again. "So, you'll make furniture, just like Pawpaw did."

"When I was working on your bookcase—and even Nellie's tables—I can't begin to tell you the immense satisfaction that filled me. Working with my hands again. There's all kinds of things I can do in wood besides furniture. I can make custom signs for homes and offices. Candle holders. Picture frames. Wall art. Planters. Cutting boards. Serving bowls. Jewelry boxes. Hell, even bird feeders."

Her face was filled with mixed emotions. "It sounds as if you've really thought this through, but I don't want you to look up in five months or five years and think you've made a mistake, quitting your fancy job in New York. You won't travel the world anymore, Sullivan. You won't make the kind of money you once did."

He leaned down and tenderly kissed her. "I've made enough money. What I need to do is make a life—and memories—with you."

Sullivan kissed Piper again, more deeply, and her response let him know she cared for him. Perhaps even loved him.

He broke the kiss. "I know I'm going to have to earn back your trust."

Her eyes filled with love, and a glimmer of hope began to glow within him.

"I trust you, Sullivan. I *love* you. I have for what it seems like forever. There's my life before you. And now, life with you. Don't take a hundred percent of the blame. I should've told you that I loved you before you left the Bay. I was afraid if I did, though, you would stay out of some sense of obligation. I didn't want to keep you from your life here in New York."

He framed her face with his hands. "I came back to New York and found I was miserable. All I could think about was you, Piper. I was marking time and finally decided to man up and be the man I want to be."

"What did Mr. Wagner say?"

Sullivan took her hand in his again and began walking down the street. "The old man surprised me. He actually encouraged me to go for it. To pursue you and what I love doing."

"Have you...talked to your parents?" she asked, hesitation in her voice.

"They know everything. About you and me quitting Wagner Enterprises. Mother is close to completely disowning me, but Dad was very supportive."

"Dad?" she asked. "You've never referred to him that way. You've always been so formal, calling him Father."

"I know. It was the way I was raised. The man who was encouraging me to follow my heart, both professionally and personally, suddenly became Dad. I think he admires what I'm doing, stepping away from all the expectations he and Mother put upon me and freeing me to become who I want to be for the rest of my life."

Sullivan smiled at Piper. "I'm a better man when I'm with you. I'm the man I want to be. I'm going to need some help, though. I'll need your love and support as I start this new journey and open my one-man office."

"You have it. You have *me*. Always."

Dropping to one knee, he took her hands in his.

"I've talked all around the subject, but I need to ask you a very important question. Will you be my wife, Piper? Will you love me through good times and bad?"

Her radiant smile caused a glow to start within him, and it spread throughout him.

"I'm ready to become the me I'm supposed to be, as well, Sullivan. I can't imagine doing that with anyone except the man I love. My answer is yes. A thousand, million times yes!"

Sullivan sprang to his feet and embraced her, holding her so close that he could feel the beating of her heart. Everything was finally the way it should be. He only regretted that Memaw and Pawpaw would never get to know Piper. He would do his best to tell her stories about them, though. She could come to know them that way, as well as know why he had loved them so much.

She pulled away, panic on her face. "I need to get to work!"

"Work? You already have a job?"

"Come with me," she said, rushing him back to her apartment.

When they entered, the tiny place was empty. Piper started throwing off clothes and for a brief moment, Sullivan hoped they could stay and make love.

"I've been auditioning. Two different shows. Got a job as a cook in a diner to supplement in the meantime," she said, and he heard the pride in her voice.

"Well, you do make the best scrambled eggs and greasy bacon ever."

She grinned at him. "I know, right?"

Piper finished dressing and took his hand again, pulling him out the door. "I auditioned for one show yesterday. Two new guys on the scene. They offered me the lead for their off-Broadway musical. I went in and read the book today and looked at the show's songs, but it wasn't good enough. I turned it down. Didn't want to be associated with that show, which I think will bomb spectacularly."

They turned the corner, and he saw a sign which said Edie's Diner. That must be their destination.

"I also auditioned for a revival of a musical on Broadway, coming in November. Got a call back. It's sometime next week."

They arrived at the door, and Piper came to a halt. "But I'd rather be with you in the Bay than singing on Broadway."

That didn't sit well with him. "Piper, if your dream is to be on Broadway, we can flip the script here. I wouldn't go back to Wagner Enterprises, but I can rent some workspace and build my furniture here. You can sing and dance on Broadway and fulfill that dream."

Her eyes misted with tears. "You would do that for me?" she asked softly.

"Honey, I'd lasso the moon and pull it down to earth if you asked me to."

She burst out laughing. "That's about the most Texas thing you've ever said." She kissed him hard. "And I love it. Come inside. Let me cook you breakfast for dinner."

They entered the diner, and she went up to a woman in her late fifties. "Edie, this is Sullivan." She paused, beaming at him. "My fiancé."

Edie harrumphed. "Guess I'm losing me a cook."

"I'm afraid so," Piper said, laughing. "I will work tonight's shift for you. I'll keep coming in until you can find a replacement for me."

Edie shook her head. "Cooks and servers come and go. Fiancés? Not so much. Grab on to love while you can, Piper. It doesn't always come calling twice."

Piper stood on tiptoe and kissed him. "Go find a booth. I'll whip you up something you'll enjoy."

He watched as she hurried back to the kitchen. Sullivan could catch sight of her working through the pass-through window.

Edie came over and placed a glass of ice water in front of him. "Anything else to drink?"

"Coffee's always good," he told her.

The woman studied him a moment and then said, "You're the greasy bacon guy, aren't you?"

He puffed with pride, knowing Piper had told Edie about him. "Yes, ma'am. My memaw in Maine fried it up that way, and I taught Piper how to do it."

"Keep greasing those wheels of love, kid," Edie said, leaving him and then returning with a large mug of coffee, which Sullivan doctored the way he liked.

A few minutes later, he saw Piper put a plate in the window and knew what it would contain. When it arrived at his table, he had wet scrambled eggs. Greasy bacon. An English muffin toasted to perfection. Plus, a new item. Hash browns. Piper must have learned how to make them after he'd left the Bay.

He glanced up and saw her at the pass-through and blew her a kiss.

Sullivan stayed for several hours. He switched from drinking coffee to water as he watched people from the diner come and go. At a quarter to ten, Piper appeared at his table, pulling the hair tie from her ponytail and tousling her hair with her fingers.

"Do you have any auditions tomorrow?" he asked.

She shook her head. "I've got nowhere to be tomorrow." Her eyes lit with mischief. "Except your bed."

"Want to go back to my place for the night then?" he asked. "At least, I don't think Zane has emptied everything out of my bedroom yet."

She laughed. "Let's go, Prepster."

They went to his apartment and found Zane sitting on the sofa with a glass of wine in his hand. If he were surprised to see them together in New York, his friend didn't show it.

"Good to see you again, Piper." Zane's eyes flicked to Sullivan.

"You're addressing the future Mrs. Shepherd," he informed his best friend.

Zane came to his feet and hugged Piper, kissing her on the cheek. He turned to Sullivan and enveloped him in a bear hug, slapping him heartily on the back.

"So, when's the wedding?" he asked. "I'm assuming it'll be in the Bay."

Sullivan looked to Piper. "We haven't worked out the details yet, but we'll let you know, Best Man."

He took Piper's hand and led her to his bedroom. Immediately, they were in a frenzy to shed their clothes. They fell onto the bed, and he kissed her with a hunger he knew would always be satisfied, now that they had committed to one another. He was excited to start a life with this woman. One he could be proud of, knowing she was by his side, supporting him in every endeavor, as he did for her.

After they made love, they lay entwined, talking about their future. Sullivan insisted that Piper attend her callback next week, saying, "If you land a Broadway show, we'll stay here through its run. If you want to keep auditioning after that show, I'm fine with it. If you prefer going back to the Bay, that's good, too."

"Thank you for being so supportive," she said, kissing him tenderly.

They fell asleep in one another's arms, and Sullivan looked at today as the start of the best chapter in his life.

Chapter Twenty-Six

TEN MONTHS LATER...

Piper woke and stretched lazily. The bed was empty beside her because Sullivan had spent the night at their house.

No, their *home*.

He had been incredibly supportive of her career, especially when she landed the Broadway role she'd auditioned for. He encouraged her to sign the contract for the six-month run and that it would be up to her whether she renewed it or not. Rehearsals had been exhausting, but she had thrived on performing on a Broadway stage.

The revival had opened the first week of November, and Piper had stepped into the lead's role when the woman came down with COVID the week of Thanksgiving. That meant not only had her parents seen her perform in a secondary role, but their trip had coincided with watching their daughter take the stage as the top-billed performer in the cast. Spying them in the audience as she took her curtain call and seeing the look of pride on their faces meant the world to her.

Piper had moved from her cramped Brooklyn apartment

into Sullivan and Zane's spacious one. In a move which surprised everyone, Zane married very quickly, leaving them the apartment and finding a new one—in the same building. Sullivan went back and forth between New York and Texas, overseeing the construction of the dream home that they had discussed and designed together.

He had also opened his design studio and spent about four days a week in the Bay, building his business and producing custom pieces, returning to New York for long weekends so he could catch at least one of Piper's performances before spending all day Monday with her when the theater was dark and no performances occurred.

Though the producers encouraged Piper to extend her run in the musical, saying she was one of the chief reasons it had received such rave reviews and did great at the box office, she had accomplished that professional goal. Besides, her man—and a new life—waited for her back in Driftwood Bay.

She rolled out of bed and went through a half-hour of Zumba before jumping in the shower. She had stayed the night in a lavish suite at Tidewater, and their wedding guests had also been offered rooms at the luxury resort. The rehearsal dinner had been held last night in the restaurant Ty headed. Her old friend was also in charge of the food for today's reception, which would also be held in the same restaurant. While the rehearsal dinner had been a sit-down affair, today's fare would consist of various stations, from a brisket carving bar to a taco bar to a mashed and sweet potato station. Ty had also included a charcuterie board, two seafood stations, and a gelato bar. They had FaceTimed several times leading up to the wedding, tweaking the menu, and she thought their guests would enjoy the selections prepared for them.

Mila was the first of her bridesmaids to arrive. She had

bounced back from her pregnancy and looked much the same after giving birth to Jessica last October. Although Piper had been unable to come home to see Jess at the time, being back in the Bay full-time would give her plenty of opportunities to play with the baby and watch her grow up.

Layne sailed through the door next, carrying Alicia in her arms. Her friend had given birth two weeks ago, and Piper had arrived in time to be at the hospital to meet the baby when Keaton brought her out to introduce the newest Maxwell.

"I've got to feed Alicia now," Layne said, "then Dotty is going to take over. It was so generous of Zane to provide a room for kids, as well as babysitters."

"I know," Mila said. "I dropped Lily and Jess off and promised Dotty that I'd stop by to check on them between the wedding and reception."

The baby latched onto Layne's breast and began sucking enthusiastically. Piper felt a maternal wave wash over her, and she hoped that she and Sullivan would start a family in the next couple of years. Her first move, however, was going back to college. They had discussed it at length, and her fiancé had encouraged her to finish her degree since it meant so much to her. She was registered for the upcoming summer session at a university in Corpus, and Piper knew she would feel better about herself by having that degree in hand, no matter what she chose to do upon graduation.

She put on her makeup, talking with Mila and Layne as she did so. Kylie, her third bridesmaid, arrived in the middle of this. Kylie truly had become d'Artagnan, the fourth musketeer to their tight trio of three. Since Kylie also lived in New York, they saw one another when they could, and Piper was thrilled that her newest friend had found lasting love the way the rest of them had.

Layne went to take Alicia to where the children were staying during the ceremony and reception. Not only had Zane provided space for that, but he had thought of everything. Provided rooms for their guests for the weekend. Picked up the cost of both the rehearsal dinner and wedding itself. She knew there had been no way her parents could have afforded the cost of a wedding held at Tidewater, but Zane assured her that this was his gift to the newlyweds. It meant a great deal to Piper and Sullivan that they would wed at a property he had designed, one where they had spent happy times together.

Piper's mom showed up, complimenting her daughter on how beautiful she looked as tears misted her eyes.

"Everything is ready downstairs," Mom said. "They're simply waiting on the bride and her party to show up."

"How is Dad holding up?" she asked.

"Pacing a hole through the carpet."

"Then let's go, everyone," Piper said.

They rode the elevator downstairs and went to the room which had been decorated with abundant flowers. It had glass walls on two sides, so that it almost seemed as if the wedding took place outside. Dad brightened as he spotted her.

"There's my girl," he said, beaming proudly at her.

Piper slipped her hand through the crook of his arm as her bridesmaids lined up. She saw the harpist looking in their direction and nodded to her. The music began, and her friends went down the aisle, one at a time. She had wanted a low-fuss wedding, so each bridesmaid wore a dress of her own choosing in varying shades of purple, Piper's favorite color. She herself wore a simple, A-line wedding gown in soft ivory.

As the last bridesmaid left them, Dad said, "I hope you aren't disappointed that I passed on performing the ceremony, honey. I would've blubbered through the entire thing and made a mess."

She squeezed his forearm. "I like you being right here in this role, Dad. Father of the Bride."

Now that all bridesmaids had arrived at the other side of the room, Dad stepped into the center of the open doorway as the harpist struck up *Here Comes the Bride*. Her gaze immediately was drawn to her groom. Sullivan had never looked more handsome, wearing a dark blue suit and the biggest smile she had ever seen. Dad led her toward her groom, and Piper's heart almost burst with joy. She had never been happier.

The local minister from her parents' church asked who was giving away the bride, and her dad replied, "Her mother and I."

He brushed a kiss along his daughter's cheek and then placed her hand in Sullivan's before he took a seat next to Mom on the front row.

Piper grew warm under Sullivan's loving gaze.

"You are incredibly beautiful," he said huskily, looking as if he might shed a few tears.

Trying to lighten the mood a bit, she whispered, "You clean up pretty well yourself, Prepster," and winked at him.

His sunny smile grew wider, and she could feel him relaxing next to her.

The ceremony moved along quickly. They hadn't wanted it to be lengthy, only meaningful. A quarter-hour later, they were pronounced husband and wife.

The preacher then announced to those gathered, "I give to you Mr. and Mrs. Sullivan Shepherd."

Their guests applauded heartily as she and Sullivan sailed down the makeshift aisle. For the first time, she was aware of the videographer who stood at the door, capturing that first walk as man and wife.

They posed for several pictures, both with family and friends, and then Zane said, "Chef Chastain is waiting for you. Please follow me."

Guests began filing from the ballroom until only Piper and her new husband remained. Sullivan kissed her tenderly, his fingers caressing her cheek.

"I missed having you sleep next to me last night, Mrs. Shepherd."

"I missed you more. Especially in the shower," she said saucily, causing him to laugh aloud.

"Let's go to our reception and celebrate," he said.

They had agreed to a late morning wedding when Zane told them it would be easier to close the restaurant and have Ty cater the reception if they held the wedding at eleven and reception at noon. Piper hadn't minded because it meant she got to marry Sullivan even sooner than she'd expected.

They made their way to the restaurant, and Ty greeted them himself, saying, "Welcome, lovebirds. I hope you're going to enjoy everything my staff and I have prepared for you."

Just like last night's rehearsal dinner, the food turned out to be exceptional. The pastry chef had created a three-tiered wedding cake, which was almost too pretty to cut into, but they did so together. Zane had remembered how much Piper loved Blue Bell ice cream, and scoops of it accompanied each slice of the wedding and groom's cakes.

While they tasted everything offered at each station, they spent time going around to each table to visit with each of their guests. The last table they reached was the table which seated her parents, Sullivan's parents, and Alexander Wagner. Instead of standing, they slipped into seats so they could visit longer.

Piper actually liked Oliver Shepherd a great deal. She had met him several times during her months in New York. He had also attended her musical twice. The second time, he brought his wife along, saying he wanted her to see how talented Piper was.

Her eyes flicked to Jacqueline Shepherd now. The woman would never be a warm, loving mother-in-law, but at least she had agreed to attend her son's wedding at the last minute.

"Who would have thought that I came from the Bay and I'd be back here, celebrating the marriage of a man who has been almost like a son to me," Mr. Wagner said. "This is a very happy occasion, Sullivan and Piper, and I'm thrilled that we're here together today, celebrating you and your love."

"Thank you, Mr. Wagner," Sullivan said.

"Did you know I spent some time at Sullivan Design Studio yesterday, Piper?" Wagner asked her.

"No, I didn't, but I'm thinking that you found something you wanted while you were there."

"I had no idea how talented Sullivan was with his hands. I commissioned a new dining table and chairs for my house on Martha's Vineyard. I entertain quite a bit there, and the table is going to be larger than my current one."

"It'll seat twenty-four," Sullivan said. "I'll be working on this commission for months to come."

Zane strolled up and said, "I predict once Dad's friends see it, they'll all be clamoring for a custom piece from you. Just make sure you charge Dad a fair price. Don't give him some kind of family and friends discount."

Zane's words caused everyone—except Jacqueline Shepherd—to laugh.

"I think we're going to say our goodbyes now," Sullivan told those seated at the table. He looked to his parents. "Thank you for making the trip from New York. Piper and I appreciate that you came to our wedding."

Jacqueline nodded stiffly, while Oliver said, "We wouldn't have missed this for the world, son."

"Thanks, Dad," Sullivan said, and Piper was happy that the

two men had reached a new level of closeness in their relationship.

She hugged her parents and was pleased to see Sullivan do the same. Mom and Dad had Sullivan over once a week for dinner while she'd been in New York, and he had grown close to them, telling Piper how much he enjoyed being in their company.

They excused themselves and went to find Ty, thanking him and his staff for putting together such an amazing reception.

"Not only was the food outstanding, but I know you cooked from the heart for an old friend," Piper said. "We're so grateful you were a part of this day."

They exited the kitchen, and Sullivan got the attention of their guests.

"We're saying our goodbyes now. Remember, as guests at Tidewater, you have access to all the amenities on the island. I hope you'll take advantage of the golf course this afternoon. The pools. Even coming to the club tonight and being entertained there."

He turned his gaze to Piper. "As for Mrs. Shepherd and me, we've got some catching up to do."

They left the restaurant, the friendly laughter wafting out behind them.

In the elevator, the groom took his bride in his arms and gave her a lingering kiss.

"Ready to start the next chapter in our lives together, sweetheart?" he asked. "I hope you're going to enjoy Maui."

That was their honeymoon destination, which they would squeeze in before she started classes. They would leave Tidewater now and take the ferry back to the mainland, going straight to the airport and their evening flight to Hawaii.

"I hear that Maui is heaven on earth, but I've already found that in your arms, Sullivan."

"Good answer, Mrs. Shepherd," her new husband said, kissing her again.

Happily ever afters do come true, Piper thought.

And they would be living theirs every single today. Together.

Epilogue

SEVEN YEARS LATER…

Piper watched from the wings as the last few minutes of *Grease* unfolded for the final time this season. This afternoon's Sunday matinee performance would close out the third season of the Driftwood Bay Summer Playhouse, a dream she had brought to reality.

She had decided when she returned to college that she didn't want to pursue a theater degree. She had plenty of experience in that area, so she set her sights on a business degree to fill in the gaps. Starting up a summer theater program in her hometown was ambitious, but visitors who came to the Texas coast needed to find things to do after the sun set—and Piper had decided opening a playhouse would be a great way to give back to the community, as well as entertain visitors to the Bay. They also drew a decent nightly crowd from those who stayed at Tidewater. After only three years in operation, her playhouse was beginning to gain attention and recognition beyond the Texas coast.

Sullivan had helped her put together a partnership, which was responsible for purchasing the building. He had helped lead the renovations and pitched in that first season in designing and building the sets. Without her husband's help, Piper could not have accomplished so much in such a short amount of time.

She had gone to her university in Corpus, along with talking with the local community college reps and Driftwood Bay High School drama teacher, drawing from their resources to get the playhouse up and running. Students from these three departments served as actors, technicians for lighting and sound, and costume designers. The musicians for each musical had also come from these groups, as well as students who handled marketing, the playhouse's website, and even ushers, ticket sellers, and concession workers. All these students were offered school credit for their volunteer work, and the program had only grown since it began.

Piper hired a stage manager who also served as the playhouse's chief fundraiser. Another paid position had been the stage manager, who coordinated rehearsals and performances and served as the front-of-house manager, while she took on the role as the director for each musical. That first year, she had also choreographed the musical numbers, as well as handling vocal director duties. All that was accomplished while she was a new mother to Lizzy, named after *Pride and Prejudice*'s Elizabeth Bennet.

Her last semester in college, Piper had been as big as a barn door, scheduled to deliver her firstborn three day after graduation. Lizzy had a different idea about how she would come into the world, however. Piper had just walked across the stage and received her diploma and was headed back to her seat when her water broke. Since, as a Shepherd, she was among the S-students graduating, she waited until the ceremonies ended and a few pictures had been taken before she whispered to Sullivan that they needed to head to the hospital.

She rubbed her baby bump now, thinking she looked as if someone had slipped a basketball under her shirt. Baby Number Two was due in less than a week, and Piper was happy today's musical was now concluding. She hadn't wanted to give birth before the season ended and she put her playhouse baby to bed.

Thunderous applause sounded, and actors went out for their curtain calls. Then she heard her name being chanted, and the actor who played Danny Zuko came to get her, leading Piper to the center of the stage, where she was given a bouquet of red roses. She usually said a few words at the end of each season, never planning ahead of time what she would say. Piper had learned to speak from the heart in these moments.

Gazing out at the audience, she saw so many of her friends and people she knew from the Bay, which filled her with a sense of satisfaction and pride.

"Thank you," she began, quickly collecting her thoughts. "When I started the Driftwood Bay Playhouse, I had no idea it would grow into what it's become. Four years ago, I was a recent college graduate with a newborn—and a dream. My husband, Sullivan Shepherd, helped support me making my dream a reality."

She swallowed, her gaze meeting his, love for this man filling her.

"The first year, I ran myself ragged, putting on four shows. The residents of Driftwood Bay, along with the numerous visitors to the Texas coast, really turned out and made that inaugural season a roaring success. I was able to arrange for others to handle the choreography and vocal direction, in subsequent seasons, thanks to the partnerships our playhouse has formed with our high school and local universities. Now, students earn college credits for their participation at the playhouse. I only directed two of the six shows we put on this season. The others were helmed by graduate students working toward their MFA in directing."

The lights were hot and the roses' scent a little too strong, so Piper turned and handed the bouquet to a nearby actor.

"We're already accepting audition tapes for next season. Performers are eager to be in a production at the Driftwood Bay Playhouse. I try to choose musicals which are fresh and exciting, ones which will attract top actors and directors. At the same time, I also try to blend in musicals familiar to our audiences. I aim to attract audiences of all ages, which is why we put on *Shrek* and *The Wizard of Oz* for our younger fans this year, while still featuring classics such as *Mamma Mia, Little Shop of Horrors,* and *My Fair Lady.*"

Piper smiled at the crowd. "Thank you to my husband, Sullivan Shepherd, for all his support in everything I do, as well as my parents and our friends. I hope one day I might even see my daughter Lizzy up here, singing and dancing her heart out." She rubbed her belly. "Or the newest Shepherd, who should be making his appearance any day now. And to you, our loyal fans, thank you for supporting our playhouse and for making this the biggest and best season yet."

A rousing cheer sounded, and she waved to the crowd. Suddenly, a familiar feeling swept over her, with a quick whoosh.

"Not again," she said under her breath, shaking her head.

Sullivan must have realized what happened. He scooped up Lizzy, who sat in his lap, and placed her in her mom's lap and said something quickly. Then he strode to the stage and hopped on it.

Grinning at her, he said, "Come on, pretty mama. We've got a date with an OB—and we better not be late. I've learned from our friends that second babies can come awfully fast."

He led her offstage, adding, "I handed Lizzy off to Mom and told her we'd call them from the hospital."

"You think of everything," she said, still thinking how much this man made her swoon.

They reached his car, and he tucked her into the passenger's seat before racing around and jumping behind the wheel. Piper was already texting her OB, who told her to come straight to the hospital. She laughed at the rest of the message.

"What's so funny?" Sullivan asked.

"Dr. B said we might beat her there. She's at the beach with her family and said she'd leave now. That she'd be the one in the room smelling of sunscreen and salt."

He threaded his fingers through hers. "We're going to have a baby again."

Love washed over her. "Yes, we are."

"I kinda miss that baby smell," he told her. "With Lizzy walking and talking so much, it'll be nice to have a baby again."

"I hope her nose won't get too far out of joint," Piper said. "She's used to being the main act."

"She'll love her little brother," Sullivan assured her. "Will she boss him around? That's a definite. But she'll take to him."

They arrived at the hospital, and Piper was placed in a wheelchair. She was taken up to a room while Sullivan filled out some paperwork.

She wanted him not to take too long and said, "I've been timing my contractions. We don't have long."

"I'll be up fast," he promised. "I'll bring your suitcase with me."

He had insisted on putting her packed suitcase in the car every time they went somewhere for the last two weeks. Now, she was glad he had done so.

She reached the labor and delivery floor and was taken to a

room and prepped. Her OB arrived, and Piper updated Dr. B on her contractions.

"Where were you when your water broke?" the doctor asked. "A better story than last time?"

Piper shook her head. "I'd just finished delivering my farewell to the season speech on stage. At least we got in the last performance before I went into labor." She groaned. "This is a big one."

Dr. B checked her as Sullivan rushed into the room, wearing a hospital gown, his hairnet sitting jauntily on his head.

"How is she, Dr. B?"

"Piper is fine. The head is crowning. Stand by—because we're going to have a baby join us very soon. Piper, next contraction, push for your life."

"Got it," she said, gritting her teeth as Sullivan joined her and took her hand in his. The wave of pain struck her, and she bore down hard, gripping her husband's hand tightly.

"Good job. The head is through," the OB said. "Give me another great push to get the shoulders to pass."

She did her breathing, Sullivan panting along with her in unison, and pushed again with all her might with the next contraction.

"Nice work, Piper," the doctor praised. "Ooh, slippery little thing. He's all the way out. And as handsome as they come."

Sullivan leaned closer for a better look. "Yup. He's a keeper."

The baby's Apgar score was nine both times it was taken by his pediatrician. He was cleaned up, along with Piper, and a nurse placed the newborn in her arms.

"We'll give you some family time now," Dr. B said. "Congratulations, Shepherds, on your new addition to the family."

The room emptied, leaving them alone, and Sullivan took his son's small fist, brushing a kiss on his brow and then Piper's.

"So, Regency Romance Queen, what are we going to name this one?"

Her husband had been understanding when Piper hadn't wanted to choose names for their firstborn months in advance. She'd told him she wanted to actually see their baby before picking a name for her. When she'd held their daughter, she just knew the baby was an Elizabeth, who would go by Lizzy, named after her favorite character from *Pride and Prejudice*.

Piper gazed with love at their newborn son, who opened his eyes and stared steadily at her. In that moment, she knew he would be calm and steadfast and had the perfect name for him.

"He's going to be Brandon, after Colonel Brandon in *Sense and Sensibility*." She looked to Sullivan. "If that's all right with you."

Although Sullivan hadn't read any Jane Austen, he had watched several movie versions of Austen novels with her, and he nodded approvingly.

"Brandon Shepherd. I like it." He bent and kissed the baby's head. Brandon yawned and closed his eyes. "And I like you, Piper Shepherd."

Her husband's lips touched hers, and joy filled Piper. They had added another child to their family.

And they were continuing to live their happily ever after, one day at a time.

Also by Alexa Aston

COASTAL DREAMS

Second Chance on the Shore

The Art of Healing

Crafting Love

Tides of Trust

HEARTS IN HAWTHORNE

Heartstrings and Helmets

Heartbeat Harmony

Agent of the Heart

Hearts and Hooves

Hoops and Hearts

LOST CREEK, TEXAS HILL COUNTRY

The Perfect Blend

Painted Melodies

Script of Love

Love in Every Bite

Whispered Melodies

SUGAR SPRINGS

Shadows of the Past

Learning to Trust Again

A Perfect Match

A Fresh Start

Recipe for Love

MAPLE COVE

Another Chance at Love

A New Beginning

Coming Home

The Lyrics of Love

Finding Home

HOLLYWOOD NAME GAME

Hollywood Heartbreaker

Hollywood Flirt

Hollywood Player

Hollywood Double

Hollywood Enigma

LAWMEN OF THE WEST

Runaway Hearts

Blind Faith

Love and the Lawman

Ballad Beauty

SAGEBRUSH BRIDES

A Game of Chance

Written in the Cards

Outlaw Muse

KNIGHTS OF REDEMPTION

A Bit of Heaven on Earth

A Knight for Kallen

SUDDENLY A DUKE

Portrait of the Duke

Music for the Duke

Polishing the Duke

Designs on the Duke

Fashioning the Duke

Love Blooms with the Duke

Training the Duke

Investigating the Duke

SECOND SONS OF LONDON

Educated by the Earl

Debating with the Duke

Empowered by the Earl

Made for the Marquess

Dubious about the Duke

Valued by the Viscount

Meant for the Marquess

DUKES DONE WRONG

Discouraging the Duke

Deflecting the Duke

Disrupting the Duke

Delighting the Duke

Destiny with a Duke

DUKES OF DISTINCTION

Duke of Renown

Duke of Charm

Duke of Disrepute

Duke of Arrogance

Duke of Honor

SOLDIERS AND SOULMATES

To Heal an Earl

To Tame a Rogue

To Trust a Duke

To Save a Love

To Win a Widow

THE ST. CLAIRS

Devoted to the Duke

Midnight with the Marquess

Embracing the Earl

Defending the Duke

Suddenly a St. Clair

STANDALONE ROMANTIC THRILLERS

Leave Yesterday Behind

Illusions of Death

About the Author

USA Today and Amazon Top 100 bestselling author Alexa Aston lives with her husband in a Dallas suburb, where she eats her fair share of dark chocolate and plots out stories while she walks every morning. She enjoys travel, sports, and binge-watching—and never misses an episode of *Survivor*.

Alexa brings her characters to life in steamy historicals, contemporary romances, and romantic suspense novels that resonate with passion, intensity, and heart.

Keep up with Alexa

Visit her website

Newsletter Sign-Up

More ways to connect with Alexa

OLIVERHEBERBOOKS

www.ingramcontent.com/pod-product-compliance
Lightning Source LLC
LaVergne TN
LVHW090438160826
845672LV00019B/1038